More praise for the novels of

CANDACE CAMP

"Entertaining, well-written Victorian romantic mystery."
—*The Best Reviews* on *An Unexpected Pleasure*

"A smart, fun-filled romp."
—*Publishers Weekly* on *Impetuous*

"Camp brings the dark Victorian world to life.
Her strong characters and perfect pacing keep
you turning the pages of this chilling mystery."
—*Romantic Times BOOKreviews* on *Winterset*

"From its delicious beginning to its satisfying ending,
[*Mesmerized*] offers a double helping of romance."
—*Booklist*

A
Dangerous MAN

CANDACE
CAMP

HQN™

ISBN 13: 978-0-373-77136-3
ISBN-10:   0-373-77136-3

A DANGEROUS MAN

www.HQNBooks.com

Printed in U.S.A.

Also available from Candace Camp and HQN Books

An Independent Woman
An Unexpected Pleasure
A Stolen Heart
So Wild a Heart
The Hidden Heart
Swept Away

Other books by Candace Camp

Winterset
Beyond Compare
Mesmerized
No Other Love
Promise Me Tomorrow
Impetuous
Indiscreet
Impulse
Scandalous
Suddenly

**Watch for Candace Camp's enthralling
new historical romance series,
The Matchmakers, beginning with
THE MARRIAGE WAGER in September.**

A
Dangerous
MAN

PROLOGUE

THE FUNERAL PYRE WAS arranged on the beach, a simple bier of wooden planks resting on two branches at either end, crossed and nailed into disproportionate X-shapes. Below the bier, the wood was stacked—a jumble of hewn logs, branches and smaller pieces of driftwood gathered from the beach itself, all soaked with kerosene to make them burn fast and hot. On the two wide planks rested a still figure, wrapped round with a sheet, the shape of a man but faceless, and all the more stark and lonely for that.

The widow stood at some distance, tall and statuesque, imposing in her severe black mourning. It was as close as they would let her stand. The authorities had tried to dissuade her, even sending a priest to counsel reason. It was too upsetting for delicate feminine sensibilities, they explained, too harsh a thing for her to witness.

"Rather more harsh for my husband, I imagine," Eleanor, Lady Scarbrough, had answered in the flat way that would have warned anyone familiar with

her that the lady's mind was made up. "I will see him through to the end."

The Italian authorities had had no experience with her, but eventually they, too, learned that Eleanor Townsend Scarbrough rarely lost an argument, and finally they had had to accede to her wishes—though they had not budged on the place where she must stand, finally dropping their delicate phrasings in exasperation and pointing out bluntly that the smell would be overpowering any closer up.

So she now stood on a hillock, still and straight, gazing across the sand to where Sir Edmund Scarbrough's body lay in its final resting place. The wind molded the long black mantle to her body and whipped her veil, and she shivered, thinking bitterly that it should not be so cold on the sunny coast of the Kingdom of Naples.

The short, rotund man beside her glanced at Eleanor uneasily. In less somber circumstances, they would have looked comical side-by-side, she so tall and straight, he so round and short, especially given his ineffective efforts to play the role of male protector. He touched her arm, then dropped his hand, which hovered at her back, not quite daring to place it upon her unyielding form. Finally he glanced at her and then at the scene playing out below them, and his features contracted in dismay. He quickly glanced away.

"I do not think…you must be cold… Please, Lady Scarbrough…"

Eleanor spared him a brief glance. "It is all right, Signore Castellati, you need not stay. I will be perfectly fine."

The man's round face reflected his horror. "No, no, no." He burst into impassioned Italian, too fast for Eleanor to follow entirely, but she understood enough to get the gist of his speech, which was that the opera impresario had no thought for himself but only for the lady's discomfort and distress. He ended with a quick glance at the pile of wood, putting the lie to his own words.

"Thank you, Signore," Eleanor said sincerely, reaching out and patting the short man's arm. However silly the man might seem, he was standing fast in his determination to see her through this moment, despite his obvious dislike, even fear, and that, she thought, was very brave of him. "You have helped me a great deal."

It was true. Castellati had been at her side throughout the last few days, ever since Sir Edmund had not returned from his afternoon of boating. While it was true that Castellati had a vested interest in Edmund's welfare, as he was in the midst of producing Edmund's opera, and while at times Eleanor had wished him elsewhere, he had been helpful in dealing with the Italian authorities.

Of course, Dario Paradella, Sir Edmund's closest friend in Naples, had been by her side, as well, but he, caught up in his own grief, had been of little help. In

any case, Dario, she well knew, was not on the best of terms with the Neapolitan government, as he had some rather liberal leanings that did not sit well with them.

"Ah, *ma donna bella...*" Dario, standing on the other side of Eleanor, turned toward her and took her hand, squeezing it tightly. "It is so sad...so sad... such a genius."

"Yes."

They lit the funeral pyre then, the flames licking to life along the kerosene-soaked logs, dancing and setting the smaller pieces of driftwood alight. The men who had set it afire moved back hastily, several of them crossing themselves.

It was a macabre scene—the lifeless, covered form, the flames crawling up the wood toward it. A shudder ran through Eleanor's body.

How had it come to this? Edmund should not have died so soon. Guilt and regret welled up in her. *Had she been wrong to bring him here?*

She had been so certain that she could help him. Improve his life, his health. She could see now what utter gall it had been on her part, what false pride she had indulged in, to think she could cheat death of its intended victim.

She had brought Edmund to Naples for his health, hoping that the warm Italian climate would prove salubrious. There was no cure, of course, for consumption, but the doctors had agreed that the damp English weather could only make him worse. But

here, she had thought, where Edmund would have warmth, gentle ocean breezes, freedom from the demands of his persistent family and all the time in the world to create his music, in the country where opera was most revered, he would thrive.

Instead, he had died.

The pyre was burning fiercely now, the long form atop the bier engulfed in flames. Despite the distance, the odor of burning flesh was unmistakable. Beside her, Signor Castellati raised one gloved hand to his face, pressing a handkerchief over his nose and mouth, and turned his head away from the sight. Even Dario lowered his gaze.

But Eleanor would not let herself look away. She would not excuse herself from this last duty. It was all she could do for her husband now.

She would watch the fire consume his earthly remains, and she would take his ashes from the fire. And then, once his work was brought to completion, his opera performed in Naples, she would take his ashes home to England.

CHAPTER ONE

ANTHONY, LORD NEALE, sliced through the seal on the note that the footman had just handed him and read through it quickly. He sighed. His older sister, Honoria, was informing him that she planned to visit him that afternoon. Knowing Honoria, he suspected that her carriage would arrive not long after the messenger.

He was aware of a cowardly impulse to send a note to the stables to saddle his horse and pretend that he had not been there to receive Honoria's message. But he knew, with a sigh, that he could not. It had been only six months since Sir Edmund's death. Annoying as his sister could be, he could not bring himself to be rude to a grieving mother.

Tossing the letter onto his desk, he rang for the footman and sent a message to the kitchen, informing the butler that his sister would be with them for tea…and perhaps supper.

He walked over to the window and stood looking out on the front drive. It was his favorite view, offering a sweeping expanse of the front yard, the

drive and the trees beyond, but at the moment, he scarcely saw it. His thoughts were turned inward, to his nephew and the young man's death six months ago. He had not been close, he supposed, to Edmund; he was not, he admitted, close to any of his relatives—a fault, no doubt Honoria would tell him, of his own nature. But he had been fond of Edmund, and had thought him a man of great talent and promise. Anthony had been saddened by the news of Edmund's death, and he was certain that the world would be poorer for the music that it had lost.

It had been clear for years that Edmund would not have a long life. He had always been sickly. But to have lost him this way, in a sudden accident, seemed even more wrong. Anthony could not help but wonder if the young man would still have been alive if it had not been for that stubborn woman he had been foolish enough to marry.

At the time, despite his dislike for Eleanor Townsend, now Lady Scarbrough, he had approved of their moving to Italy, thinking that the warm, sunny clime would be better for Edmund's consumption than the damp winters of England. Nor, he had thought, would it hurt the young man to be farther away from his mother's frequent complaints and demands.

But ever since Edmund's death, Anthony had been weighed down by the guilty thought that he had failed his nephew by not trying to persuade him to remain in England. Only Anthony knew how much

of his decision not to talk to Sir Edmund about it had been due to his reluctance to go to Sir Edmund's house, where he might once again run into Lady Eleanor.

Anthony felt the same uneasy sensations that he always did whenever he thought of Lady Eleanor—a volatile blend of annoyance and sharp physical hunger, as well as a fierce stab of anger at his seeming inability to control those emotions. The devil take the woman, he thought. She was impossible in every way, not the least of which was that she was impossible to forget.

It had been a year since he had first seen her, but he could remember every moment of it perfectly....

ANTHONY KNOCKED on the door of Eleanor Townsend's house and waited, wishing he were somewhere else, anywhere else. He regretted telling his sister he would talk to the woman Sir Edmund intended to marry.

Anthony had not wanted to do as his older sister asked; everything within him rebelled at the idea of messing about in his relatives' lives. He was a man who preferred to live his own life free of others' interference, and he liked to return the favor.

But Honoria had pleaded with him, hands clasped dramatically to her heaving bosom. He must save her only son from the clutches of a money-hungry harpy, she had told him. Edmund was so young and inex-

perienced that he had asked an American adventuress to marry him. Eleanor Townsend, Honoria was convinced, had tricked her son into it. Anthony, she had decided, must call upon the American siren who had ensnared Edmund and convince her not to marry him. An offer of money, in Honoria's opinion, would speak volumes with the adventuress.

Honoria, who was in fact his half sister, had, of course, reminded him of his duty as the head of the family and especially of his duty regarding her. She had been fourteen years old when his mother had died giving birth to him and had, at least according to Honoria herself, practically raised him. And, she pointed out, he of all people should know the harm that could be done by a beautiful adventuress who lured a rich man into marriage.

Anthony was well aware of his responsibilities to his family; it was a lesson that had been pounded into his head from childhood. However, he was also quite aware that for his sister, the earl's duties usually coincided with her own wishes. And since he knew that Honoria had married and left the house when he was five years old, and that he had been primarily raised by his old nurse and a succession of governesses until he was old enough to be sent away to Eton, he was generally unmoved by Honoria's claims to have been "almost a mother" to him.

Ordinarily, he would have turned down her request, disavowing that one of his responsibilities

was meddling about in the private life of a grown man of twenty-four years of age.

But Sir Edmund was different. There was a child-like innocence to him that one rarely saw in an aristocratic young gentleman, and he was possessed of a talent that both awed and puzzled Anthony. He suspected that Edmund was a musical genius, but the young man's experience with the world—and his ability to deal with it—were as small as his talent was large. Anthony, being fonder of the young man than he was of most of his relatives, had hated to see him crushed between his mother and his fiancée.

Besides, Honoria was right about one thing: He *did* have a wealth of personal experience in the area of the harm wrought by a beautiful, money-hungry woman. His father had married one when Anthony was sixteen, and she had managed to drive a wedge between Anthony and his father that had almost destroyed their relationship.

So, finally, Anthony had agreed to her request, and here he was, standing on Eleanor Townsend's doorstep. He allowed himself a small, vain hope that no one would answer the door.

At that moment the door swung open, revealing a man who looked like no other servant Anthony had ever seen. He was short and squarely built, the muscles of his chest and arms straining against the cloth of his jacket. One ear was peculiarly mis-shapen; his nose appeared to have been broken at

least once in the past, and there were two or three small scars on his face. He looked, Anthony thought, more like a pugilist or a ruffian than a servant.

"Lord Neale," Anthony told him, extracting a calling card from his case and extending it to him.

Unlike a proper British footman or butler, the man did not hold out a small silver tray for him to place the card upon but simply took it from Anthony's hand. He examined it somewhat suspiciously, then nodded to Anthony.

"I'll tell her you're here," the man told him and strode away, leaving Anthony standing in the entry hall.

Anthony watched him leave, astonished. It was the first time he could remember ever being left to wait in the hall when he called upon someone. His title and wealth usually earned him a deferential bow, after which he was escorted to the best drawing room.

Another man might have been offended. Anthony found it rather amusing.

Well, Honoria *had* warned him that Miss Townsend and her household were decidedly "off." She was, first of all, an American. Secondly, she was an unmarried woman living in London without any sort of proper chaperone—unless one could count a young Indian *amah* for the two children who traveled with her, which Honoria clearly did not. Thirdly, as Honoria had found out by setting one of

her own servants to spy on the house from across the street, Miss Townsend's household consisted of a hodgepodge of people from a variety of countries, including not only the two children whose parentage was decidedly unclear—one of them was American and the other apparently French—and the aforementioned Indian girl who cared for the children, but also an African man who wore not the livery of a servant but the suit of a gentleman and who was, according to the gossip Honoria's spy had heard in a nearby pub, Miss Townsend's man of business.

Anthony glanced around him as he waited, taking in the spare yet elegant décor. Whatever else could be said about Miss Townsend, her taste was impeccable.

He wondered if the woman was the grasping harpy his older sister had portrayed her as. Honoria was not only given to dramatic excess, she was, in Anthony's opinion, far too protective and clinging where her son was concerned. Edmund had been frail from childhood, given to coughs and catarrh. More than once the doctor had assured Honoria that her beloved son would not last through the winter.

As a result of this—and her innate personality— Honoria had coddled Edmund all his life, keeping him at home with her until, as a grown man, he had finally insisted on moving to London and living on his own. Even then, Honoria had kept him running to her side for one reason or another, alternating her

coddling with pleas for him to help her with this problem or that. She had, Anthony thought, ignored her daughter, Samantha, and her late husband in her obsession with her son—which was, he reasoned, probably a good thing as far as the daughter was concerned.

Honoria would not easily give up her son to another woman, and Anthony suspected that even a saint would not have earned the elder Lady Scarbrough's approval.

However, he could not dismiss her suggestion out of hand, either. Edmund's title and fortune, while not as great as Anthony's own, were enough to lure any fortune-hunting female. Moreover, given Edmund's frail constitution and the frequency with which he suffered from debilitating fevers and lung ailments—which Edmund privately feared was deadly consumption, not just the weak constitution that Honoria believed—the aforesaid fortune-hunting female could feel assured that she would not have to play the role of loving wife for long but would within a few years be a wealthy widow.

At the sound of footsteps, Anthony turned and went absolutely still. The woman walking toward him was stunning.

She was tall and statuesque, with thick jet-black hair and vivid blue eyes. Her firm jaw and prominent cheekbones were, perhaps, a trifle too strong, but those features were softened by a soft, full-lipped mouth and

large, compelling eyes. She was dressed in peacock blue, too bold for a proper maiden, and she carried herself with confidence, head up and gaze straight.

A wave of pure physical desire swept through Anthony, so intense and hot that it stunned him. He was a man used to being in control of himself, and at thirty-five years of age, he considered himself long past the adolescent days of being swept this way or that by sheer lust. But this woman…

He took an unconscious step toward her, then stopped, realizing what he was doing. By sheer strength of will, he tamped down the surge of desire.

Clearly, he thought, this was the woman who had captured Sir Edmund's heart. And, just as clearly, his sister had been correct in her assessment that Miss Eleanor Townsend was a fortune hunter. There was no way a woman like this would be marrying his inarticulate, inexperienced nephew out of love. Indeed, it was astonishing that she had not set her cap for a wealthier man or one of higher title.

She was a beauty of the kind who could inspire poets or start wars. And she had the confident carriage of a woman well aware of her power. Had she been some timid soul, a sweet girl fresh from the country, he could have believed that she had fallen in love with his nephew, dazzled, perhaps, by his genius, or filled with the maternal urge to take care of him.

But this was no naïve girl. This was a woman in the full flush of her beauty, strong and self-assured.

It was ludicrous to think that she could have fallen in love with Edmund.

Anthony, much to his regret, was quite familiar with manipulative beauties and the ways in which they ensnared men too weak or lonely to see past their looks.

"Lord Neale?" Eleanor Townsend said, and there was a certain wariness in her eyes that made him feel even more certain that she was an adventuress. An innocent female, surely, would not be so guarded when meeting her fiancé's relative. "You are Edmund's uncle?"

He nodded shortly, irritated by the fact that her voice, low and throaty with just the trace of an American inflection, made his loins tighten. "Yes."

Her eyebrows rose a fraction at his response, and he knew that he had sounded rude. He was not a man who was particularly at ease in social situations. While he enjoyed intelligent conversation, he had never mastered the art of polite small talk. Indeed, he had never tried, disdaining both trivial conversation and the social occasions at which it was employed. He was considered blunt and rather antisocial, and the only reason he continued to be invited to all the best parties, even though he rarely attended, was because of his title and his fortune. But on this occasion, he knew, he was even stiffer than usual, rattled by his body's intense reaction to this woman.

"Why don't we converse in the drawing room?" she suggested, gesturing down the hall, then turning and starting in the direction she had indicated. "I am sorry that Edmund is not here."

"I didn't expect him to be." It was, after all, not yet noon, rather early for anyone to be visiting. "I came to see *you*, Miss Townsend."

"Indeed? I am honored."

Anthony did not miss the slightly ironic twist to her voice as she said the words. She sat down in a chair, motioning him to do likewise, and waited, watching him coolly.

Lord Neale shifted uncomfortably beneath her gaze and finally said abruptly, "Lady Scarbrough, my sister, asked me to speak with you."

"Ah." Eleanor said nothing else, giving him no encouragement.

"She—I—you cannot marry Edmund," Anthony blurted out, realizing even as he said it that he had been even more maladroit than he usually was. He felt a flush starting in his cheeks. *Damn the woman!* She made him feel as awkward as a schoolboy.

"Indeed? Why not? Is there some impediment?" Eleanor responded, her voice cool and faintly sarcastic.

He had expected indignation, and he was aware of a curious disappointment at her lack of dismay. It was obvious that she had expected him to say something of the kind.

"Only common decency," he snapped.

"I should think it would be more indecent if Edmund resided in my house without the benefit of marriage, don't you?" Eleanor replied, her blue eyes challenging him.

The look in her eyes was like a spark to tinder, and anger flared to life in Anthony, quick and hot.

"You must have known his family would object to this marriage," he retorted, nettled.

"Of course. No doubt it will be quite a loss to you," Eleanor told him.

Her tone carried a sting. Anthony was not quite sure what she meant by her words, but her contempt for him was clear. It would be useless, he knew, to try to persuade or reason with her. So he went straight to the point.

"I am prepared to pay you."

"Pay me?" Eleanor's eyebrows soared, and her voice became almost a purr. "You are offering to pay me not to marry Edmund?" She crossed her arms, considering him. "Just how much are you prepared to offer?"

For an instant he thought she would accept. Hope surged up in him, mingled, strangely, with a kind of disappointment, and he named a figure far higher than he had originally intended.

Eleanor rose to her feet, her movement not quick but with a kind of regal grace and power that made him realize suddenly how mistaken he had been in

thinking she might accept his offer. He had, he saw, gravely underestimated his opponent.

"It is interesting to learn," she said bitingly, "that your concern for your nephew is solely monetary. I shall not tell Edmund about your offer, as he inexplicably admires you, and I do not like to see him hurt."

She was fairly vibrating with fury, her blue eyes blazing at him, and, much to Anthony's surprise and self-disgust, lust coiled in his loins in response.

"I am sorry," Eleanor went on in a clipped voice that clearly said she was no such thing. "But I must decline your offer. Pray tell Lady Scarbrough that it is too late. Her son is out of her grasp now. Sir Edmund and I were married yesterday by special license."

Anthony had not seen Eleanor, Lady Scarbrough, again. Two months later, she and Sir Edmund had sailed for Italy. A year later, Sir Edmund was dead.

THE SOUND OF WHEELS on the driveway outside roused Anthony from his reverie. His sister's carriage had arrived. He watched as a footman hurried forward and let down the step of the carriage, opening the door to help his sister down.

Honoria, Anthony saw, was dressed all in black, her figure still slim, though she had reached middle age. She looked touchingly fragile. A heavy mourning veil was draped over her hat, but as she came up

the steps, she reached up and turned it back, so that it fell down on either side of her face in a flattering manner. Honoria always wanted to make a statement, but not, of course, to the detriment of her looks.

Anthony repressed the cynical thought, reminding himself that his older sister had recently lost her only son and had every right to be in the depths of sorrow—even if she did mourn Sir Edmund to the utmost effect.

He strode out into the entryway to greet her, schooling the impatience out of his face and voice. "Honoria."

"Oh, Anthony!" Tears filled her limpid blue eyes, and she held out both her hands to him, her body somehow bending a little in such a way as to hint that she might faint.

Anthony took her hands in his, and led her quickly into the drawing room and over to the sofa. He had had enough experience with his sister not to allow her to develop her scene to its fullest extent.

"What brings you here today?" he asked, cutting to the heart of the matter.

"Oh, Anthony," the older woman repeated, one hand going to her heart. She looked up into his face. "That woman murdered my son!"

CHAPTER TWO

HIS SISTER'S WORDS LEFT Anthony speechless.

He did not have to ask what woman she meant. There was only one—at the moment—who earned the title of That Woman, always pronounced in the most scathing of accents. However, even for Honoria, the accusation of murder seemed excessive.

Anthony frowned. "What basis do you have for thinking that? You cannot go about accusing people without any reason."

"She has written me. She is coming back here."

"It would seem the natural thing to do, Honoria," Anthony pointed out, wondering if this could possibly be all that had set his sister off.

"Natural? There is nothing natural about any of it," Honoria snapped, in her annoyance casting aside the mantle of wilting sorrow. "She is bringing Edmund's ashes. His ashes!"

"But, Honoria, isn't this where you would want Edmund to—"

"Yes, of course, this is where I want my son." She

raised the handkerchief to her eyes again. "This is where I want him *buried*. But she has denied me even that solace. She burned him, Anthony!"

"Yes, Honoria, I know."

"Do you understand the horror of that? There is not even the shell of him left to bury in the Scarbrough mausoleum. It was wicked of her. Wicked! First she took him to that awful country, so far from home. And she did it only to spite me. I know it. And now...now that he has been taken from me forever, she deprives me of even this comfort. It is outside the bounds of decency. It is sacrilegious!"

There was, Anthony knew, a good deal of religious feeling against the immolation of a body. However, it was the first time he had heard of his sister being in any way religious.

He said only, "Wouldn't you rather have his ashes here than have his body buried in Naples?"

Honoria cast him an irritated look. "That is not the point. He should not have been there in the first place. He should have been here where I could look after him. That is why she took him to Italy—to keep him from me. She knew that if she separated him from me and his family, no one could protest anything that happened to him. If only he hadn't gone to Italy, none of this would have happened. He wouldn't be dead now."

She began to weep again. Anthony sighed.

"Edmund was a grown man, Honoria. She could

not make him go. And we could not keep him here," he pointed out.

"You could have made more of a push to stop him."

"How was I to foresee that Edmund would be in a boating accident there?" he replied reasonably, his words as much for himself as for his sister. "I had never known him to show a preference for sailing."

"That is just it!" Honoria said triumphantly, her eyes lighting now with fervor. "Edmund abhorred such activities. You know that. You remember how he was about riding. Or any sort of sport."

"Yes."

"Well? Don't you see? How do we know that Edmund died in a sailing accident?" His sister went on. "All we have saying so is the letter that *she* wrote me!"

Anthony hesitated. His sister was often hysterical and given to dramatics, but he could not help but think that she had a point. It was very odd that Edmund would have taken up sailing. Edmund had found the desire for outdoor activities largely incomprehensible in others and absurd for himself. His lungs had always been too weak for him to engage in any strenuous physical activity, and the thought of perhaps injuring his hands and being unable to play his music had filled him with horror.

"Why else would she have had his body burned?" Honoria saw Anthony's hesitation and pressed her

advantage. "It is bizarre. Unnatural. Why would she do it—unless she had something to hide? A dead body can be dug up. Poison can be found in a person's body even after they are dead. I have heard it."

"Yes, that's true."

"But if there is no body to exhume, no one could ever find the poison. Or a crack in his skull or some other injury. No one could prove that he did not die in a boating accident."

"But why would she kill him?" Anthony found it hard to believe that Eleanor, however grasping she might be, was a murderer.

Honoria sent him a scathing look. "His money, of course."

"She already had that. And I cannot imagine that Edmund was a demanding husband."

"What reason does any woman have to do away with her husband?" his sister replied matter-of-factly. "Because she has found another? Because she no longer wants to have to ask him for money? Because he refuses to allow her to do exactly as she pleases? It would not surprise me that when she married him, she thought his weak lungs would carry him off within a few months, but then Edmund did not die. So she decided to help him along."

"Honoria…"

"I am not being foolish, Anthony. Stop being a man, and look past her pretty face and elegant

figure. Women are capable of killing to get what
they want."

"I am sure they are. But there is no reason to
think that *she* did."

"I believe Edmund had discovered what she was
like. Anthony, he cut her out of his will. Why else
would a man do that except that he knew she was a
rapacious harpy who married him for his money? Or
that she was having an affair with another man?
Perhaps both."

"Edmund cut her from the will?"

"Yes. He did not leave her a cent."

Anthony scowled. It would take something very
compelling to make a man like Edmund leave his
wife nothing to live on. "Still, Honoria, that would
argue against her killing him. She would get
nothing."

"Well, she may not have known that before she
murdered him. She might not have realized he had
changed his will. Besides, there is a way that she can
get to his money. Edmund left everything to his
sister—outside of his entailed estate, of course,
which goes to Sir Malcolm. Why he would have
done that, I do not know. I am his mother, after all,
and—"

"He left you nothing?" Anthony asked skeptically.

"Oh, he left me a bit," Honoria allowed, waving
it away. "A mere pittance, really. However, that is a

mother's lot, I suppose." She released the sigh of a martyr.

"But how does this help Lady Eleanor?" Anthony asked, dragging Honoria back to the subject at hand.

"He left control of the trust to her!" Honoria said indignantly. "Even though I am Samantha's mother, he did not make me guardian of her money until she comes of age. He left That Woman as sole trustee!"

"Why would he cut Lady Eleanor out of his will, then put her in charge of Samantha's money for the next six years?" Anthony asked.

"I don't know. Edmund was never one who understood money."

Anthony thought that her statement was a bit of the pot calling the kettle black, but he wisely refrained from pointing this out.

"You have to see what an opportunity this presents for her to siphon off money from the trust," Honoria told him. "She wrote me saying she would 'explain' the trust to me when she brings poor Edmund's ashes home. I do not need any 'explanation.' It is quite clear to me what she intends to do. My poor daughter and I will live in poverty, while she bleeds Samantha's trust dry."

"Honoria, calm yourself. I will not let that happen," Anthony promised her grimly. Even allowing for Honoria's usual gift of hyperbole, Anthony was troubled by what she had told him. It did not make sense, really, but neither could he

ignore Honoria's theories. If Lady Eleanor did indeed have control of Samantha's money, she could easily take out a great deal of it without anyone's noticing. And there *were* several suspicious things about Edmund's death.

"But how can you stop her? She has gotten away with murder, and she has control over Samantha's money."

"I will go to see the woman," he told Honoria. "And I will make sure she realizes that if anything is amiss, she will have to answer to me."

ELEANOR STEPPED DOWN out of the carriage and simply stood for a moment, looking up at her house. It was an elegant white stone structure, with clean, symmetrical lines, and it warmed her heart to look at it again. It had been almost a year since she had been here, and it wasn't until she saw it again that she realized how much she had missed it.

The children bounced out of the carriage after her, letting out a whoop at the freedom after being confined in the carriage all day. "Look! We're home!"

Their *amah,* a small, quiet Indian woman named Kerani, followed them at a more sedate pace. "Wait, please," she called after them softly, and it was a measure of their affection for her that they waited at the bottom of the stoop, bouncing up and down, as she walked over to join them.

The front door was opened by a grinning

footman, who stood aside to let Bartwell exit the door first. "Miss Eleanor!"

Bartwell's well-worn face was creased with a smile. One would have thought, Eleanor told herself affectionately, that it had been months since her old friend and butler had seen them, rather than the few days it had actually been. The servants had gone ahead to open the house and prepare it as soon as their ship had pulled into port, while she and the children had stayed behind for a few days. It had given the children a much-needed respite from traveling. The days cooped up on the ship they had taken from Italy had left them bored and full of pent-up energy. It had also served, much to Eleanor's delight, as a means of breaking free of the smothering company of Mr. and Mrs. Colton-Smythe.

Hugo Colton-Smythe, a middle-aged cousin to a minor baron and a lifelong civil servant, and his wife, Adelaide, had been traveling on the same ship home from Naples to England as Eleanor, and they had taken it upon themselves to provide her with their respectable chaperonage. Only six months a widow, she was not, they were sure, up to dealing with all the exigencies of life, even the restricted sort of life aboard ship, and certainly she should be shielded from the importunate advances of the other passengers, many of whom were foreigners, and several of whom, they were sure, were adventurers seeking out a vulnerable wealthy widow.

Eleanor knew that kindness had been their main motive—and ignored the uncharitable thought that they were almost as interested in being able to drop into conversation little tidbits, such as, "When we were traveling with Lady Scarbrough…." However, she had found it an ever-increasing chore to put up with their mundane conversation and stultifying outlook on life.

She had been afraid that they would want to ride on with her to London, and for that reason, the thought of spending a few extra days in port while Bartwell saw to the house had seemed a godsend to her.

"Bartwell," she greeted the butler with a happy smile and a quick hug. Most people, she knew, found her choice of butler strange. He was a retired pugilist who had worked for her father since Eleanor was a child, and he was as fond of her as if she had been his own daughter. He had accompanied her when her father had sent her to school in England when she was fifteen, and she had been grateful for his companionship as much as for his protection. "I trust everything is in order."

"Oh, the usual, miss," he told her with a grin. "That Frenchified cook of yours is throwing a fit. But we've got the house all tidy and ready for you and the little ones."

He turned to the little ones in question, nodding his head in polite greeting to the shy, soft-spoken Indian woman before inviting Nathan to show him

his boxing form, holding up his hands as targets, then admiring Claire's new bonnet.

Eleanor reached back into the carriage and pulled out the teak box that had traveled on the seat beside her all the way from the coast. It was dark, made of the finest wood and beautifully carved, and its hinges and fastening were fashioned of gold.

Swallowing the lump that rose in her throat, Eleanor murmured, "You're home at last, my dear."

"Miss Elly," a deep voice behind her said. "Welcome home. Here, let me take that for you."

Eleanor turned, smiling. "Hello, Zachary. It is good to see you."

Zachary was another of her employees whose presence in her household was the focus of much gossip, Eleanor knew. His skin was dark—not much lighter, in truth, than the box she held in her hands—and because of this, the *ton* found it scandalous that Zachary was not a liveried servant but Eleanor's man of business. Zachary and his mother had been slaves, belonging to a Southern man whom Eleanor's father had been visiting. Eleanor's father had purchased both the boy and his mother, and had freed them when he returned home. Zachary's mother had become the cook in her father's home, but Mr. Townsend, seeing the young boy's intelligence, had paid for Zachary to be educated. He had worked for Mr. Townsend after he had gotten out of school, and upon her father's death a few years ago, he had come

to work for her, handling the details of Eleanor's business affairs.

She handed the box over to her business assistant without hesitation. Zachary and Bartwell were two of the people she trusted most in the world, the other one being her dear friend Juliana. Moreover, Zachary had admired her husband's talent and had spent more than one evening discussing music with him. "Put this in the music room, please."

"Of course."

Eleanor went into the house, the others following her, and there she found the remainder of the servants lined up to greet her. She was tired, but she was not one to shirk her duty, so she spent time with each of them, greeting the ones who had returned with her from Italy by name and letting Bartwell introduce her to those whom she did not know.

The children ran off upstairs, and Eleanor, after handing her hat and light traveling cloak to a footman, went down the hall to the music room. She closed the door after her and stood for a moment, simply looking around. This was the room where Edmund had spent most of his time, and it was the one she most closely connected with him. She felt a pang of sadness, looking at the piano and not seeing him sitting there, as he had a hundred times in the past.

She walked over to the piano and sat down on the padded bench. The music stand was empty, the can-

delabras holding unburned candles. Clearly the room had been kept up—there wasn't a trace of dust upon the instrument—but it had the empty feel of a place unoccupied.

Eleanor thought about the first time she had seen Sir Edmund. It had been at a musicale at Francis Buckminster's home. Eleanor had long been a patron of the arts. Though she did not possess any sort of artistic talent herself, her soul thrilled to the works of those who were talented in those areas, and she had always used part of her fortune to patronize the arts. Wherever she had lived, New York or London or Paris, she had been well-known for her fashionable salon attended by other patrons of the arts, as well as by the writers, composers and others whom she admired. She did not move among the most aristocratic circles in London, for despite her years at a finishing school in England, her American background and the trade-based origins of her family's wealth would forever make her socially inferior to the elite who ruled London society. But she had a broad circle of friends and acquaintances that consisted of artists and their patrons, so she enjoyed a lively social scene frequented by people from all strata of society.

Sir Edmund had performed one of his sonatas at the musicale, and Eleanor had been struck not only by his virtuosity on the piano but also by the beauty of the piece, which had brought her almost to tears.

She had realized almost immediately that this pale, frail blond man was a musical genius.

Over the course of the next few weeks, the two of them had become friends. Unlike most of the artists she knew, he was not in need of financial help. But as she had gotten to know him better, she had realized that he was nevertheless in great need. His health was obviously precarious, for he was wracked by fits of coughing that left him weak and suggested to Eleanor that he was likely consumptive. The damp climate of England could not be good for his health, she thought, but when she had suggested that he travel to sunnier climes, he had only smiled wistfully and told her that he could not.

The reason he could not move, Eleanor soon learned, was his mother, a grasping, demanding, domineering woman who both leaned upon and dominated her only son. Whenever Sir Edmund left his home in the Kentish countryside to live on his own in London, he was soon bombarded with notes from his mother, all filled with problems that only he could solve or accounts of her loneliness without him. This servant or that was stealing from her; the estate manager would not give her enough money to run the house; his younger sister cried into her pillow at night, missing her dearest brother. The result was that Sir Edmund would go rushing home every week or two, abandoning the opera upon which he was working. Worse still, Lady Scarbrough would come

to London to visit, and when she was there, she demanded that her son accompany her to balls and soirees, escort her to Almack's and meet a number of marriageable women, all handpicked by Lady Scarbrough herself.

Sir Edmund invariably did as his mother bid, again neglecting his music to perform a number of chores that could have been done by any ninny, in Eleanor's opinion. To make up for the lost time, once she left he would then work late into the night on his music, free at last of his mother's presence. As often as not he forgot to eat, which did little to improve his health.

His servants were sloppy, his household poorly run, and he seemed to have only the vaguest idea about his income, whether from the estate that came with his title or from the money that had been left to him by his maternal grandfather. Such inattentiveness to the necessary details of his life did not surprise Eleanor; she was accustomed to artists and the way they often muddled through the practicalities of life.

She wished that she could simply take charge of his life. It was difficult for her to stand aside and watch people's lives run off course, and taking hold of a situation and making it work right was something she was extraordinarily good at. There were those, she knew, who termed her bossy and difficult. But she was also quite aware that the people who called her these things

were never the ones whom she had stepped in to help, but rather those who were benefiting from the muddle.

Eleanor had been certain that she could put Sir Edmund's life in better order. The problem, of course, was that she had no right to do any such thing. Edmund was a grown man, not some poor orphan or servant at the mercy of others. She could advise him what to do, of course—and generally did, if the opportunity presented itself—but Sir Edmund's abhorrence of any sort of conflict, along with his artist's lack of concern over mundane matters, generally kept him going in his usual rut.

Finally, one afternoon Edmund had come to her, looking drawn and gaunt, wracked by coughs and worried because his mother had written him, describing her loneliness in heart-wrenching words and adding a long list of things she needed to have done for her. Eleanor, alarmed at the state of his health and furious at Lady Scarbrough's selfishness, had been struck at last by the solution to the problem.

She had decided to marry Sir Edmund. As his wife, she could whip the household and his finances into shape, and see to it that he slept and ate properly. Most of all, she could shield him from his mother.

Of course, she did not love him in the way that a woman loved a man. Theirs would be, truly, a marriage of convenience. But Eleanor did not care about that. She had long ago decided that the sort of marriage other girls dreamed about was not for her.

The men who had pursued her were generally only interested in her fortune, and she was too clever and realistic to be fooled by their honeyed words. And the sort of men who were not interested in her wealth did not court her. They might be drawn by her beauty, but she had found that they quickly abandoned the chase.

She was too headstrong, her stepmother Lydia had told her, too stubborn and too capable. A man wanted a more willing wife, a softer woman, the sort who turned to him to solve problems for her instead of charging in herself to solve not only her own problems, but those of everyone else, as well.

Eleanor, frankly, had had no interest in marrying the sort of man who wanted that sort of woman for a wife. She had found most of the men who pursued her to be foolish or greedy or entirely too domineering—sometimes all three. She had no desire to become a wife who was subject to her husband's decisions, giving up control of her money and her life to him. At twenty-six, she considered herself a confirmed spinster and did not regard the prospect with dismay. She had come to believe that the romantic love other women swooned over was something they simply made up in their heads.

Marrying Sir Edmund had suited her perfectly. She would be able to take care of him and nurture his tremendous talent. She would make it possible for the world to be blessed by his music. And she

would take great enjoyment in once again setting a life in order.

Edmund had been equally willing. He admired Eleanor's strength and determination, and loved her as much as he was capable of loving anything besides his music. He was a passive creature, his strongest passions reserved for his art, and he was delighted to have Eleanor shoulder the burdens that had plagued him and kept him from his primary love.

Everything had worked out as she had planned. Edmund had moved into her well-ordered and smoothly-running household, and devoted himself to composing. Eleanor had seen to it that his finances and his health were both improved, and she had taken on his mother. The result, of course, was that Lady Scarbrough despised her, but Eleanor did not care for that. They had moved to Naples, and in the warm climate there, Sir Edmund had grown better daily. Eleanor had been quite pleased with what she had done.

And then Sir Edmund had died.

Tears sprang into Eleanor's eyes, and she ran her hand lovingly over the shining wood of the piano. It seemed too cruel a twist of fate that she had made such strides with Edmund's health, only to have him fall prey to a foolish boating accident.

She turned and went to the carved wooden box where her husband's ashes lay. Unconsciously, she

smoothed her forefinger over the intricately carved patterns. She had spent the past six months making sure that Edmund's last work, the glorious opera he had written, had been produced with all the care and dignity it deserved. But now that it was over, now that she had made sure Edmund's memory would be preserved in the music he had written, she felt empty and at loose ends.

The sadness she had helped to keep at bay with work had seeped in, and on the long voyage back to England, often alone in her cabin to avoid the company of the ubiquitous Colton-Smythes, she had had to face the fact that, despite the children and her friends and the people who worked for her, she was lonely. There was an emptiness in her life, she thought, one she had never even realized was there. And while she might have become aware of it since her husband's death, she knew it had been there long before that.

Eleanor caught the direction of her thoughts and gave herself a mental shake. She was not going to dwell on such things. There were still things to be done for Edmund. She must take his ashes to his estate in the country and see that they were interred in his family's mausoleum. And she must meet with his mother and sister, and explain in more detail the provisions of Sir Edmund's will.

She could imagine how Honoria Scarbrough had reacted to the news that Eleanor would be the

guardian of her daughter's estate until she reached the age of twenty-one. It would be a difficult visit, followed by six more years of difficulty in dealing with the woman. It was not a duty she looked forward to, but she would do it. It was the last thing that Edmund had asked of her, and she would follow it through.

With a sigh, Eleanor turned and left the music room, going upstairs to her bedroom. The footmen were in the process of bringing in her trunks, and two maids were bustling around, putting her things away. She moved out of their way, going to the window and looking out at the street scene below.

Dusk had fallen. Down the way, she could see the lamplighter lighting the street lamp. The street was deserted except for him as he made his way toward her. He illuminated the light directly across from her house, and as it sprang into being, a form was revealed standing beside the tree across from her door. It was a man, motionless, staring straight up at her window.

With a startled gasp, Eleanor stepped back, away from his sight, her heart pounding. Quickly, she recovered her composure and stepped back up to the window. The dark form was gone.

She glanced up and down the street, staring intently into the darkness, but she could see no sign of him. *Had he been watching her house? Or was it only happenstance that she had looked out just as he*

had glanced up? Eleanor would have liked to believe the latter, but there had been something about the way he was standing, a stillness in his body, an intensity in his face, that hinted that he had been there some time. And he had left as soon as she saw him. That in itself indicated that he had not been there for a legitimate purpose.

Eleanor frowned. She was not usually the sort to worry. But she could not help but remember the odd incident a week or so before she had left Naples, when the house seemed to have been entered— things shoved out of place, a lock broken on one of the windows. Nothing had been taken, which in itself seemed strange. She had dismissed it, but now she could not help but wonder. *Why would anyone be watching her house?*

A little shiver ran down her spine. There was no reason to be afraid, she told herself. And yet, she realized, she was.

ELEANOR SPENT THE NEXT DAY settling in. She told Bartwell to make sure that the locks on all windows and doors were engaged, and that the house was secured at night. Then, having taken precautions in her customary way, she put the thought of the man watching her house out of her mind. Instead, she concentrated on the myriad details concerning her business that had sprung up in the days she had been out of reach on board the ship, as well as the small

but necessary items that were involved in getting the household running again. She penned a note to her friend Juliana to let her know that she was once more in town.

Juliana had been her closest friend for over ten years, from the time they had met at school. Eleanor's widowed father, with whom she had been very close throughout her childhood, had remarried when she was fourteen, and Eleanor's stepmother, jealous of the bond between them, had convinced Eleanor's father that only a finishing at a refined young women's academy would turn Eleanor into a proper and marriageable young lady. The girl's willful nature, she had assured him with a soft, dimpling smile, would doom her to a life of unhappy solitude if he did not make a push to change her. So Eleanor had been shipped off to the school in England, a desperately lonely girl in a foreign land.

Eleanor had found herself an outcast at school, ostracized for her American accent, odd ways and, most of all, lack of English lineage. Her loneliness had ended, however, when she found Juliana. Juliana, too, had been snubbed by the other girls, because it was well known that even though her birth was impeccable, her father had died when she was young, leaving her and her mother penniless. They had lived ever since on the generosity of their relatives, and Juliana was at the school only to look after her cousin Seraphina.

Eleanor and Juliana had quickly found in each

other a similar streak of independence—even, at times, of rebellion—as well as a common sense of compassion and a lively sense of humor. They had become inseparable, and in the years since they had left school, they had maintained their friendship, despite periods of separation. Juliana had stayed with Eleanor now and then; Eleanor would have welcomed her to live in her household, but Juliana had been too proud to accept Eleanor's generosity. Instead, she had worked as a paid companion for several years. Then, six months ago, just after Eleanor and Edmund had gone to Italy, Juliana had married Lord Barre. Eleanor had met Lord Barre, and though she did not know him well, she liked what she had seen of him. She was looking forward to seeing both of them again soon.

After she wrote to Juliana and sent the note off with a servant, Eleanor started on the mail that awaited her. As she was working, one of the footmen brought in a piece of paper, folded into a square and sealed with the wax imprint of some sort of heraldic device, just delivered, he explained, by a liveried servant.

Eleanor's eyebrows went up. Her friends and acquaintances were generally less formal—and less monied—than the sort who sent liveried servants with missives. Moreover, it seemed strange that anyone could know that she was once again in residence. Juliana had known that she was returning at

some point, but even she would not know that Eleanor had actually arrived until she received the note Eleanor had only just now sent her. It seemed unlikely, if not impossible, that her friend could have already received it and sent her a reply.

She took the envelope from the silver salver that the footman extended to her and broke the seal. Her eyes went immediately to the signature at the bottom, a bold scrawl that took her a moment to decipher. *Anthony, Lord Neale.*

Eleanor set down the piece of paper, startled. She felt suddenly flushed, and her pulse sped up. The reaction irritated her, and she grimaced. Just the sight of a person's name should not affect her so, she told herself. Other people had been rude and condescending to her—she had, after all, dealt with the English *ton* since her days at school—and she had learned to shrug off their snobbish attitude. Besides, she was quite aware of the fact that the man's dislike of her stemmed from his own self-interest. He was Edmund's uncle, Lady Scarbrough's brother, and Eleanor suspected that he had relied on Edmund's generosity to supplement Lady Scarbrough, so he could maintain a hold on his own fortune for his own amusements, whatever they might be. Or perhaps, even worse, he, too, had lived off Edmund's fortune and had intended to use Edmund's own money to bribe her. It was little wonder that he had reacted

poorly to the news that Edmund had married Eleanor.

When he had come to see her a year ago to forbid her to marry his nephew, she had been disappointed. Until that point, she had harbored some hope that Lord Neale would welcome her to the family. After all, Edmund obviously admired his uncle and had assured her that Anthony would like her. But when she saw Lord Neale waiting for her in the entryway, she had quickly relinquished all such illusions.

He was, she had been surprised to see, not the older gentleman she had expected, but a tall, virile-looking man no more than a few years older than she was. Obviously, he was the much younger brother of Sir Edmund's mother. He was not what one would call handsome, exactly; his face was too square, his features too hard, for that. But there was a strength in him that drew her gaze and held it. His brows were straight, dark slashes across his forehead, and the eyes beneath them were cool and gray, defined by thick dark lashes.

In other circumstances, Eleanor would have labeled his face compelling, and she had felt a startling and distinct attraction to him, a reaction so unusual and so unwanted that she had come to a sudden halt, feeling oddly girlish and unsure. But then she had noticed the cold, polite set of his attractive face, and she had known that this man was her enemy. She had seen the expression on his face too

many times before—the cool hauteur of an English gentleman, convinced of his own superiority over everyone else in the world. She had known that he would not be pleased at the idea of his nephew marrying an American who could not trace her ancestors back to the Norman conquerors, and even less pleased at the idea of her putting an end to Edmund's easygoing habit of giving money to his relatives.

She had been right, of course. Lord Neale had told her bluntly that she must not marry Edmund, and she had been pleased to inform him that his was a lost cause, as she and Edmund had married the day before by special license. This last announcement had come after a sharp exchange of words during which Lord Neale had accused her of being a fortune-hunting harpy. By the time he left, Eleanor had been trembling with fury and filled with a deep, passionate dislike of Lord Neale.

Clearly, she thought, a year's absence had not lessened that feeling. Just remembering their meeting filled her with a nerve-jangling irritation. Taking a calming breath, she began to read. His note was short and peremptory, a terse request to call upon her to discuss matters.

Eleanor's mouth twitched with the beginnings of a smile. She had a good idea what "matters" the man wanted to discuss. Edmund, despite his love for his mother, was well aware of her spendthrift qual-

ities, and he had wanted to make sure that his sister had enough money to make her independent. His faith in Eleanor was as deep as his trust of his mother was not, so he had appointed Eleanor trustee of the money he left to Samantha.

No doubt Lady Honoria had kicked up a fuss when she had learned the terms of her son's will, and that would be the reason for Lord Neale's wish to speak to her. Eleanor took out a sheet of fine vellum and quickly wrote a note equal in length to the one Lord Neale had sent her, informing him that she was not receiving visitors. Her spirits somewhat lifted by this exercise, she signed and sealed the missive, and handed it to one of the footmen to take to Lord Neale. She sat back in her chair, a smile playing on her lips, envisioning the man's face when he got the letter.

Her spirits were further raised an hour later when she received an answer from her friend Juliana, who, thrilled to have Eleanor in London again, invited her to dinner that evening. It would be, Juliana assured her, a private dinner, quite suitable even to one in mourning.

Eleanor immediately sent back her acceptance. Even if she had still been in full mourning, she would have gone to visit Juliana. As it was, after six months of wearing all black, she had gone into half-mourning. There were those who insisted on a full year of mourning after the death of a loved one, but neither Eleanor nor Sir Edmund had been sticklers

for such traditions. Love and respect, as well as missing someone, were not, in her opinion, things that could be measured by the cloth one wore nor the length of time one wore it.

LATE IN THE AFTERNOON, a little after tea, Eleanor's butler stepped into the room, saying, "There's a gentleman here to see you, miss."

Eleanor raised her eyebrows, surprised. "Who?"

"Master Edmund's uncle, miss." Bartwell's scowl left little doubt as to how he felt about the man, a fact that was confirmed by his ensuing words. "I left him waiting in the entry and said I'd see if you wanted to speak with him."

Eleanor smothered a smile. She could imagine how well the proud Lord Neale would have taken that snub. She doubted if he was ever left to cool his heels in the hallway when he called on someone, much less was told bluntly that the butler would check to see if he would be received.

Of course, Lord Neale was no stranger to rudeness. He had shown quite a bit of it himself by calling on her only a few hours after she had sent him a note expressly telling him that she was not receiving visitors. Obviously he was not accustomed to people turning him down.

"Please remind Lord Neale that I am not receiving visitors, as I have already told him," Eleanor said crisply.

Bartwell's lips twitched with satisfaction, and he said, "He won't like that much, I'll warrant."

"I daresay not." Eleanor grinned. "But if he is rude to you, you have my full permission to throw him out of the house."

Bartwell's eyes lit up, and Eleanor knew he was hoping that the man would be recalcitrant. There were times when Bartwell considered his present life a trifle too dull.

After he left, Eleanor listened for sounds of an altercation, but she heard none, so she assumed that his lordship must have left peacefully enough. She wished she could have been there to see his face when Bartwell delivered her message. Indeed, she had been tempted to see Lord Neale just to tell him to his face that she did not care to talk to him. But, of course, that would have defeated the whole purpose of the message.

After that, Eleanor found it difficult to concentrate on anything. Her mind kept returning to Lord Neale and his unmitigated gall in coming to call on her this afternoon, wondering whether he would attempt to do so again and whether he would be with his sister when Eleanor met with Lady Honoria. Finally she gave up trying to work and went upstairs to dress for her dinner that night with Juliana and her husband.

After some consideration she chose a half-mourning white dress with a modest black train that

fell from the shoulders in back. Her maid dressed her hair simply, winding a black velvet ribbon through her dark curls, and her only ornamentation was a black stone brooch that Edmund had given her not long before he died. Made in the Italian *pietra dura* style, the center was a cluster of white and pink flowers, each tiny piece inlaid into the dark stone. Though it was not precisely a mourning brooch, as it contained colors, Eleanor had worn it as such because Edmund had given it to her. After he died, she had remembered how he had put it in her palm, folding her fingers over it and saying earnestly that she must wear it for his sake. At the time she had found his solemn manner odd, but also rather sweet and touching. Afterwards, she had wondered if he had suffered some premonition of his death…or, even worse, if he had known that his death would come because he had planned it.

Eleanor pushed the dark thought away. She would not let it intrude on this happy evening, when she was going to see her friend again after a year's separation.

Quickly she pinned the brooch onto her dress and took a last glance at herself in the mirror. She was, she knew, a statuesque woman, far from the ideal of the dainty pink-and-white, fair-haired English beauty. Though her eyes were fine and her skin creamy, her features were too large, her mouth too wide, her jaw too strong. But she looked, she

thought, attractive tonight. Simple styles in dress and hair always suited her, and the prospect of an enjoyable evening ahead had put color in her cheeks and brightened her eyes—something that had been missing in her recently.

Eleanor picked up her fan from the dresser and allowed her maid to drape her light evening cloak about her shoulders, then went down to the carriage that waited outside. Her coachman tipped his hat to her as Bartwell helped her up into the carriage, a task he reserved to himself whenever possible.

Eleanor settled against the soft leather back of the seat as the carriage rattled away from the house. They stopped at the next corner, then turned onto the cross street, and as the carriage began to move, the door suddenly opened and a man swung inside.

CHAPTER THREE

ELEANOR SUCKED IN HER BREATH sharply, her heart pounding, every nerve standing on end. Her mind flew to the pistol that she carried concealed in a compartment beside the seat, but even as she thought of it, she recognized the man who had entered her carriage in such an unconventional manner. Her intruder was Lord Neale.

She had seen him only one time, but he was not an easy man to forget. Eleanor relaxed. She disliked Neale thoroughly, but at least she felt sure that he had not entered her coach to rob or attack her. The fear that had rushed through her at his intrusion turned in an instant to an anger just as intense. He was, she thought, a perfectly loathsome man. No doubt he had intended to frighten her and thus gain the upper hand.

Well, he would find out that Eleanor Townsend Scarbrough was made of rather sterner stuff, she thought grimly. Tamping down her anger, she kept her expression cool and unruffled, simply gazing at

him with raised eyebrows for a long moment while she gave her heart a chance to stop racing.

"Lord Neale," she greeted him calmly. "To what, may I ask, do I owe this unexpected visit?"

His lips twitched—she wasn't sure if it was with a smile or in chagrin. Eleanor's gaze was drawn to his mouth, and she noted the sensually full lower lip, the sharply cut upper lip. His was a very appealing mouth. Quickly, a trifle shocked at her own thought, she pulled her gaze back up to his cool gray eyes. He was a handsome man, she thought, in a hard sort of way, with fiercely jutting cheekbones and an unyielding jaw. She had told herself over the course of the last year that he had not been as attractive as she remembered. But she realized now that he was, if anything, more good-looking.

"Nothing surprises you, does it?" he asked.

"Is that what you hoped to do?" Eleanor countered. "Inspire terror in my poor maidenly heart? Is that the reason for your, shall we say, unorthodox entrance?"

"No," he replied with some irritation. "The reason for my jumping into your carriage is that you refused me when I asked to call upon you earlier."

"I notice that it did not stop you from coming to my house anyway," Eleanor put in tartly.

"No," he admitted without even the semblance of shame. "But it was of little help, since you still would not see me." He shrugged. "I had to find some other way."

"So you feel I haven't the right to choose whom I will see and when?" she asked.

His fierce black slashes of eyebrows drew together in a scowl. "Of course you have the right. I, however, have the right to find a way to reach you."

"By accosting me?"

"'Accost' is a rather harsh term," he responded, something that was very close to a twinkle warming his eyes.

"And what would you call it?"

He smiled faintly. "I am merely bringing myself to your attention."

Eleanor refused to respond to his smile. It was bad enough that he had forced his way into her vehicle. She certainly was not about to let him charm her out of her anger now. She crossed her arms and gazed back at him, keeping the aloof look firmly fixed on her face. "All right. Now that you have my attention, what is so urgent? I assume that you are once again acting as your sister's messenger."

She had not told her husband about the first time that Lord Neale had come to visit her; Edmund would have been upset about the insult offered her, and it would have been to no purpose. After all, she had married Edmund precisely to shield him from these sorts of worldly problems. Besides, Edmund had held an affection for his uncle. He had once told her that Lord Neale was a "bang-up fellow." He was,

Edmund had assured her, one who did not fuss and interfere, and he was the one to go to if one had a problem. Anthony, he said, always knew just what to do, and he would not run to Edmund's mother about it, either. So, not wanting to cause her husband disappointment, Eleanor had refrained from telling him what manner of man she had found Lord Neale to be. But, privately, she was certain that he was either securely under Lady Honoria's thumb or in league with her, even living, as she did, off Edmund's generosity.

The brief hint of a smile disappeared from his face. "Lady Scarbrough is in great distress over the death of her son."

Eleanor simply waited, saying nothing. It seemed to her the normal reaction of a mother to the death of her son—even though she cynically suspected that in this case it was the loss of her son's largesse that Lady Honoria regretted the most.

Lord Neale paused, as though choosing his words carefully, then added, "Edmund was always rather frail, but none of us expected his death to come as it did."

"Nor did I," Eleanor agreed, still wondering why he should jump into her carriage to tell her such obvious things.

"I never knew him to go sailing," he went on finally, his eyes intent on her face.

"He took it up in Italy," Eleanor explained. "I was

somewhat surprised myself. I suppose it was because it was so much warmer there...and his health had improved considerably."

"Then he was doing better?" Lord Neale asked.

"Yes, certainly." She refrained from adding that that was precisely what she had thought would happen and why she had insisted on going to Italy despite Lady Honoria's objections. "His coughing was diminished, his color improved. He became more active. He made several friends and went out with them frequently. Actually, it was they who got him interested in sailing."

"You did not go with him?"

Eleanor shook her head, still at a loss as to what Lord Neale's interest in all this was. "He went with his friend Dario Paradella, usually." She shrugged. "And others."

"Was he with this Paradella fellow when he died?"

"No. He was alone." Eleanor frowned. "Why are you asking these questions? What is it you want to know?"

"The name of someone who can confirm your story," he replied bluntly.

Eleanor stared at him. "Confirm my—" She stopped, finally understanding the direction of his conversation. "My *story?*" she hissed. "You dare to imply that I—that I made it up?"

"Did you?" he responded, watching her coolly.

"Of course not! Why would I make up such a—" Fury swept through her, white-hot. Her eyes flashed. "You are accusing me of murdering Edmund?"

Lord Neale did not deny her words, simply continued to look at her levelly.

"How can you be so vile?" Eleanor was so consumed by anger that she could barely speak. "You are inhuman! A monster! A—" She could think of no word bad enough to describe him.

"I notice that you have not denied the charge," he commented calmly.

"I have no obligation to answer to you!" Eleanor spat. "I don't have to prove anything to you just because you have a low, suspicious mind. Edmund died exactly as I told his mother. Clearly the Italian authorities had no questions about his death."

"Unless their heads were turned by beauty," he murmured. "Or money…"

Enraged, Eleanor swung at him with all her might, no ladylike slap, but a doubled-up fist. Lord Neale, however, was faster than she, and his hand flew out and wrapped around her wrist, stopping her swing in midair. His hold was like iron, biting painfully into her flesh, and Eleanor could not move her hand. She glared at him, and he stared back at her with a gaze equally hard and bright. The very air between them seemed to vibrate.

They remained frozen in position, his hand hot on

the bare flesh of her arm. His eyes bored into hers, then dropped fractionally to her mouth, and for a brief, crazy moment, Eleanor thought that he was about to kiss her.

Abruptly he released her arm and sat back in his seat. Her hand dropped numbly into her lap. "Get out of my carriage! Now!"

"Calm down and listen to me."

"Calm down? You jump into my carriage and accuse me of killing my husband, and you tell me to calm down?" Eleanor exclaimed.

"I did not actually accuse you of anything."

"You accused me of making up a story about how he died," she shot back. "You implied that I—that I—"

"Got rid of an inconvenient husband?" Anthony finished for her, his eyes intent upon her face.

She was pale, except for the bright spots of color that rage had put in her cheeks. Her vivid eyes were huge, midnight blue in the dim light of the carriage. She was startlingly beautiful, he thought. Thinner than when he had last seen her—too thin, really. Her cheekbones were too prominent in her face; her wrist had felt impossibly small in his hand.

He shoved down the sympathy that rose involuntarily in him. If his sister was right, this lovely creature had cold-bloodedly murdered his nephew.

Anthony went on roughly. "You married a frail man, one obviously dying of consumption. But then

you moved to Naples and his health improved. That was a miscalculation on your part, wasn't it? Now you were faced with a husband who might live for several years or more. You would have to put up with his demands. Or perhaps there was another man, someone you wanted, and your husband had become an inconvenience. Whatever the reason, you decided to hurry his death along. You killed him, then made up the sailing story to tell his grieving mother. Then you burned his body so that if anyone became suspicious, they would not be able to tell how he died."

Anthony watched her closely as he spoke, alert for any telltale sign of guilt.

Eleanor let her hand fall back into her lap. Her eyes were dark with disgust. "You and Lady Honoria certainly have vivid imaginations. What do you expect me to do now? Cry and confess my sins?" Her lip curled in contempt. "You are an even greater fool than I thought you were."

Neale's stomach tightened. She still had not denied his statements. "Why? Because I thought you might act honestly?"

"No. Because you are so hungry for Edmund's money that you are willing to say anything to get rid of me."

"I don't give a damn about Edmund's money," he retorted. "But if he was killed, I *will* see his murderer punished. I can promise you that."

His eyes were hard as stone. Eleanor gazed back at him with an equally obdurate gaze. Her dislike of this man was so intense that it was like a huge ball in her chest, fiery and hard, threatening to explode. She curled her gloved fingers tightly into her palms, struggling to retain her usual calm self-possession.

She wasn't sure why Lord Neale's accusation enraged her so. She knew that he and Edmund's mother thoroughly disliked her. It shouldn't surprise her that Lady Scarbrough and her brother would go to such an extent to discredit her. But his words had sliced through her like a knife.

"A very noble sentiment," Eleanor said scornfully. "Since there is little likelihood of your having to follow through, as Edmund was not murdered. But no doubt it will sound good to the others at your club. And, of course, there is the added benefit of blackening my reputation. Everyone will repeat your vile rumors, even though there isn't the slightest shred of evidence, merely the fevered imaginings of a pair of greedy relatives."

His nostrils flared at her biting words, and he opened his mouth to refute her. But at that moment the carriage came to a stop, surprising them both. Eleanor glanced out the window and saw that they had halted in front of an elegant town house of pale yellow stone. Her driver jumped down and opened the door.

"Barre House, my lady," he intoned. Then his

gaze fell upon Anthony sitting in the carriage, and he goggled at him. "My lady! How—who—"

"Lord Neale joined me along the way, as you can see," Eleanor said with heavy irony. She got up and stepped out of the carriage, saying, "Perhaps you will take him back to his house while I am visiting Lord and Lady Barre."

"No need to go to the trouble," Anthony said behind her, jumping lightly down to the ground beside Eleanor. "I will escort Lady Scarbrough inside."

He offered her his arm, and when Eleanor gaped at him in astonishment, he picked up her hand and tucked it into the crook of his elbow. "Come, my lady, I am sure our hosts are waiting."

"What do you think you're doing?" Eleanor snapped, trying in vain to tug her hand from his grasp. "You cannot go in with me."

"Ah, but I already am," he responded with an irritating coolness. "You see, I intend to stay with you until you give me a satisfactory answer to my questions."

"Questions? Accusations, rather! I have no intention of talking to you, now or at any other time. You know there is no truth to what you are saying, and I certainly would not lend any credence to your absurd accusations by trying to defend myself."

He shrugged as he walked up the steps. "Then I fear you will have to suffer my company for some time."

A liveried footman opened the door before they reached it and bowed to them. "Lady Scarbrough?"

"And Lord Neale," Anthony added calmly, handing his hat to the man.

Eleanor, struck speechless by the man's audacity, handed her wrap over to the footman. It was an unaccustomed position for her to be in, but, frankly, she was at a loss as to what to do. If she told the footman that Lord Neale was not supposed to be there and he should throw him out, she would be putting the poor footman in an untenable position. Her own servants would readily toss out anyone at her command, noble or ruffian, but the average London servant would be horrified at the idea of laying hands on a peer of the realm. Besides, it was such an absurd thing to say that, frankly, she was too embarrassed to utter the words.

As the servant turned to lead them down the hallway, Lord Neale offered his arm to her again, but Eleanor did not take it, clasping her hands together.

"Are you mad?" she whispered at him as they followed the servant. "You were not invited. You cannot simply barge in on someone."

He cocked an eyebrow. "Can I not? They might, perhaps, think it rude of you not to have informed them that I was escorting you, but..."

"Rude? *You* are the rudest man I have ever met, and I shall be happy to tell them that you forced your way into my carriage."

"Really?" He looked at her quizzically. "You want to explain all this to them?"

Eleanor set her jaw in irritation. He was right, of course; she certainly did not want to embroil Juliana and her husband in this situation. However absurd Lord Neale's accusations were, and however little Juliana would believe them, it would place her friend in a very uncomfortable position. And though Eleanor had met Lord Barre on a few occasions, she did not know him well, and she had no idea how he would take such accusations. What if he, like a true aristocrat, chose to believe Lord Neale? Eleanor had no desire to be the cause of any friction between the newlyweds.

"You know I do not," she said in a low voice, charged with emotion. "You are an unfeeling—"

She cut off her words as the footman stopped at an open doorway and announced their names. He stepped aside to allow Eleanor and her companion to enter. Across the room, Juliana was seated on a blue velvet sofa, a tall, dark man beside her. At the footman's announcement, Juliana bounded up from the sofa and hurried toward them. Her husband, Nicholas, followed somewhat more slowly.

"Eleanor!" Juliana threw her arms around her taller friend and hugged her. "Oh, I am so happy to see you. It has been so long."

"Juliana!" Eleanor's irritation with Lord Neale disappeared under the force of her affection for her friend, and she hugged her back. "I've missed you...."

Finally Eleanor released Juliana and stepped back a bit to stare at her. "You look very well."

It was the truth. Juliana had always been attractive, but she positively glowed with happiness now, and it was this, more than the expensive dress or the fashionable hairstyle, that made her beautiful. Her large, gray eyes were alight, and her creamy skin was rosy with pleasure. Her face, Eleanor noted, was softer and rounder than before, and as Eleanor's eyes dropped down her friend's figure, she saw that Juliana's formerly slender body was now roundly curved.

"Juliana!" Eleanor gasped, her eyes flying to the other woman's questioningly.

Juliana nodded, with a happy laugh. "Yes, I am."

"Why did you not write to me?" Eleanor cried, grinning, and enveloped the other woman in another hug. "I am so happy for you."

"I started to, but when you wrote that you were returning, well, I wanted to surprise you."

"You have indeed."

Juliana could not seem to stop smiling, but her eyes flickered a little curiously to Lord Neale, standing a bit behind Eleanor, politely waiting.

"Oh, I'm sorry. Allow me to introduce you to Lord Neale." Eleanor turned toward the man, her manner coolly polite. "Sir Edmund's uncle. He was kind enough to offer to escort me here. I hope you will not mind."

"Of course not," Juliana responded quickly, flashing a smile at Anthony. "You are quite welcome, my lord. I know that Eleanor appreciates your help and support in her grief."

"Neale," Juliana's husband said in greeting, nodding to Anthony.

"Lord Barre. Good to see you again."

"Then you two know each other," Juliana said, pleased.

"We have run into each other now and then at White's," Nicholas Barre answered. "Neither of us, I fear, is a terribly regular member."

"No. In general, I prefer the comforts of my own home," Anthony agreed with a smile.

One would have thought Lord Neale a perfectly amiable sort, Eleanor thought sourly, to hear him. It galled her to have to go along with his charade. Still, there was little she could do except return Lord Barre's greeting politely.

They sat down, exchanging casual small talk until the meal was announced. Lord Neale, though polite and polished, offered little conversation except in response to others' remarks. Eleanor was uncomfortably aware of his penetrating gaze upon her throughout the conversation. She felt sure he was judging her, looking for some chink in her armor, some remark or gesture that he could use against her. It was irritating to realize that she was watching her words, examining them for any way in which they

could be misinterpreted, before she spoke, aware that any laugh or smile on her part would doubtless be evidence to him that she had not loved Edmund.

Damn his eyes, she thought, borrowing one of her father's favorite curses. She had never cared what people thought, and she was not going to start now. She refused to let some arrogant British lord rattle her. Eleanor turned toward him, lifting her chin and giving him a long, cool look. And though there was no movement in his face, she saw a subtle change, and she knew that he had seen her defiant look and acknowledged it.

After that, she did her best to maintain a polite indifference to the man, ignoring him and concentrating on the pleasure of once again visiting with her best friend. Amazingly enough, the evening moved along easily. Eleanor and Juliana rarely lacked for topics of conversation, and after Eleanor's long absence, there was much to catch up on. Juliana and Nicholas filled her in on all the major scandals and on-dits among the fashionable *ton,* as well as in the government, and the state of the theater and opera was thoroughly rehashed. Lord Neale, though he did not speak a great deal, kept his remarks on a light and lively plane. He was knowledgeable on a variety of topics, and his opinions, often tinged by sarcasm, were incisive and accurate. Eleanor had to acknowledge that had he been anyone else, she would have found his company enjoyable and invigorating. In

fact, on more than one occasion, she had to remind herself why he was there.

Of course, she thought grimly, Lord Neale would not let her forget it. She knew that his steady regard throughout the evening was meant to keep her aware of his intent, as was the faintly ironic undertone to his words whenever he spoke to her. When the evening was over, she would have to face him alone again, and he would insist on answers to his questions. No doubt he hoped that threat would frighten her. Well, he would soon find out that she was made of sterner stuff.

After the meal, the two men retired to Lord Barre's library, as was the custom, leaving Eleanor and Juliana alone together for a good long talk, which suited them both admirably.

"I am so happy for you," Eleanor told her friend, her gaze going to Juliana's gently swelling belly. "When are you due?"

Juliana smiled broadly. "A little more than three months. I wanted to have my lying-in at the family home in Cornwall, where Nicholas lived until his parents died. But he insisted that we remain in London, where I could have the care of the best doctors." Her smile turned fond. "He worries far more about me than is necessary. I am healthy as a horse."

"Of course he does," Eleanor responded. "He obviously dotes on you. Which is just as it should be."

Eleanor had met Nicholas Barre a year ago, just before she and Edmund had left for Naples. He had asked Juliana to marry him, and though Juliana assured her that his proposal was merely evidence of his kindness and fondness for a childhood companion, Eleanor had suspected that it was love for Juliana that lay at the base of his offer of marriage. He might have been hiding it from Juliana and even from himself, but Eleanor had seen the truth in the way he looked at Juliana. It was clear, watching them tonight, that she had been right.

Juliana and Nicholas clearly adored one another. It was, Eleanor thought, the sort of marriage that young girls dreamed of, the kind of love made famous by poets. Watching them through dinner, seeing the love that shone in their eyes when they looked at each other, that expressed itself in a brush of his fingers along her shoulder or the way her hand curled around his arm as he escorted her in to dinner, Eleanor had felt an unaccustomed pang. She had never known such love, and she was realistic enough to admit that she probably never would. The fond admiration and caring she had felt for Edmund had held none of the depth and passion that lay in Juliana and Nicholas's love.

Eleanor did not normally wish for such a feeling in her life. She knew that she was simply too practical and levelheaded for such dramatic emotion, and, quite frankly, she liked the way she lived her

life. But at a moment like this, she could not help but give a little inward sigh and wonder what it would be like to love as Juliana and Nicholas did.

Juliana let out a happy little laugh at her friend's words. "Yes," she admitted. "He does. And I love him just as much. Oh, Eleanor, sometimes I have to pinch myself, my life seems so much like a dream. A year and a half ago, when I was working for that odious Mrs. Thrall, I could not have imagined that I would be so happy today."

"It is no more than you deserve," Eleanor told her firmly.

"But enough about me," Juliana said now, leaning in confidentially. "Tell me about you and Lord Neale."

Eleanor looked at her friend. She had always confided in Juliana, and she wanted to tell her exactly what had transpired between her and Lord Neale. But it seemed even worse, now that she knew Juliana was pregnant, to drag her into the middle of Eleanor's own problems.

"There is nothing to tell, really," Eleanor said with a shrug. "I did not ask him to escort me here this evening. He more or less invited himself. And I did not want to create a scene. I apologize for thrusting him upon you uninvited."

"It was no problem, I assure you. I am glad that you had someone to escort you, frankly. London is not a safe city. Perhaps he was simply concerned

about you," Juliana suggested. "He seemed terribly attentive to you."

"Oh, yes, he is attentive—in the way an eagle is attentive to a rabbit."

Juliana's brows went up. "Whatever do you mean? Is something amiss?"

Eleanor firmly squelched her desire to pour out the whole story and said, "No, not really. It is just that I dislike dealing with the man. He has always been quite rude. He did not consider me an appropriate match for Edmund."

"Then he was a fool. But perhaps now he realizes how wrong he was. Perhaps he is trying to make it up to you, and that is why he wanted to escort you."

"Perhaps," Eleanor responded noncommittally, looking down at her hands. She did not see the shrewd gaze that Juliana turned upon her.

"He is a terribly handsome man," Juliana said after a moment.

"Is he?" Eleanor grimaced. "I hadn't noticed."

Juliana laughed. "Surely you don't expect me to swallow that fib."

"He is…handsome, in a harsh sort of way," Eleanor admitted. "'Tis a pity that his nature does not match his appearance."

"Yes." Juliana sighed, looking disappointed. "I had hoped…"

"Now, Juliana, do not turn matchmaker on me, I pray. What is it that makes a woman want to marry

off her friends as soon as she gets married herself?" Eleanor's smile took the sting from her words.

Juliana chuckled. "I am guilty, I confess. It is just that I am so happy, I want you to have the same sort of happiness."

"Well, I do not think I will find it with the odious Lord Neale—nor he with me. I do not need a husband. I am fine just as I am, I assure you."

"I know. I have no doubts that you handle everything perfectly," Juliana told her. "It is only love that I wish for you."

"But I have love. I have Claire and Nathan and you."

"That isn't the sort of love I meant," Juliana pointed out. "And you are well aware of that."

"I do not think I am destined for the sort of love you are talking about. I do not think I am a woman who would be happy married. I am more accustomed to telling others what to do than to being told."

"You think Nicholas tells me what to do?" Juliana asked indignantly.

"Does he not?"

Juliana started to answer, then stopped and let out a little laugh. "Well, yes, he does—but it is nearly always out of concern for me. He wants to protect me even when I haven't the slightest need for it. However, that does not mean that I follow his orders or that he tries to force me to. I have even on

occasion given him my opinion of what *he* should do. 'Tis a natural enough thing between husband and wife." She looked at Eleanor a little quizzically. "Surely you know that. You were married."

"Edmund and I had a…different sort of marriage. He needed my help. I do not think that Lord Neale does."

"Perhaps he just does not know it."

Eleanor cast her friend a sardonic glance, one eyebrow raised. "Why are you so set on Lord Neale?"

Juliana shrugged. "I am not *set* on him. It is just that there seemed to be…I don't know. I cannot explain it, really. There was just something between the two of you this evening."

"I think it is called mutual dislike," Eleanor responded.

"You may call it that if you wish. But I have never noticed dislike putting such a glow on a woman's face as I saw on yours tonight."

Eleanor's eyes widened in surprise, and she was suddenly at a loss for words. She was saved from having to respond to her friend by the arrival of Juliana's husband and Lord Neale, who strolled into the drawing room and sat down with them.

Nicholas suggested that Juliana play for them, so she moved to the piano and played a few songs, insisting that Eleanor join her. Eleanor turned the pages for her and added her passable alto voice to

Juliana's melodious soprano. Eleanor was grateful for something to do. She would have been hard-pressed to carry on a decent conversation, the way her mind was whirling from Juliana's words.

Her friend was wrong, of course, she told herself. If there was any special glow on her face this evening, it had sprung from anger, not any sort of interest in Lord Neale. Perhaps, she admitted, she had felt some small tug of attraction to the man when she first met him, but that had been before she talked to him, before she found out what a rude and thoroughly dislikeable man he was. And if her pulse had picked up tonight when he entered her carriage, it was only because he had startled her. It had nothing to do with his well-modeled lips or clear gray eyes.

She glanced at him as she sang. He was leaning back in his chair, long legs stretched out in front of him and his arms crossed, watching her. She stumbled on the words and turned quickly back to the music, a blush rising in her cheeks. *The devil take the man!*

She was careful not to look at him again.

Not long after that, Eleanor took her leave, thanking Juliana and Nicholas for the evening and the meal. She had, despite Lord Neale's presence, enjoyed it. Neale, of course, was quick to offer his escort.

"Thank you, but it is not necessary, my lord," Eleanor told him without any real hope that he would agree. "I can manage quite well, I assure you."

"No doubt. But I insist." His gray eyes gazed into hers challengingly.

"Of course." Eleanor thrust her hands into her gloves with a trifle more force than was necessary.

She took the arm he offered and, with another farewell to their hosts, walked with him out to the waiting carriage. She allowed him to assist her into the carriage and watched, resigned, as he settled onto the seat across from her.

"Well?" he asked, as the coach rattled over the cobblestone streets. "Are you ready to answer my questions?"

Eleanor set her jaw. Her pride made her want to refuse. His very questions were an insult, and to answer them seemed to admit that he had some sort of right to question her. She hated to give him the satisfaction of explaining anything to him.

However, she had been thinking about the problem all evening, and she knew that it would be foolish to let her pride dictate to her in this matter. If she did not quash this story of his right at the beginning, she knew that he and his sister would spread the rumor all over the city. While she cared little for the opinion of the *ton,* she knew that this sort of story would travel into the set among which she and Edmund had socialized. She *did* care what many of that group thought of her, and such a rumor, once started, was difficult to dispel. Moreover, it would embroil Juliana in exactly the sort of situation in

which Eleanor did not want to involve her. Juliana would, of course, defend her friend; Eleanor knew how loyal she was. And that would put her at odds with the aristocratic society in which her marriage to Lord Barre had placed her.

Above all, she did not want Edmund's memory to be touched in any way by a scandal. His death had been a tragedy for the world of music, and she refused to let that fact be submerged under a storm of gossip and innuendo.

"I will not be questioned by you like a criminal," Eleanor told him coldly. "However, I have no intention of allowing you to drag Edmund's name or mine through the mud of scandal. So I will show you exactly how wrong you are."

"Very well."

They continued their ride to Eleanor's house in stony silence.

When they pulled up in front of the elegant white townhome some minutes later, Eleanor saw to her surprise that it was blazing with lights. A little prickle of unease ran through her, and she hurried down from the carriage, ignoring Lord Neale's proffered hand. He followed her as she swept up the steps and through the front door.

Instead of the tranquility of a houseful of inhabitants retired for the night, as one would have expected at this late hour, the front hall was a hubbub of people and noise. Two children in their night-

gowns sat on the stairs, interestedly watching the scene below them, where several servants in varying states of dress milled around, everyone seemingly talking at once. At the center of the activity was a dark, attractive young woman wrapped in a blue sari, her liquid dark eyes large and frightened, as she talked in a low voice to the two men before her. One of the men, a rough-looking sort whom Anthony remembered as Eleanor's butler, handed the woman a small glass of an amber liquid. The other man, a tall African dressed in a suit, was on one knee before the woman, looking anxiously into her face.

Eleanor's voice cut through the hum of talk. "What is going on here?"

Everyone turned and began to talk at once, their voices rising in a babble, until finally Lord Neale's voice rang out, overpowering all the others. "Silence!"

In the ringing quiet that followed, Eleanor said, "Bartwell?"

The rough-looking man replied, "A thief got into the house, Miss Elly."

The African man, who had risen and turned, but stayed protectively by the Indian woman's side, added, "And he assaulted Kerani."

CHAPTER FOUR

"WHAT!" Eleanor gasped, and swept forward toward the young woman. The servants parted quickly before her. She scarcely noticed that Lord Neale stayed at her side. "Kerani, are you all right?"

"No, no, it was not as it sounds," the woman replied softly, standing up and inclining her head in a little bow to Eleanor. "He only pushed me aside as he ran away. I stumbled and fell."

The man beside her snorted and said, "You would excuse the devil himself, ma'am. Pushing you down is an attack."

"Yes, of course it is, Zachary, but you are scarcely helping the poor girl standing over her glowering like that," Eleanor told him. "Now, Kerani…" She reached down and took the smaller woman's hand in hers and looked into her face. "Tell me what happened."

"I—" Kerani drew a shaky breath and straightened her shoulders, seeming to draw strength from Eleanor's grasp. "I had just put the children to bed,"

she went on in her soft, lilting accent. "I was going down to the library. I wanted to read a bit before I went to bed and—I walked by your room, my lady. I saw a man inside. I—he was standing in front of the dresser. He was turned away from me. But I gasped, I think, and he turned and saw me."

The woman began to tremble, and Eleanor slid a comforting arm around her shoulders. "It's all right, Kerani. He's gone now. You are safe."

"I know. I am sorry. It is just…he looked so—so frightening. His face—it was not human."

"What?"

"He looked, um, it was all white, with holes, and his eyes behind them."

"A mask?" Anthony suggested, and Kerani glanced at him, surprised.

"Yes," she said hesitantly. "I think it was. But not just over his eyes, as I have seen before."

"A full mask, then, and all white?" Anthony said, his voice so gentle and reassuring that Eleanor looked at him, surprised.

The Indian woman nodded. "Yes. It does not sound like much, but it scared me. It was as though he did not have a face at all."

"I can imagine," Eleanor commented. "It's not at all surprising that he frightened you."

"I screamed when he turned around. And he ran toward me. I could not get out of his way fast enough, and he shoved me hard. I stumbled and fell

down. Then everyone came. But he had run down the stairs and out of the house."

"Did no one else see him?" Anthony asked.

Zachary, after a questioning glance at Anthony, said, "No. I wish I had. I was in the office when I heard her scream, and I came up the back stairs, as they were closer. He went down the front."

"I did," one of the footmen admitted, lifting his hand somewhat shamefacedly. "I heard Miss Kerani scream, and I went running to the stairs. But that bloke was barreling down the stairs, and he ran straight into me. Knocked me halfway across the room, and by the time I got to me feet, he was out the front door. I went after him, but..." He shrugged. "I couldn't see him."

"No one else was about, Miss Eleanor," Bartwell put in. "Everyone was back in the kitchens or already gone up to bed."

"Well, at least no one was hurt," Eleanor said. "Did he take anything?"

"I don't know, miss. He made a mess in your room, but it was hard to tell if anything was gone."

"Why don't we go up and look?" Anthony suggested.

Eleanor thought about pointing out that this whole matter was none of his concern. But, frankly, it was strangely comforting to have his large, calm presence beside her, so she made no comment as he took her arm and went up the stairs beside her. The others followed them.

On the way up the stairs, they met the two children, who popped up to greet them. "Eleanor! Was it a thief? Did he take anything? Who do you think it was? The same as before?"

"The same as before?" Anthony turned to look at her. "This is a common occurrence?"

"No. I am sure it has nothing to do with this. It was when we were still in Naples. Someone broke into the house, but nothing was taken. That is all."

"I see. You are doubtless right. It was not connected."

Eleanor turned back to the children. "You two should be in bed. It is long past your bedtime."

"How could we sleep?" the girl, Claire, asked reasonably.

"It's far too exciting," Nathan agreed. "We want to see if he took anything."

"Very well. But then you will let Kerani take you straight back to bed."

"Yes, ma'am."

Eleanor continued up the stairs and to the doorway of her bedroom. "Oh, my." She stopped and looked in some dismay at her room.

The drawers of her vanity and dresser stood open, as did the doors of her wardrobe, and clothes were scattered about, spilling out of the drawers, as though someone had rifled through them hastily. A chair had been turned upside down, and the pillows of the bed had been tossed aside, the mattress shoved

halfway off. A music box stood on its side and open on the dresser, as well as a small chest, its lid up, necklaces spilling down the side of it. Earrings, brooches and such lay tumbled across the top of her dresser.

Eleanor walked over to the dresser, and Anthony followed her, glancing around the room. Eleanor turned the small music box upright and closed it, then looked through her jewelry box, picking up all the pieces and putting them back where they belonged.

"Is anything missing?"

"I—I'm not sure. Offhand, I don't think so. No, wait, there is a brooch gone. A silver one. Oh, and a cloisonné locket." She frowned. "It's very odd. They were not even the most valuable pieces in this box. My garnets are still here, and they are worth more. And this is just my everyday jewelry. All the really valuable pieces are downstairs in the safe."

She turned to Bartwell, who was standing inside the door. "What about the safe? Was anything taken?"

"No, miss. Nothing happened to the safe. I was working in the butler's room right next to it, so I'm certain of that. The silver plate is all still there in the butler's pantry, as well. I looked around downstairs, and none of your pictures or doodads are missing."

Anthony cast Eleanor a questioning look at the butler's words, and a faint smile touched her lips. "My pieces of art, he means."

"Anything of Edmund's?" Anthony asked.

Eleanor looked faintly alarmed and turned to Bartwell. "Did you look in Sir Edmund's room?"

"No, miss, I didn't think about it."

Eleanor hurried out of the room and across the hall, opening the door into a room the twin of hers in size and shape, where Edmund had briefly stayed before their move to Italy. The furniture was heavy and dark, richly carved. It was a tidy room, obviously kept dusted and ready, but there was an empty quality to its neatness that spoke of the lack of an occupant.

The light from the hallway revealed that this bedroom had not been ransacked, but Eleanor went to the desk in the corner and laid her hands on a rosewood box. She opened it, then closed the lid and turned away, seemingly satisfied. "I don't think anything was disturbed in here."

They left the room and stood for a moment in the hallway. Eleanor glanced around at the waiting faces, all watching her expectantly. "Bartwell, why don't you set the maids to putting my room back in order? Kerani, take the children to bed. And perhaps we had better set up a watch for the night, just in case."

"I will take first watch," Zachary offered.

"And I'll relieve you," Bartwell added.

"Very well." Eleanor nodded. They were the two whom she trusted most. "Thank you." She turned to

Anthony. "Now, Lord Neale, if you will join me in my office…"

She turned briskly and led the way down the stairs to her office. Anthony followed her, ignoring the curious looks of the household.

Once inside the office, Eleanor went to a small cabinet on which sat two cut glass decanters and an array of glasses. "Would you care for a whiskey?"

"Yes, thank you," Anthony responded, somewhat surprised. He was even more astonished when he saw Eleanor pour another glass for herself.

She handed him one of the glasses, and, seeing the askance glance he sent toward the one she held, she smiled. "The best remedy for shock, my father always said."

"What? Oh, yes. I suppose it is." Anthony took a drink, watching as Eleanor sipped at the amber liquid, grimacing a little at its strong taste.

She shivered, and Anthony reached out to lay a hand upon her arm. "Are you all right?"

She looked up at him. The whiskey lay like fire in her stomach, sending its heat throughout her body. Though it was meant only as a comforting gesture, she was very aware of his hand on her bare skin. She remembered the moment in the carriage when she had thought he was about to kiss her. The air was once again charged between them, as it had been then, and her flesh tingled where his skin touched hers. Eleanor tilted her head back to look up at him.

His eyes gazed down into hers, capturing and holding her as surely as if he had taken her in his hands.

Anthony took a half step closer, his hand sliding up her arm, sending prickles of sensation through her. Her breath caught in her throat, and she stared at him, unable to look away. This time he *was* going to kiss her, she thought, and unconsciously lifted her face toward him.

Footsteps hurried along the hall outside, cracking like shots on the wood floor, and the noise seemed to break the spell. Eleanor took a hasty step backward, a blush rising in her cheeks. She turned away and walked around her desk before she turned to face Anthony again, the large wooden expanse lying between them.

"Well. I am sorry that you happened upon such a scene. Our household is normally much quieter."

"Thieves are not usually the routine in any household, I imagine," he replied mildly. He glanced around the room, taking in its spaciousness and comfort, the glass-doored shelves and locked cabinets, the pile of ledgers upon the desk and its well-used look.

"This is, um, your office?" he asked. Certainly he could not imagine Edmund in a place such as this.

Eleanor nodded. "Yes, it is where I work."

She looked down at the desk, somewhat distractedly arranging the pencils in a row. The discovery of her ransacked room had disturbed her more than she

cared to admit. "Why did he tear apart my bedchamber that way? Nearly everything valuable is down here."

"Doubtless he did not realize that. Perhaps he simply started in your room, expecting to find jewels, and then he planned to work his way downstairs. He wasn't counting, I'm sure, on your, um, maid discovering him."

"*Amah*," Eleanor corrected. "Kerani looks after the children for me." She looked up at him, her gaze hardening a little, offering him a challenge. "No doubt you find us a rather unusual household."

He shrugged. "Somewhat."

He found himself wanting to ask who were all the people whom he had seen—why her household contained an African man who spoke perfect English and wore a gentleman's suit, as well as an Indian woman, two children, and a butler who looked as though he would be more at home in a dockside tavern than in a butler's pantry. And what did a woman do in an office like this? Why had someone ransacked her bedroom—surely not the pattern of a common thief, no matter what he had told her?

But Anthony knew that such thoughts were entirely beside the point. There was no reason for him to be wondering about this woman and her life any more than there had been any reason a moment earlier for him to want to kiss her. So he said nothing, and silence stretched between them.

"Well, that is not why you came," Eleanor said briskly, turning away and going to a cabinet and unlocking it. "You want to know about Edmund's death."

She picked up a piece of paper inside the cabinet and turned, bringing it back and laying it down on the desk close to where Anthony stood, turning it so that he could see it. It was an official-looking document, complete with stamps and seals, written in Italian.

"This is the death certificate the Italian authorities wrote for Edmund. Can you read Italian?"

"A little," he replied, picking up the document and perusing it. He felt uncomfortable, almost embarrassed.

"It says that his death was due to drowning," Eleanor told him flatly, pointing with the tip of a pencil to the appropriate line. "Of course, if one believes that the Italian officials are corrupt and lied on the death certificate, I suppose that is not proof enough. There was also an article in the Italian newspapers about his death, since it was an accident." She handed over a folded piece of newsprint, again in Italian. "There."

Anthony's eyes ran down the story. His Italian, never fluent, was rather rusty, but he recalled enough to see that the article was indeed about Sir Edmund Scarbrough and his drowning.

"His health improved so much in Naples that

Edmund was much more vigorous than he was here. I am not sure why he grew interested in sailing. I think it had more to do with his friends being interested in it than anything else. Usually he sailed with Dario Paradella or one of his other friends. Dario had been supposed to go, but he had to cancel, and Edmund went by himself. He said he needed to think. When he did not return by nightfall, I grew worried, and I sent a servant to the docks, but his boat was not there. I grew increasingly worried, of course, and I sent notes around to his friends. I sent servants to the various places that he might have stopped, but he was nowhere to be found. So, eventually, I contacted the authorities. Two days later, his…" Eleanor paused, her throat tightening. She swallowed hard and continued. "His body washed up on shore."

Looking at her quietly pained face, Anthony found it difficult to disbelieve her grief. He wanted to tell her not to talk about it any longer. He wanted to put his arms around her and let her head rest against his chest, just as he had wanted earlier to protect her from the burglar who had ransacked her room. He felt sure that such a reaction was how most men felt about her. She was beautiful, and no doubt she was well used to using that beauty to manipulate men into doing whatever she wanted. Believing whatever she wanted.

He firmly quashed his feelings of sympathy and asked, "Why did you burn his body?"

"It certainly was not to hide anything!" Eleanor snapped, her eyes flashing with anger and resentment.

"Then why? It goes against all decent behavior. What about his poor mother, grieving for him, with no grave to go to for comfort?"

"We were in Italy. She would have had no grave to go to, if I had buried him there, either. At least now she can put his ashes in the family vault. I would think she would prefer to have some reminder of him," Eleanor retorted. She shook her head, holding out her hands as if to stave off any further dispute. "It does not matter, in any case. I had no say in the matter. The Italian authorities are responsible for that decision, not I."

"What?" Anthony asked skeptically. "It was they who burned his body?"

Eleanor nodded. "It is some archaic Italian law, a holdover from the days when plague ran rampant throughout Europe. Any body washed in from the sea must be burned immediately, right there on the beach. It is the way Percy Shelley died, and his body, too, was burned on a funeral pyre on the beach. They say his chest split open, exposing his heart, and one of his friends snatched it out and gave it to Mary Shelley to keep. They say she put it in a box and brought it back home."

"Bloody hell," Anthony murmured.

Eleanor smiled faintly. "Yes, I found it rather odd

when Edmund told me about it. But, then, there is much about the Shelleys that was odd—even to me, as peculiar as most hold me to be."

Anthony wanted to believe her. It would not be surprising to have some medieval law still hanging about on the books, and doubtless during the time of the plague it had made sense to burn any body washed up on shore. Doubtless there was nothing to Honoria's fears and suspicions.

Still, merely the fact that he wanted so much to believe Eleanor, that as he looked into her clear blue eyes, he could not believe that they would hold deceit, made him hold back. He set his jaw, firmly ignoring the heat that burned deep in his loins and the subtle tingling in his fingertips that made him itch to touch her again.

"What about the inheritance?" he asked abruptly, his tone rough with the effort of suppressing his instinctive desire for her.

Eleanor's face tightened. "Ah, yes, the inheritance. It always comes back to that, does it not?"

"Yes, I am afraid so."

"I cannot see how you can think that I would have murdered Edmund to get his money since, as you must know, I inherited none of his wealth. The entailed estate went to his cousin, Malcolm Scarbrough, and the bulk of his personal fortune was left to his sister."

"It strikes me as odd that a man would cut his wife out of his will," Anthony countered.

Eleanor's eyebrows rose skeptically. "You wish me to believe that you are concerned for me?"

"I am merely saying that it would seem to me to indicate that such a man was estranged from his wife, that he had reason to feel she did not deserve to be left his fortune."

"Or that she had no need of it," Eleanor countered. "Even you must see the folly of that argument, my lord. If my husband intended to leave me no money and it was money I sought, it would make much more sense for me to keep him alive."

"You are the trustee for his sister's fortune. Even though you were left nothing, you would have ample opportunity to take what you want from her funds."

Eleanor smiled thinly. "And that is the crux of the matter, isn't it? Managing the money that was left to Edmund's sister. I would think that any man of reason would clearly see that if Edmund had distrusted me or been estranged from me, he would never have appointed me as the guardian of his sister's fortune. But you are not interested in reason. You and Lady Scarbrough are interested only in the fortune. Why do you think Edmund left it in my care? Because he knew that I would administer it fairly and well. He knew that I would see to it that his sister's money was invested wisely, and that it was not all spent on his mother's extravagances. Edmund had little head for business, but he was quite aware of how his mother would have mishan-

dled the trust if he had left it in her hands—and how much of those funds would have been used for Lady Honoria's expenses, not Samantha's."

It was infuriating, but Anthony could scarcely dispute Eleanor's words. What money his sister did not bungle away with bad investments, she would use for her own benefit, arguing that she was, after all, Samantha's mother and in charge of her upbringing. He would personally never have recommended putting Honoria in charge of Samantha's funds.

"Did you think I did not know that was what this whole charade was about?" Eleanor went on bitingly. "That you and Edmund's mother want to get your hands on Samantha's money? That is the reason for this 'suspicion' regarding Edmund's death—you hope to spread enough rumors that I killed him that my reputation will be ruined and my life made miserable. No doubt you hope that I would then flee the country to escape the vicious rumors and turn the money over to you and Lady Honoria to manage."

"What?" Anthony gaped at her, stunned. "How dare you—"

"Oh, I dare anything, Lord Neale," Eleanor said, leaning forward and placing her hands on the desk in front of her. Her blue eyes were bright and challenging, her very stance pugnacious. "Didn't you know? I am that odd American woman who pays no attention to conventions, who cares naught for the 'proper' way to do things. I go out unescorted. I

manage my life and my funds without the guidance of a man. I travel where and when I please, without answering to anyone. You will not break me with rumors, my lord. I shan't run weeping because I am not received at some foolish aristocrat's house. You will not get your hands on Edmund's money!"

Much to Eleanor's surprise, her adversary let out a short, sharp bark of laughter. "You must be mad. As if I am interested in Edmund's money! Obviously you do not know me."

"Oh, I know you, my lord," Eleanor retorted. "I know you very well. All you are interested in is money. The only times you have ever been to this house, it has been because of money. The first time it was to keep Edmund from marrying me and turning his fortune over to me instead of giving it to his mother and you. You never considered whether marrying me would make Edmund happier or healthier. All you cared about was that it might lighten his pocketbook. You never expressed any concern or affection for him. And now you come to see me because you hate my control of his sister's money. I see no sorrow in you over his death."

"You know nothing about how I feel," Anthony responded tightly.

"Why did you never call on Edmund before we left for Italy? It would have pleased him, I am sure. For some odd reason, Edmund liked you. He trusted you. He even told me once that if I ever needed

anything, I should turn to you." Eleanor's mouth curled bitterly as she added, "I never told him that you would be the last man I would call on for help if I ever needed it."

Her words struck Anthony like a blow. It was unreasonable, of course; he was quite aware of the woman's dislike of him. It should not surprise or hurt him. The feeling, after all, was mutual. He might have this strange feeling of physical attraction to her, but he had only disdain for her as a person.

"I did not call on Edmund here because I did not care to see the two of you together," he told her honestly, his voice clipped. "I talked to Edmund at his club."

"Oh. I see. You avoided only me. Of course." Eleanor turned away, surprised by the slash of hurt that had cut through her. It was no surprise, after all, she told herself. She knew how much the man despised her.

"My only concern was for Edmund's well-being," Anthony went on stiffly. He had seen the hurt in Eleanor's face, but he steeled himself against it. "However much you think you know about me, I can tell you that you know me not at all."

"And you, sir, know as little about me," Eleanor retorted, lifting her head proudly.

"I may not know you," he said, his voice sharp as glass. "But I know women like you. I know what a woman as beautiful as you are can do to a man. How

you can turn him against the people who love him. How you can twist him inside out so that he does not care about anyone or anything but you."

His eyes were intent upon her face as he spoke, and he moved toward her, as if drawn by the force of his words. His voice dropped, almost caressing the words as he went on. "I know what it does to a man when you smile at him…how he hungers so for the taste of you, the touch, that he will do almost anything."

Eleanor remained frozen where she was, unable to move or speak, held in place by the husky flow of words as surely as if he held her there physically. Her head tilted back as he came closer, looming over her now. Hunger burned in his eyes, and Eleanor felt an answering hunger rising in her, filling her with heat and yearning.

"Nothing else matters, then," he went on, his eyes boring into hers. He leaned toward her, saying, "Nothing and no one. Only you and the sweet lure of your mouth, the satin feel of your skin…"

He lowered his head and kissed her. Eleanor instinctively went up on her toes to meet him. His lips were soft, a velvet heat, and desire shook her at their touch. She pressed her mouth against his, feeling a yearning she had never experienced before. Anthony wrapped his arms around her, pressing her up into him, hard bone and sinew against her feminine

softness. The contrast stirred Eleanor more than she would have thought possible.

Her breasts were full and aching, her nipples tightening, and fire flooded her loins. No man had ever kissed her like this before, teeth and tongue and melting passion. No man would have dared. And Eleanor, who had always believed herself immune to desire, found herself locked in its hot grip. She trembled, clinging to him, and wanted more.

At last he released her, his arms falling away as he took a quick step backward. For a long moment they simply stared at each other, both of them too stunned to speak or act. Then his hands went out, taking her arms to pull her to him again. Eleanor saw the intent in his hot gaze. She did not move, pride and hurt rising in her to hold her back.

"Aren't you afraid I will ruin you?" she asked bitterly.

"God help me, I don't care," he muttered, and pulled her close.

"No!" Eleanor jerked away from him, anger flooding in and wrapping around her heart. She held her head high, her cheeks flaming with color. She would not let desire carry her away as if she were some mindless thing, a slave to her passion. She refused to respond to a man who not only did not care for her but, indeed, despised her.

He looked at her, his jaw clenched, a struggle of his own playing across his face. "Eleanor…"

"Leave me," she told him in a charged voice. When he hesitated, she snapped, "Go! Get out of my house."

With a nod, he turned and walked out the door.

Eleanor realized that her legs were trembling so much that she could barely stand. She turned and sank down into the chair behind her desk. Her breath rasped in her throat.

Whatever had possessed her? She would have said that she disliked Lord Neale above all others. Yet when he had kissed her, she had melted in his arms.

She pressed her hand to her mouth. Her lips, she noted, were still warm and damp from his kiss. She had kissed him wantonly, she thought, and her cheeks flamed at the memory.

"Anthony," she murmured, trying his name out on her tongue.

For the first time in her life, she had felt passion. And it was for the one man who was implacably her enemy.

CHAPTER FIVE

ELEANOR WAS READING through her correspondence the next morning when Zachary entered the room. He hesitated at the door, as though not wanting to disturb her, but Eleanor was glad for the interruption. She had spent a largely sleepless night, and this morning she was having a great deal of trouble concentrating on anything.

"Zachary. Come in," she said, smiling.

"John said you wished to see me."

"Yes. Sit down." She gestured toward the chair on the other side of her desk, and he sat down, crossing his hands and looking at her expectantly.

"I have a task for you."

He inclined his head. "Of course. I am working on the books. That can wait."

"Good. I want you to find out what you can about Lord Neale."

Zachary's dark face registered surprise. "The man who was here last night? Sir Edmund's uncle?"

"Yes. I—I do not entirely trust him."

Zachary frowned. "You think he had something to do with the intruder?"

"What? Oh, no." Eleanor paused, thinking. "At least, I had not thought about it. I don't presume so. I—surely that was simply an ordinary thief."

Zachary shrugged. "Perhaps. But I find his behavior odd. Why did he break into the house so early? While people were still up and about? And why did he start in your bedchamber? An ordinary thief, I would have thought, would wait until everyone was asleep and then he would sneak in downstairs and steal the valuables in the butler's pantry and the safe."

"That seems logical," Eleanor agreed. "Do you have a theory why he acted as he did?"

"I wonder if he behaved so because he specifically wanted something from your room. And he knew that you were out of the house at the time, so he could search your room. Any later, and you might come home from your evening. He could have been watching the house and seen you leave in the carriage."

Eleanor nodded thoughtfully, her stomach dropping in realization. "Or he could have known because he had a confederate with me."

"Lord Neale?" Zachary clarified.

Eleanor nodded. It made her feel a little sick to think that Anthony might have orchestrated the attack on her room. "But what would Lord Neale—or

anyone else, for that matter—hope to find in my room?"

"I do not know. If it wasn't valuables, perhaps it was something that would be otherwise important. Some sort of document, perhaps?"

"I don't keep anything like that in my bedroom."

"He wouldn't necessarily know that."

Eleanor shook her head. "Still, I can think of nothing of that sort that would be of any interest to anyone."

Could Lord Neale have wanted to take Edmund's will? But that made no sense. He could have seen what was in it merely by asking. Eleanor was, after all, going to show Lady Scarbrough the document, and she would have showed him, as well. Perhaps he thought she would not, but it seemed an extreme measure just to look at the will. Of course, if he were able to find it and destroy it…

Well, Eleanor was not sure exactly what would happen. Without a will, Edmund's money would be distributed as the law prescribed. Eleanor was not conversant with English law, but she assumed that surely Edmund's widow would get some portion of that. But perhaps the rest would go to his mother or to his sister, in which case Honoria could easily get her hands on it. Without the trust that Edmund had set up, Samantha's mother would certainly be appointed as the girl's guardian.

She frowned, wondering if this *was* in fact the reason for the intruder last night.

"Perhaps they weren't really wanting anything but to frighten you," Zachary suggested.

"But why?" Eleanor asked, but even as she said it, she knew the answer. Like rumors and gossip, fear might drive her to leave the country and hand over the trust to Honoria or Anthony.

Her stomach tightened at the thought. Every path her thoughts took seemed to lead back to the idea that Anthony had engineered the break-in. It seemed less and less a matter of coincidence that he had been with her last night while the intrusion took place. It had given him a rock-solid alibi in case she suspected him.

"Or perhaps it was simply a thief," Eleanor reiterated, turning her thoughts away from the path they had taken. After all, she had no proof of any of this, only the merest speculation. "In any case, I think we need to take precautions. I have already told Bartwell to check every window and door before bed, and we should have a couple of footmen on watch, at least for the time being."

Zachary's jaw went rigid. "I agree. We are just lucky that Kerani was not more badly hurt last night."

Eleanor cast a speculative glance at her man of business. "Does Kerani know how you feel about her?" she asked quietly.

He looked at her, startled. "No. What do you mean?"

Eleanor raised an eyebrow. "You know what I mean. You care for Kerani. I think you have from the moment you met her."

He looked alarmed. "Blast it, Eleanor," he began, dropping the carefully cultivated air of employee deference that he tried to maintain with her and reverted to the man who had played with her when they were both children. "You must not tell her. Promise me you will not."

"If you do not wish it, I won't. But I do not understand why you won't let her in on the secret. How can you ever hope to win her hand if she has no idea how you feel?"

"There is little chance of that. I am not…someone she would ever consider."

"I don't know how you can know that," Eleanor countered. "Since you never give her a chance. I think she is fond of you."

"She is grateful to me, just as she is grateful to you, because we rescued her from *suttee*."

He spoke of the custom in India of placing a dead man's widow on his funeral pyre to burn with him, a practice that the British had not succeeded in stamping out. When they were in India, looking at a ruby mine that Eleanor was thinking of buying, Eleanor, Bartwell and Zachary had happened upon one such funeral pyre. Kerani had been tied beside her husband atop the stacked wood, waiting for the torch to be put to it. Bartwell and Eleanor had held off the

irate members of the funeral party with a brace of pistols, while Zachary had climbed onto the pile of wood and cut the poor frightened woman free. Kerani had fled with them, knowing that she no longer had a home among her own people. She had insisted on making herself useful by looking after the children.

"It has been several years since then," Eleanor pointed out. "She has come to like you as a person, not just as her rescuer."

"She is of a high caste. I do not think she would look upon me as an equal."

Eleanor grimaced. "I would not think that, after her experiences, she would cling to her people's beliefs. Besides, you do not give yourself enough credit. You are a nice-looking man, well-employed, and if I know you, you have set aside a pleasant nest egg."

He offered a faint smile at her statement. "I have been saving my money, you are right. But it is not yet enough for me to be able to offer marriage."

Eleanor knew it was useless to argue with Zachary, so she mildly said, "You might consider what Kerani would think about it. It's possible that she would value the time spent with you more than a house or the services of a maid."

Zachary shook his head, frowning a little. "'Tis not so easy for some of us as it is for you. You are always certain, whatever you decide. I am not so sure."

Eleanor knew that everyone thought this of her, and generally it was true. She acted with confidence.

But for once, regarding Lord Neale, she was, in fact, quite undecided.

"I will not press you," she told Zachary. "Will you look into the matter of Lord Neale?"

"Yes, of course. What exactly is it you wish to know? His financial circumstances? Personal information?"

"Whatever you can find out that seems pertinent. Primarily his finances, I suppose. Anything that might show whether he could have been behind what happened last night."

"Of course. I will start right away."

After Zachary left, Eleanor sat for a moment, letting her mind drift. She was sitting there, head on her hand, staring off into space, when a footman arrived to announce a visitor.

Anthony! Her stomach grew tight, and she rose to her feet. "Who is it, Arthur?"

"Foreign sort, my lady." He extended a calling card on a silver platter.

Eleanor took it and read the name there. "Dario Paradella? Dario?" A smile broke across her face. "Show him to the drawing room, Arthur. I will be right there."

The man waiting for her in the drawing room was about Eleanor's height, slender and handsome, his dark hair cut short—though it was not enough to entirely hide the curls. He was impeccably dressed and quite handsome, with large, liquid-brown eyes

set into a smooth olive-skinned face. He smiled when Eleanor entered the room, and stood up, coming forward to bow in a courtly manner over her hand.

"Lady Scarbrough. It is a delight to see you."

"Lady Scarbrough? How formal, Dario. You were wont to call me Eleanor."

He grinned, giving a little shrug. "I was not sure. Perhaps in England things are different."

"*I* am not different." Eleanor smiled at him. It made her feel happy and a little sad all at once to see Dario. He had been Edmund's best friend when they were in Italy, and it had been he who had gotten Edmund interested in sailing. A wealthy gentleman of leisure, he was a patron of the arts, and fond of long intellectual and artistic discussions. Seeing him brought to mind the many evenings she and Edmund had spent with Dario and others, talking and laughing until late into the night.

"Come. Sit down. May I offer you some tea?" Eleanor gestured toward a chair. "Or coffee. You would prefer that, yes?"

"I am fine. Go to no trouble. It is enough for me to see you. You look lovely. How are you?"

"Thank you. I am well. I miss Edmund, of course." She gave a little shrug. "But life goes on." She smiled. "But tell me about you. What are you doing here in England?"

"What can I tell you? Life in Naples was dreadfully dull once you left."

Eleanor chuckled. "Flatterer."

A white grin flashed in his tanned face. "I speak only the truth. I was bored. So I decided to travel. What better place to go than to England? My friend always spoke of it with such love. 'I am better here, Dario,' he would tell me. 'But my heart will always be there.'"

"A lovely sentiment," Eleanor said. She did not add that she doubted Edmund's words had been as sweet, but they probably had expressed what he had felt.

"So here I am," Dario finished.

"For how long?"

"A few weeks. A month. I am not sure."

"Until you are bored again?" Eleanor ventured.

"You know me too well."

"Well, we shall have to make sure that you are well-entertained, then, so that you will not wish to leave," Eleanor told him. "I am attending the opera tomorrow night. You will find it a poor substitute for the opera in Naples, of course, but if you would like to accompany me…?"

"It is my dearest wish," Dario assured her, one hand on his heart. "I will be honored to escort you."

IT WAS GOOD to be out in society again, Eleanor thought to herself as she swept into the opera house on Dario's arm the following evening. It made her think a little wistfully of the operas that she and Sir

Edmund had attended together, but there was more sweetness in the memory than pain. And she realized how much, during her semi-seclusion after Edmund's death, she had missed the panoply and bustle of such an event. She paused for a moment, drinking in the noise and the movement of the throng, the glitter of jewels and the sumptuous richness of brocades, velvets, satins and silks, ranging in every color from the demure white of debutantes to the vibrant hues of fashionable matrons.

Eleanor herself had opted for half-mourning again, an elegant satin evening gown in black with white accents, with a pendant necklace of diamonds as clear and sparkling as ice and a matching scatter of diamonds pinned in her dark hair. She knew, even before Dario's exclamation, that she looked her best, and she could not help but wish that Lord Neale would be at the opera that night, just so he could witness her splendid entrance. He would see that she was not cowed by him or anyone else—and she could not help but think with smug satisfaction that the sight of her might have a deleterious effect on his pulse.

Not, of course, she reminded herself, that that had influenced her decision to go. After all, Anthony might very well not even be there. And she was not, she added as she glanced all around the spacious lobby, looking for him.

Eleanor could see heads turning toward them as

they made their way up the marble steps and around to her box. They made, she knew, an arresting couple. Dario was a handsome man in his black evening suit and white shirt, with a snowy white cravat centered by a pigeon's blood ruby the size of Eleanor's thumb, and his obviously foreign air and looks would have made him stand out in any case.

There would be gossip, of course. She had been given a grudging entrée into the *ton* by virtue of her marriage to Sir Edmund, but she knew that she was not considered one of them and never would be. There would doubtless be those here tonight who criticized her for forsaking full mourning after six months. She wondered how much Lord Neale and his sister would add to the rumor mill.

When she and Dario had settled in their seats, Eleanor took out her opera glasses to peruse the rest of the audience, much as everyone else was doing. She saw the dreadfully dull Colton-Smythes, who had sailed from Italy to England with her. They were standing in a box across the way from her, talking to a middle-aged man who looked vaguely familiar to her. He was handsome, with dark eyes and a rather ascetic face, his black hair silvering at the temples.

Colton-Smythe was watching her, and when his eye caught Eleanor's, he bowed to her in greeting. She inclined her head to the couple, knowing that

at intermission they would doubtless make their way to her box.

Eleanor turned toward Dario to tell him about the couple and found him watching them already, his eyes narrowed.

"Do you know Mr. and Mrs. Colton-Smythe?" she asked, faintly surprised.

"That woman in the unfortunate colored dress?" he asked. "What do you call that?"

"Frightful," Eleanor replied. "But I think the name of the color is puce. It is not a color most people should wear. The woman is Mrs. Colton-Smythe, and the balding man beside her is her husband. You looked as though you recognized them."

"They are, perhaps, somewhat familiar, but I do not know them, really. It is the man with them I have the misfortune to know. Alessandro Moncari, Conte di Graffeo."

"Ah." Eleanor recognized the name. Dario was one of the earnest, intellectual young men of Naples who desired a more democratic government for that city-state, as well as a unified country of Italy, rather than the collection of small states that now prevailed there. The Conte di Graffeo was one of the conservative aristocrats who strongly supported the king of Naples and the present government.

"He is despicable," Dario said with a bitter twist of his lips.

Eleanor was a little surprised by the depth of Dario's dislike. She had not realized, she supposed, how deeply committed he was to the movement of democracy and unification for Italy.

Dario saw her glance and forced a smile. "We do not agree on many issues."

Eleanor, who had heard many a discussion among him and Edmund and their other friends regarding the many political ills of the Kingdom of Naples, smiled faintly. "Yes, I know. I remember that Edmund disliked the man also."

She had been sympathetic to the ideas of the liberally-minded young men of Naples. They had hoped, after Napoleon was defeated and driven from their country, that they would have a new, more democratic government. Much as they had disliked Napoleon's conquest of their city, they had had little affection for the autocratic kingdom that had existed before Bonaparte. However, the Congress of Vienna had done its best to put everything back the way it was before Napoleon had taken over most of Europe, and as a result, the old Kingdom of Naples was reinstated. The king had continued an autocratic rule, quelling all hope of the blend of monarchy and democratic rule that existed in England.

Eleanor had not felt the same sort of passion for the subject that Edmund had. And she did not particularly want to plunge into the matter right now.

She felt in much too good a humor to talk about politics.

So Eleanor returned to her opera glasses, leaving the matter of the Conte di Graffeo. And there, suddenly, looming up in her glasses, was Lord Neale.

Eleanor let out a little gasp and lowered her glasses immediately. Her heart was suddenly pounding. Dario turned toward her curiously.

"Are you feeling unwell?" he asked.

"No. Oh no." Eleanor gave a half laugh. "I just saw someone I know. I did not really expect him to be here tonight."

She looked back at Anthony. He was in a box down and across from them, sitting alone. He cast a glance around the opera house, his gaze disinterested. Then he saw Eleanor. He straightened, staring across at her. Eleanor inclined her head toward him, moving just the polite amount and no more. She could feel her cheeks flush under his regard, but she hoped he could not spy that clear across the theater from her.

He nodded back to her; then his gaze flickered over to Dario, sitting beside her, and remained for a moment. He looked back at Eleanor, but she could not read his expression. Her hand tightened around her fan, and she made herself turn her attention toward the stage—anywhere, really, so long as it was not at Lord Neale. She waited for a moment, consi-

dering the heavy red velvet curtains across the stage-front with a great deal more interest than they warranted.

After a long pause, she turned her head, letting her gaze wander across the boxes, moving over Anthony again. He was no longer looking at her but idly watching the seats below, in the center of the house. Eleanor looked at him for a moment, unnoticed, then firmly turned her gaze back to the orchestra, where the musicians were tuning up.

Dario, thankfully, was quiet during the performance. Eleanor hated to sit with most fashionable opera-goers, who were more interested in carrying on conversations about clothes, furnishings and the other attendees—often in tones that far exceeded a whisper—than they were in watching the opera.

At intermission, of course, the real purpose of the evening for most of the patrons began. Everyone began to get up and move. Some men went to fetch refreshments for the ladies with them. Others, both men and women, paraded up and down the hall outside the boxes, looking and being looked at. And still others strolled around to pay their respects to those who remained in their boxes, often hoping to be asked to sit with them for the rest of the show.

It seemed to Eleanor that every guest whom she knew in the slightest came by her loge. It would have been more gratifying if she had not thought that the majority of them came more out of curiosity than out

of any real liking for her. And most of the curiosity, she suspected, at least among the women, was for Dario.

She dutifully introduced him to them, and watched with some amusement as they flirted and laughed with him. Dario, of course, reacted just as she expected, smiling in a way that was guaranteed to break a few hearts, flattering them outrageously and sending smoldering glances from under his thick black eyelashes.

Mr. and Mrs. Colton-Smythe appeared, bringing with them Conte di Graffeo. Eleanor cast a quick glance over at Dario, unsure how he would respond to this man whom he obviously disliked. However, he was polite, if rather stiff and uncharacteristically taciturn.

The count bowed over Eleanor's hand with Latin charm and grace. "Lady Scarbrough. It is a pleasure to meet you at last." His voice was warm and deep, somewhat at odds with his cool, restrained mien.

"Conte," Eleanor responded. "Perhaps you know Mr. Paradello, my late husband's friend?"

He spared a glance and a short nod for Dario. "Yes, of course. *Buona sera, signore.*"

Dario made a terse reply, and the count turned back to Eleanor. "Allow me to offer my condolences on the death of your husband, my lady. The music here cannot compare to that of Sir Edmund Scar-

brough. He was a genius. He will be much missed, not only here, but in Italy, as well."

His words were perfectly polite, but there was an odd, almost watchful, expression in his eyes as he talked to her that made Eleanor uncomfortable. It was almost as if he were studying her to see what her reaction to his words might be.

"Thank you, Conte di Graffeo," she replied formally. "We all miss him very much."

He bowed again, and there were formal goodbyes all around. Then the Colton-Smythes left with their obviously prized guest. Eleanor frowned, trying to figure out what had made her feel so uneasy about the count.

"Do not let him worry you," Dario told her in a low voice. "He is not worth it."

Eleanor glanced at him. Dario's words seemed an odd thing to say. There had not been anything worrisome in the Italian count's words, despite the unease she had felt. Had Dario sensed her mood, or had he heard something in the man's condolences that bothered him, too?

Before she could open her mouth to ask Dario what he had meant by his comment, there was a tap at the door and Anthony stepped in.

Eleanor stiffened, her hand tightening on her fan, all thoughts of the Conte di Graffeo fleeing her head. "Lord Neale."

"My lady." Anthony nodded at her, then turned to look at Dario. His glance was swift and encompass-

ing, and when he turned back to Eleanor, there was a question in his eyes.

It was obvious that he was waiting for an introduction to the man. So, with just a trace of wryness, Eleanor said, "Pray allow me to introduce you to Mr. Paradella, my lord. He was a friend of Sir Edmund's."

"Ah, I see. And you have come to visit your friend's widow, all the way from Naples. How kind." Anthony's tone and gaze were equally cool.

Dario did not look offended, only faintly amused. "It is my pleasure, my lord, I assure you."

"Indeed. Will you be staying long?"

"I had not decided quite yet," Dario responded amiably. "It will depend, in part, on Lady Scarbrough."

Anthony made no response to this statement, merely turned toward Eleanor and said, "I understand you are planning to visit Honoria to discuss Edmund's will."

"Yes. And to bring his ashes home to the family vault," Eleanor replied.

"Honoria has asked me to attend, as well," he told her.

"Of course." Eleanor kept her face and voice as bland as he.

"Pray, allow me to escort you," Dario put in, and both Eleanor and Anthony turned to look at him, surprised.

"I would like to see my friend's ancestral home,"

Dario said by way of explanation, adding, his voice a little roughened by emotion, "It would be good to say goodbye to Edmund there."

"Yes, of course," Eleanor replied immediately. "I am sorry I did not think to ask you earlier. I will be honored to have you escort me."

She glanced over at Anthony, who was looking at Dario now with a thinly-disguised dislike. She would have asked Dario to come in any case, for he had been good friends with Edmund, but she had to admit that Anthony's obvious disapproval of the invitation sweetened the moment.

"Then I will see you there," Anthony told her tightly, sketching a bow in her direction. "My lady."

"My lord."

She watched as Anthony turned and left the box as abruptly as he had entered it.

"Odd man," Dario commented, gazing after Anthony.

"Yes." Eleanor shrugged. "Rudeness seems to be one of his chief characteristics."

"I do not think he liked me," Dario said with a smile.

Eleanor shrugged. "He feels the same way about me, I can assure you."

"About you?" Dario looked skeptical. "I cannot believe that. I would have said the man disliked me because he was jealous about you. My guess is that he is more attracted to you than he would like."

Eleanor thought about the kiss she and Anthony

had shared the other night, and her face warmed at the memory. It had meant nothing, she told herself, just as she had many times since it had happened. It had been a brief impulse, just as quickly regretted—on both their parts. She was sure that Lord Neale wished to forget it just as much as she did.

She hoped that Dario had not noticed the blush that had touched her cheeks. She gave him a quick sideways glance but could tell little from his expression. He smiled at her warmly.

"No man could resist your beauty, my lady, even a cold Englishman. Nor can I."

Dario was a dedicated flirt, Eleanor knew. It came as naturally to him as breathing. It was hard to tell whether he was giving her those melting brown-eyed glances simply as a matter of course, or if he was actually serious. She hoped it was the former, as she certainly had no romantic interest in Dario. She enjoyed him as a friend, and she could see that he was a handsome man who would appeal to most women. But, as with most of the men she had met in her life, she did not feel any rush of emotion, any feeling of desire.

Indeed, bizarre as it was, there was apparently only one man who had inspired that sort of instant, tingling attraction.

She turned her thoughts from that unproductive path and gave Dario a noncommittal smile. "Come,

now, Dario, we both know you don't mean a word of that."

"Eleanor!" He put on a wounded expression, one hand to his heart, but then he chuckled, and they both sat down for the second act of the opera.

WHATEVER HIS MOTIVES, Dario continued to dance attendance upon Eleanor for the next couple of days, coming to call on her the following afternoon, then insisting that she allow him to walk with her as she went over to the lending library. She felt sure that there must be things he would enjoy more than taking a leisurely stroll along the city streets, but his easy chatter made the walk more enjoyable. Still, when he pressed her to attend a play with him the following evening, she declined, pointing out that his constant presence would soon cause gossip, especially given the fact that he would be accompanying her in two days to Kent.

She had been somewhat surprised by his offer to travel with her to meet Edmund's mother. He had been a good friend of Edmund's, of course, but it seemed rather a gloomy thing to do on a trip one had taken for pleasure. She supposed that even though he had attended the funeral pyre on the beach, the very oddness of the situation had left him feeling a bit unsettled. It had certainly been that way for Eleanor, who for weeks after Edmund's death had found herself listening for the sound of his piano or

thinking of something she must tell him before catching herself. She had thought that perhaps it would have been easier to accept that he was gone if there had been a normal funeral service and interment.

In any case, she was glad for the company on the journey—as well as the support in facing Lady Honoria. She was fully confident that Dario would charm Edmund's mother if anyone could. And if not, at least she would have someone to talk to besides Lady Honoria and Lord Neale.

The day before she left for Kent, Zachary took her aside, saying, "I have the information you requested."

"About Lord Neale?" Eleanor led him into her office, where they sat down in the chairs in front of her desk, facing each other. "What did you find?"

"Well, I was not sure precisely what you wanted, so I got everything I could," Zachary explained, looking down at the papers in his hand. "He is the sixth Earl Neale. They were given the earldom by Henry VII, apparently for their support. Before that they were barons. His mother was the Honorable Miss Genevieve Carruthers, also of a good family, though not of as high degree as the Neales. She was the fifth Lord Neale's second wife. The first was Lady Honoria's mother. There was a third wife, as well, for Lord Neale's mother died when he was a baby. She—the Dowager Countess, that is—is still

alive and resides in Brighton. The fifth earl died ten years ago, at which time Anthony, the present Lord Neale, came into the title."

"You are very thorough, Zachary," Eleanor commented.

"I try to be." He offered her a dazzling smile, then continued. "Lord Neale is unmarried, has never been engaged, and while regarded as prime marriage material, is also generally held to be a waste of effort in that regard. There have been rumors, of course, of relationships, but…" Zachary cleared his throat uncomfortably. "I presume you are not really wanting the details of that. In any case, there are not many rumors. He is apparently a man of great privacy."

Eleanor was, in fact, quite interested in those details, but she was not about to reveal that to her employee. She merely nodded. "Yes. Go on."

"There is some talk of an estrangement between Lord Neale and his father. It was quite some time ago, fifteen years or more, apparently, and, again, none of my sources could come up with many details. The former Lord Neale died without any reconciliation between them, I believe."

"How sad. He is a hard man, I think."

"Apparently, so was his father. He was known in the area as the Iron Earl. The son is regarded more favorably."

"Indeed?"

"As to his financial status, which I assume is the area in which you were primarily interested, he is, as best I can determine, quite a wealthy man."

"I see." The news did not surprise her. During her conversation with Lord Neale, she had begun to suspect that perhaps she had been wrong about his wanting Edmund's money. There had been an element of surprise and almost amusement in his face when he had denied her accusation that had made her begin to wonder. It was primarily because of that fact that she had asked Zachary to investigate the man.

"The Neale lands are quite large and profitable," Zachary went on. "They seem to have been a family that tended to its property. The revenues from the estate are quite good, but in addition to that, Lord Neale's mother was the only grandchild of quite a wealthy man, and upon his death, he left a fortune to her son, which Lord Neale came into upon his majority. The man is not rumored to be extravagant. Nor is he a gambler. The money is conservatively invested and has grown steadily."

"So he is more wealthy than Sir Edmund, I gather," Eleanor mused.

"Oh, yes. I would say his fortune is the equal of yours, perhaps even more."

Eleanor nodded. "Thank you, Zachary."

She stood up as he left the room and wandered over to the window, where she stood staring out at the small garden behind the house.

She was not sure exactly how she felt about what her man of business had discovered. There had been an uprush of pleased satisfaction to learn that Lord Neale was not the greedy man she had assumed him to be, that, unlike Edmund's own mother, he had not been living off Edmund's fortune.

But she could not help feeling a pang of hurt to realize that Lord Neale had not come to argue Edmund out of marrying her out of any sort of self-interest, but simply because he wanted to save his nephew from Eleanor. His only reason had been his contempt and dislike for her.

It did not bear contemplating that the only man whose kisses had deeply stirred her was a man who despised her.

Eleanor blinked away the moisture that filled her eyes. Well, there was nothing for it, she thought, except to go to Kent and face her implacable enemy. The one man she wanted and the one man she could not have.

CHAPTER SIX

TEDLOW PARK, long the home of the Scarbrough family, was a pleasant, rambling structure, timber-framed and redbricked. The center section, built in the time of Queen Elizabeth, had an uneven foundation, giving it a faintly rolling look, and wings had been added to it as the fancy struck whatever Scarbrough was living there at the time, sprawling outward and upward. The result was a mansion that was at once large and homey, with a whimsical sort of appeal.

It had been very dear to Edmund, who had grown up in it, but Eleanor had visited it only once before, when he had taken her home to meet his mother. It had been such an ordeal, with his mother alternately weeping and berating her son, then taking to her bed and refusing to even come down to eat with the new-lyweds, that Edmund and Eleanor had left the next day. Edmund had gone home by himself a few months later, just before they left for Italy, but Eleanor had remained in London.

As her carriage pulled up in front of the mansion now, she experienced a pang of regret that Edmund

had not seen his beloved home once more before his death.

Dario looked out the window interestedly. "So this is Tedlow Park," he said, nodding as he studied it. "Yes, it is as Edmund described. I could not quite picture it, but now I understand what he meant. He said it was a house touched by fairy dust."

Eleanor smiled. "Yes. I have heard him say that. It is a very charming place."

Dario alighted from the carriage and offered her his hand as she came down the steps. They stood for a moment looking at the house.

"I suppose it belongs to Edmund's cousin now, Sir Malcolm Scarbrough," Eleanor mused.

"Does his mother still live here?" Dario asked.

"I think not. Her letter to me was written from Bainbury Manor, but this is where she asked to meet with me. Her home, she informed me, was much too small to pleasantly receive guests. Don't ask me what she meant. Quite frankly, I doubt that I will be received pleasantly by Lady Honoria, no matter what the location."

"Edmund told me something about her. She seemed a very…um…needful sort of woman."

Eleanor nodded, then let out a little sigh. "I must not speak ill of the woman. Her only son has died, after all. She can scarcely be blamed for being unhappy. And I must deal with her a great deal in the

future. I can only wish that Edmund had not put his sister's fortune in my hands."

"He thought you were the most capable, I'm sure," Dario told her. "He was a little in awe of you, you know."

"In awe?" Eleanor glanced at him, startled. "But how could he be in awe of me? He was a genius."

"Ah, but you had a head for things that he understood not at all—account books, profits, investments."

Eleanor smiled reminiscently. "They gave him a headache, he said."

A footman in formal livery opened the door and ushered them into a nearby room. A middle-aged woman and a girl not yet into long skirts sat on a couch, flanked on one side by a young man sitting in a chair. But Eleanor's eyes went immediately to the man who stood apart from the others, lounging with one elbow on the mantel above the fireplace. It was Lord Neale.

His gaze went as quickly to hers, and he straightened, coming forward. "Lady Eleanor."

He bowed, and she offered her hand. She realized as he closed his fingers over it that she was trembling slightly. His skin was warm against hers, and faintly rough to the touch.

"My lord," Eleanor replied as evenly as she could. She hoped that she was not blushing, for she felt suddenly, unaccountably, warm. She tried very hard

not to think about the last time they had been together. But it seemed that the only thing occupying her mind at the moment was the thought of that kiss.

"You know my sister, I believe," Anthony was saying, turning toward the sofa. "Lady Honoria Scarbrough."

"Good day, my lady," Eleanor offered politely.

"Lady Eleanor." Edmund's mother gave her a slight nod, her face a rigid mask of sorrow.

Lady Honoria was dressed in black, with a heavy black veil turned back to expose her face. It was a dress so heavily mournful that it seemed almost comical, like a broadly-drawn character on a stage. However, Eleanor noticed that the dress itself was of the first stare of fashion, and the material was a luxurious silk. Lady Honoria was still an attractive woman, and she dressed well. Eleanor suspected that had black not suited her blond, pale-skinned looks so well, Lady Honoria would not have worn heavy mourning for so long.

Anthony next introduced Eleanor to the girl beside Lady Honoria. It was her daughter, Samantha. Though Eleanor had met her once, she would scarcely have recognized the girl, who had gone in the past year and a half through one of the growth spurts that happened to young girls, turning the chubby-cheeked child Eleanor had met into a long-limbed, slender girl teetering on the edge of

womanhood. Samantha was dressed all in black, as well, but the color did not look as good on her, the stark color washing out her very pale skin and almost white-blond hair, so that she appeared rather colorless.

"Hello, Samantha," Eleanor said, extending her hand to shake the girl's. "It's good to see you again."

Samantha smiled, lighting up her face, and Eleanor could see a resemblance to Sir Edmund in her. "Hello. It is good to see you, too."

"I hope that we can get to know one another a little better," Eleanor went on.

"I would like that, too," Samantha replied a little shyly, casting a quick nervous glance at her mother.

Lady Honoria responded with a small frown and a tightening of her lips, and Samantha's smile left her face. She cast an apologetic glance at Eleanor, and Eleanor smiled back at her reassuringly. She had meant it when she said she wanted to get to know the girl better. For Edmund's sake, she intended to be friends with Samantha and, she hoped, keep the girl from being too much under her mother's thumb. She was prepared for Lady Honoria's slights, and she knew that the woman would try to thwart any attempt she made to befriend Samantha. It would be a long process, and Eleanor wanted to avoid, if she could, making the poor girl the center of a war between herself and Edmund's mother.

Lord Neale turned toward the other man in the

room, saying, "Allow me to present to you Sir Malcolm Scarbrough, Edmund's cousin and the new master of Tedlow Park."

There was a faint resemblance to Edmund in this man, too—similar fair coloring and tall, slender build—but where Edmund's face had been alive with intelligence and interest in the world around him, this man's face was carefully controlled.

"My lady," he said to Eleanor, bowing to her a little stiffly. "Welcome to my home."

"Thank you, Sir Malcolm." She turned toward Dario, from whom Anthony had neatly separated her during the introductions. "Allow me to introduce to you a good friend of Sir Edmund's, Mr. Dario Paradella."

Dario bowed with his usual Latin flourish. "I am most honored to meet you, Lady Scarbrough. Miss Scarbrough. Sir Malcolm. Lord Neale, it is an honor to see you again. I hope you will forgive my intrusion into this time of family grief. Sir Edmund was a good friend to me, and I wished to pay my respects to him here, at his family home."

"Of course. A splendid sentiment." Lady Honoria extended her hand to him with a gracious smile. Clearly she was not immune to Dario's charm, however much she might dislike Eleanor. "We are quite pleased to have you here with us. I know Edmund would have appreciated it." She stopped, her voice catching, and dabbed her handkerchief to

her eye. "He was such a wonderful man. A blessing to have as a son. If only he had not gone away…"

Honoria began to cry. Samantha reached over to pat her hand and murmur soothing words. Sir Malcolm cast Honoria a brief glance, then looked away with a bored expression. Beside Eleanor, Anthony's jaw tightened, but he said nothing.

Dario, however, went quickly to the woman's side, offering his pristine white handkerchief for her tears and bending over her solicitously. In an amazingly swift time, his ministrations brought a watery smile to Lady Honoria's lips and her tears disappeared.

"I think it is time we went to the church, don't you?" Anthony offered. "The vicar is expecting us."

"Yes, of course." Sir Malcolm sprang up from his chair, looking relieved at the ending of the small emotional scene.

Dario helped Lady Honoria up and escorted her out to Sir Malcolm's carriage. He managed to deftly maneuver himself into the carriage with her, casting a sly glance and a smile toward Eleanor. Eleanor smiled back. She had told Dario that she wished to spend some time with Edmund's sister, and he had neatly managed to afford her the opportunity.

"Miss Scarbrough, why don't you ride with me in my carriage?" Eleanor offered. "Yours seems quite crowded, and we can have a nice chat."

"I should like that," Samantha answered quickly,

glancing toward the other vehicle, where her mother was already ensconced. She turned, hurriedly tying on her bonnet, and scrambled up into Eleanor's carriage.

"That sounds like an excellent idea," Anthony agreed. "I believe I shall join you." He swung toward the groom, giving him instructions to tie his horse to the back of the carriage, and turned back to Eleanor, offering her his hand up into the coach.

Anthony was almost as smooth as Dario had been, Eleanor thought. She should have been annoyed at his inviting himself into her chat with Samantha, but, frankly, she was aware only of a frisson of excitement.

"You have very nice horses, my lady," the girl told her politely, referring to the matched grays that pulled the vehicle.

"Our Samantha is quite the horsewoman," Anthony said, his face relaxing into a fond smile as he looked at his niece.

"Riding is ever so much more fun than boring things like geography," Samantha told him a little saucily. "Or dancing. Mama is making me take lessons with a dance tutor." She grimaced.

"You don't enjoy them?" Eleanor inquired.

"No. He smiles all the time. Like this." Samantha demonstrated, showing them a stiff rictus of a smile that looked more like a person in pain than someone being agreeable. "And he always smells of peppermints." She paused, then added judiciously, "It's not

that I don't like peppermints, but I think he does it to cover up the smell of gin. I saw him one time taking a nip out in front before he came in the house."

"Well, dancing is something that will be much more fun once you know how to do it and can go to dances," Eleanor told her.

"I know. But that is years away. Mama says I can't dance at the county assemblies until I'm seventeen, and that is two whole years. But I don't suppose it matters, because there won't be anybody to stand up with except Mama's friends and such, and they're all dreadfully old."

"My dear girl, you wound me," Anthony teased, laying a hand on his heart, his grin belying his words.

He had, Eleanor noted, the sort of grin that made one's heart flutter a little in one's chest. A long masculine dimple popped into one cheek, giving his usually stoic expression a sudden, compelling charm. Watching him, she could not help but smile, as well.

"Am I among this group of which you speak?" Anthony went on. "For I intend to ask you to dance when you reach seventeen. Perhaps even before."

Samantha giggled and dimpled prettily. "No, of course not, Uncle Anthony. You aren't old. Well, not old like General Havermore or Mr. Sotherton, or any of those other men who dance attendance on Mama."

"And are any of them gaining ground?" Anthony asked. "I have a fiver on the general, you know."

Samantha chuckled again. "No, you don't. You are being silly. You know Mama would never marry the general. He's ancient, and besides, he hasn't enough fortune." She covered her mouth, looking guilty, and said quickly, "Oh! I'm sorry. I shouldn't have said that. I didn't mean…" She trailed off, obviously not wishing to lie, but regretting what her words had implied about her mother.

"Of course you didn't mean anything bad," Eleanor told her quickly. "A mother has to be especially careful about making such decisions, and I am sure Lady Honoria is. After all, when one has a child, one has to consider her welfare above all else. Lady Honoria could not possibly consider tying herself to someone who could not support both of you in the manner appropriate to you."

Samantha looked relieved. "Yes, of course. That's right."

Out of the corner of her eye, Eleanor saw Lord Neale watching her, a considering expression on his face. No doubt he would have expected her to seize the opportunity to encourage Lady Honoria's daughter to speak ill about her. That was the sort of person he presumed her to be. Eleanor wondered, with some degree of hurt, what it was about her that had made him take such a thorough and immediate dislike to her.

Eleanor pulled her thoughts back from that unproductive path and resumed her conversation with Samantha. "When you are older and make your debut, you will be able to dance with many more people. And I can assure you that a great number of them will be young men, not old ones."

Samantha sighed. "Mama doesn't want to take me to London for my debut. She says we are quite poor now that Edmund is gone."

"What nonsense," Anthony responded, his voice edged with irritation. "Of course you will have a season when you are eighteen."

"Certainly," Eleanor agreed. "There will be ample money for that."

"Really?" Samantha's face brightened. "But Mama dislikes going to London. She says it is quite wearing."

"She will go," Anthony responded, his voice grim.

"If she does not, you can come stay with me while you make your debut," Eleanor offered.

"Truly? Do you mean it?" Samantha asked eagerly.

"Of course I do," Eleanor replied. "Edmund entrusted me with your money, and I am sure that he wanted me to do my best to take care of you in other areas, as well. I do not have enough social position myself, but I shall make arrangements, so that you are presented by someone more important in the *ton*."

"Samantha's name will ensure her a good place in the *ton*," Anthony said firmly.

"Of course," Eleanor agreed evenly. "But she needs, as well, a sponsor of the highest pedigree. Would my friend Lady Barre do, do you think? I am sure that Juliana would be happy to help me. And if she cannot, I will have no problem finding someone else of high station."

Anthony looked at her quizzically. "And how do you propose to do that?"

Eleanor gazed back at him, a challenge in her eyes. "I have found that there is always an aristocrat somewhere who has fallen on hard times and will, for an infusion of cash, be quite willing to act as one's friend."

"Such cynicism from one so young and beautiful," Anthony murmured, his eyes dancing.

His words warmed her, and Eleanor glanced away quickly so that he would not see the reaction in her face. "Anyway, Samantha, I suspect that when your mother hears about you making your debut, she will immediately realize that she wants to be the one to see you through your season. A girl's first season is the sort of memory mothers thrive on."

She noticed that the girl's face lost some of its enthusiasm at her words, but Samantha only nodded and said wistfully, "Still…'tis a long time away. I wish I could see London. It must have been so exciting to go to Italy, as you and Edmund did."

"Italy is beautiful," Eleanor agreed. "We both enjoyed it very much. And someday you shall see it, if you wish."

Samantha drew in a sharp breath. "Do you mean it?"

"Yes. I had a tour of the Continent after I left school, and I absolutely recommend it. The art, the history, the music—oh, there are so many wonderful things to see and do. It is an invaluable part of one's education." Eleanor's eyes sparkled at the memory.

She and Samantha launched into a long conversation regarding the wonders that waited for one on the Continent, taking up the rest of the trip to the village church. Across from them, Lord Neale contented himself with watching the two of them talk, offering only a comment now and then when called upon by his niece.

It was, he thought, a thoroughly enjoyable exercise. Eleanor was dressed all in black today, a plain gold locket her only ornamentation. But she was not a woman who needed ornamentation, and the severe color was an excellent foil to her dramatic beauty. Her beauty jolted him every time he saw her, just as it had the first time.

But there was more to her than beauty. She was quick-witted, as well, and a delight to converse with, whether she was extolling the virtues of Italy or exchanging acerbic ripostes with him. It was no

wonder that Edmund had fallen in love with her. The wonder, he thought, was that half the *ton* had *not*. He had always regarded himself as made of sterner stuff than many men, who seemed to be guided more by their loins than by their wits, but after a few minutes in her company, he had found himself kissing her without thought to the consequences.

Even now, thinking about that kiss, he felt lust curl through him. He was not fool enough to try to tell himself that he had not been under her spell when he kissed her. He had known he should not, but his desire had overcome his reason.

Worse, she was making him doubt his own convictions. Watching her with Samantha, he found himself wondering if he had been wrong about her all along. He had come along with the two of them because he had wanted to protect his niece from Eleanor's machinations. But she had surprised him by not undercutting Honoria's influence with her daughter. She obviously had Honoria pegged—she had phrased it nicely enough, but he had known what she meant when she said that Honoria would doubtless change her mind about accompanying her daughter for her debut in London. Honoria might drag her feet now—she always preferred the small pond of the Kentish countryside to the large pool of London, and Anthony had his suspicions that she did not like the prospect of sitting on the sidelines as a

chaperone. But let Samantha suggest that Eleanor was happy to present Samantha, and Honoria would let nothing stand in the way of keeping Eleanor from doing so.

But Eleanor had not taken the opportunity to underscore Honoria's flaws. Indeed, she had couched every reference to Samantha's mother with respect and had even offered the girl an acceptable reason for what they all knew was her mother's greedy motivation in any consideration of marriage.

It would have been easy for Eleanor to turn Samantha away from her mother and toward her. Eleanor was a much easier person to like, and she would be an adult companion who would not domineer and suppress Samantha's spirit. God knows, the poor girl needed such a woman in her life. Anthony had no illusions about his sister's qualities as a mother. Yet Eleanor had offered friendship to Samantha without using her as pawn in her struggle with Honoria.

On the other hand, his rational mind reminded him, her behavior might not be proof of anything other than her skill at manipulating people. She had laid a foundation with Samantha, and there was nothing to say that in the future she would not use that foundation to drive a wedge between the girl and Honoria. And, by behaving so circumspectly, she was causing him to wonder if he had been wrong in his evaluation of her. Winning him over would be an

essential step in any designs she had on Samantha's fortune. She would know that he was the person who would find any false figures in the books, who would realize it if she was taking money from Samantha's trust. If she could entrap him, she would have a free rein with the money.

Nor was there anything to say that she might not have her sights set on him as bigger game than Edmund. He had betrayed his desire for her with that kiss the other night. Was it not possible that she might have decided to try to lure him into marriage next?

It would never happen, of course. He was the last person to tie himself to the sort of adventuress his father had. That was a lesson he had learned well and young. No woman would ever have such control over him.

It was ridiculous to even think about it.

But Eleanor did not know that. She was no doubt a woman confident in her beauty and her skills; she would think she could turn even a man who disliked her into one panting to have her. She could hope to get a great deal more out of all this than merely skimming off money from Samantha's trust. Indeed, now that he thought about it, that was probably why she had brought that foppish Italian with her. She may have hoped to arouse his own jealousy.

"Uncle! Why are you scowling like that?" Samantha's voice startled Anthony out of his reverie.

"What? Oh." Anthony relaxed his brow. "Just thinking about a problem. Nothing important."

Eleanor, watching him, had the distinct impression that Lord Neale's "problem" was her. He had been watching her the entire time she and Samantha had been talking, and when the considering look on his face darkened into a fierce frown, she felt certain it had to do with her. He probably disliked the fact that Samantha and she were getting along well. No doubt he had come along with them precisely for the purpose of observing what she said and did with his niece. However friendly he had seemed during the ride over, she must keep in mind that it did not mean he liked her. No doubt he felt only that she must be lulled into thinking that he was no longer her enemy.

Eleanor gave him one long, cool look, then returned to her conversation with Samantha.

It was only minutes later that the carriage slowed and stopped. Eleanor looked out the window. They had arrived at the cemetery. It lay behind the village church, a gray stone structure with the Norman tower that proclaimed its age. Before them was the lych-gate, where Sir Malcolm, Dario and Lady Honoria already stood, waiting for them. Lady Honoria leaned heavily on Dario's arm, her dark veil now covering her face.

Eleanor disembarked from the carriage and turned to her coachman, who had climbed down from his high seat and now held out a teak box to

her. Eleanor's face saddened, and she reached out to take the box containing Edmund's ashes. Lord Neale quickly moved to help her, and she handed the box into his care. Whatever their dislike of each other, she knew that he, too, had cared for Edmund.

Beside her, tears welled in Samantha's eyes. Eleanor curved a comforting arm around the girl's shoulders, and they started the walk into the cemetery.

The vicar met them at the Scarbrough family vault and said a prayer over the box of ashes. After a few words from the Bible and a short eulogy for Edmund, the box was laid in the family mausoleum. It was a short, affecting ceremony, and Eleanor's eye welled with tears. Lady Honoria, predictably, sobbed through much of the eulogy, leaning against Dario's supportive shoulder. Eleanor kept her arm around Samantha, who dabbed away her tears as they slowly and quietly trickled down her cheeks. Lord Neale, not surprisingly, remained stoically inexpressive.

They left the crypt, Dario leading the way with the sobbing Honoria, and the others following behind. They stopped outside the lych-gate, standing for a moment in an awkward little group.

"It would seem rather late now for the discussion about Edmund's will," Eleanor began carefully. Nor did she feel like dealing with Honoria's histrionics. The ceremony had brought a fresh soreness to her heart as she thought of Edmund, and she feared that

his mother's sense of drama and her general obstruc-
tiveness might prod her into making a remark to the
woman that she would later regret.

"Oh, yes," Lady Honoria agreed with feeling. "I
could not face the matter now, not after…oh, my
child, my child…" Her words trailed off into a fresh
bout of tears.

Eleanor, with a quick glance at Dario, suspected
that he was growing rather weary of his role as com-
forter. "If you would direct us toward the nearest inn,
we shall meet for our discussion tomorrow."

"Nonsense. There is no need for you to stay at an
inn. The local one is quite small, and not, I am sure,
up to your standards," Lord Neale told her.

"Oh, but Anthony, I haven't room at my house,"
Honoria responded, looking alarmed, her tears van-
ishing in an instant. "You know how small my house
is, now that we have had to leave Tedlow Park."

For the first time, Eleanor saw emotion flicker
across Sir Malcolm's face. Looking irritated, he said
quickly, "Lady Honoria, I told you that you and
Samantha were more than welcome to continue living
at the Park. I would never have asked you to leave."

"No, it is no longer my home," Honoria went on
in a martyred voice. "And I could not live there, with
all its memories. Samantha and I must become used
to getting by on our own. Of course, our funds won't
enable us to live in aught but a cottage."

"The manor is scarcely a cottage, Honoria," Lord

Neale corrected her dryly. "You will have our guests thinking that you live in a hovel."

"Oh, no, it is not a hovel…" Honoria demurred without much enthusiasm.

"It is a very nice house," Samantha put in, looking embarrassed. "And, really, Mama, there are two other bedchambers."

Honoria shot her daughter a fierce look, and the girl subsided, flushing.

"Not made up, I fear," Honoria told Eleanor. "Hardly even furnished, really."

"Of course," Eleanor replied gravely, suppressing a smile. "I would not dream of putting you to the trouble, my lady. I am well able to stay at the local inn. I have weathered a few rustic places before, I assure you."

"Do not be absurd," Anthony said. "I intended for you and Mr. Paradella to be my guests at the Hall. The rooms are already made up for you."

"Oh." Eleanor, nonplussed, could think of nothing to say. She had more or less assumed that she would spend the night at an inn after the ceremony and the discussion about Samantha's trust, or perhaps at Honoria's home, but she had never considered staying at Lord Neale's house. She would have expected him to be as opposed to her presence as was Lady Honoria. "Well, yes, then, thank you. That would be very nice."

"Yes, my lord," Dario agreed politely. "It is most kind of you to offer."

Anthony glanced noncommittally at the Italian, then gave him a short nod. "All right then. If you and Mr. Paradella would follow me…"

He tipped his hat to his sister and niece, then untied his horse from the back of the carriage and mounted it. After a few brief words with Eleanor's coachman, he started off down the lane. Eleanor and Dario entered the carriage, and they rolled off after him.

Dario let out a sigh and leaned his head back against the leather squab.

"Tired?" Eleanor asked, amusement lurking in her eyes.

Dario gave her a rueful grin. "I had always thought that English ladies were unemotional. Lady Scarbrough could be from Napoli."

Eleanor chuckled. "It was very kind of you to look after her."

He shrugged. "It was not so hard. You forget, I have three sisters, a mama and several aunts. I am used to tears. It was the least I could do for Edmund…and it saved you a little aggravation, I think."

"Yes, it did. I am very grateful for it."

"Then I am glad," he replied simply.

The Hall was only a few minutes from the village church, and it did not take them long to reach it. They approached the house down a long, curving drive. Eleanor had seen grander houses. The Hall had no tier of steps leading up to a magnificent front door,

no mullioned windows, no statues ornamenting the ends of the roof beams. It was built of plain gray stone, some of it great matching blocks and others of varying shapes and sizes, some of it blackened by lichen and time. But it had a majestic symmetry, with its massive square gatehouse and battlemented wings stretching out on either side. There was a sturdiness to it, a sense of age and security, that was appealing. Over time, bushes had grown up along the walls, softening their harsh appearance, and a blanket of ivy clung to one side. The sun, now growing lower in the sky, bathed the walls with a warm golden light.

Eleanor could not help but let out a little sigh of pleasure. "How lovely."

Dario took one look at the Hall and, doubtless comparing it to the graceful red-tiled villas of his homeland, arched an eyebrow. "It looks suited to him," he pronounced.

Eleanor let out a chuckle. "Yes. It does." She cast a doubtful glance at her friend. "I hope he does not bother you too much."

Dario laughed. "Not I. I think *he* is the one who is bothered by *me,*" he commented astutely. "It is, I think, amusing to watch the oh-so-stoic British gentleman struggle with his jealousy."

"Jealous? I hardly think so. The man disapproves of me." Yet Eleanor could not deny that the other night she had thought the very same thing.

"It is not impossible to feel both at once. Which makes his struggle even more entertaining to watch."

Eleanor was glad that Dario found himself entertained by it, for all through dinner Lord Neale was at his tight-lipped British worst where Dario was concerned. It was clear that Dario annoyed him, and Dario seemed to delight in stirring the fires of Anthony's irritation, his speech and gestures growing more effusive by the minute, his compliments to Eleanor more flowery, his gazes at her more lover-like. Watching Anthony's tight-jawed face, Eleanor was unsure whether she wanted more to give Dario a kick in the shins or to laugh.

Why, she wondered, had Lord Neale invited them to stay with him? Whatever lay behind his feelings—whether it was jealousy or simply a clash of personalities—it was clear that Anthony did not enjoy Dario's company. He had made it equally clear what he thought of her, even though he had kissed her the other night and had seemed—at least in her admittedly limited experience—to enjoy it. She had felt the heat surge in him, had known the tight clasp of his arms. She did not believe she was wrong in thinking that he had experienced the same searing passion she had.

But whatever attraction he had felt, he did not like her. Indeed, he obviously held her in disdain. Lord Neale, she thought, had disliked the fact that he had been drawn to her, had despised himself for kissing

her. It seemed unlikely that he would want to be in a position where he might be subjected to the same temptation. So it made little sense for him to voluntarily place himself in her company.

So why had he not let Eleanor and Dario stay at the inn? He had done more than simply extend the invitation. He had gone to the trouble of having their rooms prepared before he ever said a word. Was it simply the British insistence on polite behavior? Had he been so embarrassed by his sister's blatant disregard for courtesy that he had felt compelled to offer his own? No, for if he was to be believed, he had intended for them to stay with him before the issue arose outside the cemetery. And it was true that their rooms were ready for them—fires laid, fresh sheets on the beds, vases of flowers on the dressers. Surely, at a large house like this, they did not keep all the bedchambers in such a state of readiness.

Whatever the reason, she could not fool herself into believing that Anthony was enjoying their presence. His face was like stone most of the evening, and every topic of conversation either of them brought up died a quick death. It was a relief when the meal was over, and she could make the excuse of weariness and go up to her bed.

Once there, however, she had little desire to retire. One of the maids came in to help her undress, but after that, she found herself pacing the floor rather

than getting into the large testered bed. She was not sleepy in the slightest.

She went to the window and pushed aside the curtain, but there was nothing to see. The night was pitch black, the sky covered with clouds so that not even the stars or a sliver of moon shone through to illuminate the landscape. Nor was there any book to while away her time.

Eleanor thought about slipping downstairs to the library to get a book to read, but the possibility of running into Anthony kept her from doing so. It would be far too embarrassing to be caught roaming about his house in her nightclothes, even if the dressing gown over her nightshift was far less revealing than many evening gowns. He might even think she was there hoping to run into him, that she wished to lure him into an indiscretion.

Finally she gave up, blew out the candle and got into bed. But she did not sleep. Instead, her mind ran round the same issues in a most aggravating way, and it was close to an hour before her eyes finally closed and she drifted into sleep.

She awoke sometime later with a start, blinking in confusion, unsure what had roused her. The room was very dark, the furniture only vague darker shapes in the general blackness. The only light came from the hallway, a dim glow that shone through a thin strip between the opened door and the doorjamb.

At that realization, Eleanor's sleepy brain jolted fully awake. The door had been shut when she went to bed, not standing open a crack. Heart pounding, she turned her head, looking across the room.

A dark form stood hunched over in front of her dresser.

CHAPTER SEVEN

ELEANOR FROZE, and for a long moment she could not breathe or move for the fear coursing through her. She watched as the figure moved stealthily across the room toward her baggage and bent over it.

Outrage overcame the momentary paralysis, and she reached over to the small table beside her bed, grabbing the first thing she could find. It turned out to be a candlestick, and she hurled it at the crouched form with all her might, letting out a loud yell as she did so.

The heavy metal candlestick landed on his back with a satisfying thump. There was a muffled exclamation of surprised pain, and the shadowy figure jumped up and ran for the door.

Eleanor scrambled out of bed after him, but her legs got tangled in the bedcovers, and she stumbled and fell to the floor. She pulled the sheets away and jumped up, running after him, screaming, "Stop! Come back!"

She ran out into the hallway, but the intruder had already disappeared from sight. She ran down the

corridor to the staircase and stopped, looking down into the darkness below. She could make out nothing, and she realized that the man could be hiding anywhere down there, waiting for her to come along so that he could knock her unconscious. Or worse.

She turned and looked back down the hallway to her bedroom. Past her chamber, a door opened, and Anthony charged out. "What is it? What happened?"

Dario popped out of his room, too. "Eleanor?"

Anthony ran to Eleanor, taking her upper arms in his hands. "Are you all right?"

His hands were like iron on her arms, and Eleanor could feel their heat through the sheer muslin of her nightshift. Nor could she escape the realization that Anthony was half-clothed. He had obviously thrown on his breeches hastily, the top button left undone, and they rode low on his hips. His feet and his torso were bare. He was half-naked and only inches from her, and it seemed to Eleanor that she could look nowhere that she did not see bare flesh.

His eyes, scanning her face, dropped down her body, and it was then that Eleanor realized she was wearing nothing but her nightshift. She blushed to the roots of her hair.

"What happened?" Anthony barked.

"Why did you scream?" Dario asked anxiously, coming up beside them. He, too, had obviously just come from bed, his hair rumpled and feet bare, shirt hanging outside his breeches and open halfway down.

"There was someone in my room," Eleanor told them. "I threw something at him, and he ran. But I don't know where he went. By the time I got out here, he was gone."

"Did he hurt you?" Anthony's brows rushed together in a fearsome scowl.

"No. No, I'm fine, just startled."

Anthony released her arms and took off toward the staircase. Dario followed, pausing long enough to duck back into his room and get a candle before he followed Anthony down the stairs.

Eleanor hurried back into her room. The first thing she did was grab her dressing gown and throw it on over her nightshift. Then she lit a candle, and went over to her dresser and her baggage to see what the intruder had done. But even as she did, her mind kept going back to Anthony.

She had never before seen a half-naked man, and the truth was, the sight had been decidedly distracting. It was obvious that the superb fit of Anthony's clothing was not owed to any judicious padding by his tailor. His shoulders were wide and his chest broad, his arms tautly muscled. Even though she had just been scared out of her wits, even though her primary concern was catching the man who had been in her room, when she had seen Anthony, she had felt a fierce jolt of desire.

Even now, remembering the sight of him, heat blossomed in her abdomen. He had looked, she thought,

the elemental male—raw and powerful. And she had wanted him, her swift hunger just as elemental.

It was mad to feel this way about him, she told herself. The two of them were at odds. He had thought her too low of birth to marry his nephew; certainly he would never consider her good enough for himself. Not, of course, that she would ever think of marrying him, either. He was the last thing she would want in a spouse—controlling, snobbish, cold.

Cold? She thought of his kiss. No, he was not cold. Underneath his exterior, fires raged. And after all, one could have a lover rather than a husband.

Sighing, she shook her head, firmly dispelling her wayward thoughts. Sitting around mooning about a man who despised her was not helping her discover who had been in her room.

Eleanor turned her attention to her dresser. It was perfectly clean, except for her silver-backed brush and mirror set. She went over to the bags that he had been searching when she startled him and squatted down beside them. They were empty; the Hall maids had efficiently unpacked everything and laid it away in drawers for her convenience.

Just as she closed the last bag, it struck her that something had been wrong about the dresser. Her locket! She had not seen her locket! With a cry of distress, she jumped up and ran over to the long mahogany dresser. Holding her candle over it, she

searched up and down the length of it, then stepped back and examined the floor, thinking that he might have knocked it off the top. She even got down and looked underneath. The locket was not there.

She let out a moan. The locket had been a simple thing, not worth a great deal, but it had held a little portrait of Edmund. He had given it to her on Boxing Day, and since his death, it had taken on new importance to her.

Eleanor hurried out into the hall, and found Anthony and Dario coming back up the stairs. "Did you find anyone?"

Dario shook his head. "There was no one."

"Tell me what happened," Anthony said. "No. Wait." He disappeared into his room and emerged a moment later, shrugging into a shirt. "Now. What happened?"

"Something woke me up. I suppose he made a noise. Anyway, I opened my eyes, and I saw someone over at my dresser."

"A man?"

"I didn't really think. I assumed it was a man." She paused for a moment, thinking, then went on. "Yes, I am fairly certain it was a man. His attire was male, and though I could not see him clearly, I think he was larger than most women."

"Tall?"

Again she paused, thinking back. "I'm not sure. He was bent over the dresser at first, and then, when

I screamed, it all happened very fast. And the light was poor. I never saw his face. His back was to me."

"Was anything missing this time?"

"This time?" Dario asked. "This has happened before? Why did you not tell me? Has someone tried to hurt you?"

"No. I was not even there the other time. I was with friends. But someone went through my jewelry, though I could not tell that they took anything other than an inexpensive brooch." She looked at Anthony. "This time he took my locket."

"The one you wore today?" Anthony asked.

Eleanor nodded. "I took it off this evening when I went to bed and laid it down on the dresser. It was gone when I looked just now. I searched all around on the floor and I could not find it. But I cannot imagine why anyone would break into my room to steal a locket. It was not very valuable, except to me."

"Whoever it is obviously is not looking for something of monetary value," Anthony commented.

"Surely it is not the same person," Eleanor protested.

"You think it is a coincidence?" Anthony asked skeptically. "Someone breaks into your bedroom at home and searches through your jewelry. Someone breaks into your bedroom here and steals a piece of jewelry."

"But how could anyone even have known I was here?" Eleanor asked. "I myself didn't know I would

be here until a few hours ago. The man tonight surely was a local thief."

"Who happened to pick tonight to break into my house?" Anthony retorted. "Who walked past my safe and my silver and went only into your bedroom?"

"Then tell me how he knew I was here," Eleanor challenged him. "Unless you are suggesting it was you who entered my bedchamber."

A light flared in his gray eyes and as quickly vanished. He said in a mild voice, "There is Mr. Paradella, of course."

At that statement Dario burst into a stream of excited Italian. Anthony turned his cool, measuring gaze on him.

"Calm down, sir. I am not actually suggesting that you took the lady's locket."

"I think not!"

"I think if you would consider the question, my lady, it is easily answered," Anthony went on. "The intruder knew you were here because he followed your carriage."

A shiver ran down Eleanor's spine. "That's absurd," she said hastily.

"The whole thing sounds absurd," Dario put in. "Why would a thief break in and take nothing? Why would someone steal your locket?"

Anthony shrugged. "Just because we cannot see it doesn't mean there is not a reason." He turned to Eleanor. "And just because you don't like the idea

that someone was following you does not mean it didn't happen."

"But why?" Eleanor flung her arms wide.

"Obviously you must have something this chap wants. Think. Is there nothing you possess that would be important to someone else, even if it's not really valuable? A…a letter, perhaps. Or something that would incriminate someone."

"Incriminate them in what?" Eleanor asked sharply. "Do you think I have evidence of crimes lying about my bedroom?"

"I have no idea," he retorted with some asperity. "But it is not my bedchamber that people are breaking into. It is yours."

"You think this is my fault, don't you? You think I have done something that has brought this upon myself?"

"I did not say that."

"You did not have to!" Eleanor cried. "It is written all over your face. I know what you think of me."

"I doubt that," he replied calmly.

Beside them, Dario cleared his throat. "Eleanor…I am sure Lord Neale did not mean that you had done anything wrong."

Eleanor cast him a dark look. "You obviously do not know his lordship. He thinks me an adventuress, a fortune hunter."

"A fortune hunter!" Dario turned a shocked gaze on Anthony.

"What do you think it is?" Eleanor swung back to Anthony. "A passionate letter from some married lord? Some evidence of scandal that no doubt I was involved in, as well? Or maybe the man is one of my former cohorts, and he thinks I took his share of whatever we swindled out of some poor widow or orphan."

"My, you have thought of more things than my poor imagination could come up with," Anthony remarked, a smile tugging at the corner of his lips.

Eleanor glared. She longed to slap him, but she remembered how easily he had fended her off the last time she had tried that.

"Eleanor, you must calm down," Dario said soothingly, reaching out to take her arm.

"Oh, don't tell me what to do," Eleanor replied irritably and shook off his hand. "I do not think, sir, that anyone took my locket with Edmund's portrait inside because they thought it would incriminate them."

To her dismay, she felt tears well up in her eyes, and she whirled angrily and stalked back into her bedroom, slamming the door behind her.

Angrily she dashed the tears from her eyes. She wasn't sure if the tears were from anger at Lord Neale or sorrow at the loss of her locket, but it humiliated her that he had seen them. She hated for him to think that he had scored some sort of triumph over her.

She took off her dressing gown and threw it on the chair. Lord Neale was the most infuriating man she had ever known. She hated him. But more than that, she knew, she hated that he thought of her what he did.

There was a knock on her door, and she swung around as the door opened and Anthony walked in. She stared at him in amazement.

"What the devil do you think you're doing here?" she snapped.

"Bearding the lioness in her den, I believe," he offered with a faint smile. He came a little farther into the room. "Actually I came to apologize."

Eleanor's eyebrows vaulted up. Nothing he could have said would have surprised her more.

"Your room was entered while you were a guest in my home. I must bear the blame for not protecting you well enough. I let my anger at that lead me to say things to you that I should not have."

He had not said, she noticed, that they were things he did not believe.

"I apologize for both," he went on.

"You apology is accepted," Eleanor replied, unbending a little. "You did not realize, after all, that you were bringing in a guest who was being stalked by a thief."

"Then you agree that it is the same man who broke into your house a few days ago?" he asked, coming over to stand in front of her.

Eleanor nodded and sighed. "It seems foolish to believe anything else. And I doubt that the culprit was you or Dario...the man in my room was scarcely naked."

This time it was Anthony whose cheeks reddened. "I apologize for my attire. When you screamed, I...well, I thought haste was in order."

She smiled a little, somewhat gratified that she had managed to embarrass him.

They stood for a moment; then Anthony said quietly, "I am sorry that your locket was taken."

"It was dear to me," Eleanor told him, sorrow lacing her voice. "Edmund gave it to me last Christmas. It had a portrait of him inside it, the only one I have of him." She looked away from him, feeling the tears threatening to well up once more.

He reached out and took her chin in his hand, then turned her face up. Eleanor stiffened, gazed up at him almost defiantly. He reached out and with his knuckle wiped away the tear that crept from the corner of her eye.

"You loved him, didn't you?" he said quietly.

She pulled her chin from his grasp and stepped back. "Of course I did. Edmund was a good man. A genius. He was a kind and gentle soul, and he was very dear to me. I know you seem to have trouble believing that, but—"

"No. I believe you." He reached out and wrapped his hand around her wrist, as though to keep her

from moving farther away from him. For a long moment, he stared down into her face. There was a tension in his long lean body, only inches from her, a heat that flickered in his gaze.

Eleanor felt breathless and flushed, and she was very aware of where his hand lay against her skin.

"But your words are those one might say about a brother," he went on hoarsely. "What about passion? Did you feel that for Edmund?"

Eleanor stiffened, and her eyes flashed. "I have found that passion is highly overrated."

"Indeed," he murmured.

His eyes darkened, and she knew he meant to kiss her. She could not let it happen again, she thought. She could not allow desire to overtake her with this man who did not love her—indeed, did not even respect her.

He pulled her closer, bending down to take her lips with his. Eleanor's free hand went up to his chest to push him away, but when she touched him, her hand curled up instead, clutching his shirt, as passion shook her. His mouth was hot and demanding, arousing responses she had never dreamed of.

Anthony's arms went around her, pulling her tightly up into him. Eleanor wrapped her arms around his neck, clinging to him. She felt as if in a fever, surging with heat, dizzy and weak. She knew she should not allow this, but she could not seem to stop herself. Normally so calm and in control, she

was suddenly all fire and hunger, her blood racing through her veins.

He made a noise deep in his throat, and she felt a shudder shake him. His hands moved down her back, gliding over her buttocks, then coming back up her sides, caressing her with long smooth strokes. The intimate movement of his hands startled her, but at the same time it sent a long curl of desire coiling through her abdomen. She felt certain she should be appalled at his familiarity, but it was fierce heat she felt instead. Indeed, she realized that, far from being appalled, she wanted to feel his hands everywhere on her body.

As if he had read her mind, one hand moved up her side and came to rest on her breast. A quiver of desire pierced straight down through her, igniting a fire in her loins.

He continued to kiss her, their lips clinging and consuming, parting only to change position, until she was breathless. And all the while his hand cupped her breast, stroking and caressing, building a hunger in her so fierce that her legs trembled from the force of it, threatening to give way beneath her.

A moan escaped her mouth, and she realized with astonishment that she wanted more of him. Her skin tingled in anticipation, longing for the touch of his lips all over her, and a sweet ache blossomed deep inside her, yearning for fulfillment. His thumb grazed gently over her nipple, making it harden, and she jerked at the sudden intense burst of sensation.

His hand went to the buttons of her nightgown, fumbling them open until he could slip his hand inside. And then her bare breast was in his hand, filling it, and he was squeezing it gently, his thumb circling and teasing her nipple.

She gasped, her mind swirling with the bombardment of sensations. His lips traveled down her throat as he toyed with her breast, evoking more and more sensual delights from her. And then his mouth was upon her nipple, and she groaned at the supreme pleasure.

Never had she imagined this sea of sensations in which she floated now. Every inch of her flesh was alive. Passion throbbed within her, and she realized that she yearned to feel him inside her.

This desire so shocked Eleanor that she pulled back, whispering, "No."

She looked up at him, stunned by the desires clamoring within her. His lips were dark and soft from their kisses, his eyes gleaming with a fierce light. They stared at each other, their breath panting in their throats.

Then he rasped out, "Do you still find passion overrated?"

His words were like a knife to her heart, and she lashed out, slapping him.

"Get out!" Eleanor pulled her nightgown up to cover her breasts, shame suddenly flooding her at her nakedness where before she had felt nothing but joy.

Every line of his body was rigid. She could see the pulse throbbing in his throat.

He turned and strode out of the room, pulling the door shut behind him with a soft click. Eleanor stood, staring at the door, humiliation warring with the heat of desire still pulsing in her.

She wanted to scream. She wished she could cry. She had never felt anything that joyous, that magical, and she hated Anthony for making her feel it.

How could desire consume her like a flame for this man, when she had never felt the slightest flicker for any other man, even Edmund, whom she had loved? It was the most awful of ironies.

Eleanor threw herself onto her bed, burying her head in her pillows. Worst of all—and what kept her awake much of the rest of the night—was the realization that even now, in full possession of her faculties, if he came back into the room, she feared that she would give herself to him.

AFTER A LARGELY SLEEPLESS NIGHT, Eleanor awoke feeling groggy and listless. She could not bring herself to go downstairs to breakfast; she could not face Anthony, at least not yet. She needed time to prepare herself.

She asked to have a tray brought to her room, then picked through the food uninterestedly, her mind on the man she was avoiding. Eleanor wished very much that she could avoid seeing him ever again.

She hated her loss of control last night and hated even more that he had been the one to cause it.

For a brief moment, the idea of simply getting in her carriage and leaving was very appealing. She could, after all, remove herself as guardian and let Lord Neale have the trust. It would be easy enough, and she no longer thought that the man was after the money.

But Edmund had entrusted her with the guardianship for a reason. Having been around his sister for a little while, she suspected that he had not only wanted Samantha's money handled well, but had hoped for Eleanor to have some influence in the girl's life. Though too kind and gentle a man to speak against his mother, Edmund was not blind to Lady Honoria's faults, and he would have wanted to give his sister some release from their mother's demands and restrictions.

Eleanor could not let Edmund down just because she had acted foolishly. And more than that, she was never one to run away from a bad situation. For her own self-respect, she would have to face Lord Neale again.

Still, it was a relief when, after bracing herself for the confrontation, she came downstairs to get into her carriage and was told by Dario that Lord Neale had ridden on ahead to Tedlow Park and would meet them there.

When they arrived at the Scarbrough estate, they were ushered into the library, where the others awaited them. Eleanor, having steeled herself to it,

greeted Anthony indifferently, giving him a brief, slightly cool nod, and moved on to greet his sister and niece and Sir Malcolm.

Dario, with his usual tact and aplomb, excused himself, saying that he would stroll around the ample and beautiful grounds while they discussed the legal matters. Eleanor, all business, turned to the ledger book and legal papers, which she had had the footman set down upon the library table.

"This is Sir Edmund's will," she began crisply, handing the legal document over to Lady Honoria.

His mother pushed it aside, saying, "Anthony, you look at it. I cannot bear to." She teared up, pressing her handkerchief to her eyes.

"As you can see," Eleanor went on, "aside from a few personal items which he left to me or to one of you, and, of course, the entailed estate, which went to you, Sir Malcolm, Edmund gave a generous bequest to Lady Honoria, and the bulk of his estate he left in trust for you, Samantha, until you reach the age of twenty-one." She smiled at the girl. "It is quite a nice amount and will keep you well for all your life."

"And precisely what assets are included in this personal estate?" Sir Malcolm asked.

Just as she had supposed, Eleanor thought, Sir Malcolm was here at the meeting to make certain that no bit of the entailed estate had slipped into the portion going to Samantha.

"I will show you," Eleanor said pleasantly,

opening the ledger book to the listing of the holdings of Edmund's estates and their current value.

Sir Malcolm studied the list intently, tugging at his lip as he read, then passed the book over to Lord Neale. Anthony ran his eyes down the column of figures, then glanced back up at Eleanor, looking surprised.

"I have seen Edmund's books in the past. I would say that his holdings are worth a good bit more than when I last saw them."

Eleanor could not suppress a smile of pride. "As soon as Edmund and I were married, I began to oversee his finances. They were, I felt, a touch too conservative, so while I left some of his money in the 'funds,' I also invested in India bonds and Exchequer bills, as well as in a few businesses here and there, which have returned rather good rewards."

Anthony studied her thoughtfully, and Eleanor gazed back at him with a bland expression. She could not keep from feeling a bit of smug pleasure at the thought that Anthony might begin to realize how wrong he had been about her. With typical aristocratic snobbery, he had assumed she was an adventuress, and while she would not have stooped to deny such a ludicrous charge, she wasn't above reveling a little in the shattering of his prejudices.

"Now, I shall send you a monthly accounting, Lady Honoria, of the funds in my charge, so that you and Samantha may go over them." She turned toward the young girl. "And I will be more than happy to

explain each of them to you, so that you can see what I did and why."

"Samantha will not need that!" Honoria exclaimed in a shocked voice. "She is a lady."

"Yes, I know. But she will inherit all this one day, and it would be a good thing for her to understand it," Eleanor pointed out reasonably.

"She doesn't need to understand it," Honoria protested. "Her husband will take care of that sort of thing for her. And until she is married, her uncle will."

Eleanor suppressed the irritated retort that first sprang to her lips and said only, "It is better, I would think, not to have to rely on others to take care of one's own fortune."

"I should like to know," Samantha spoke up, her voice a little shy but her expression determined.

Eleanor smiled at her. "Then I shall teach you."

"Samantha!" Lady Honoria glared at her daughter. "I will not have you acting like a…a Cit!"

"Honoria," Anthony said sharply. "I think it would do Samantha good to know what she owns and how it is invested."

Honoria shot him a look that said she considered him a traitor. "That is precisely the sort of thing you *would* say. But it is simply not acceptable behavior in a girl. It is entirely unladylike."

She turned and looked meaningfully at Eleanor.

Eleanor simply said, "Perhaps you would like to

talk about the money I will be sending you each month."

Honoria looked immediately more interested. However, when Eleanor named the figure that she would be supplying Honoria for the household allowance, the woman let out a shocked gasp.

"That is all?" she wailed. "We cannot live on that!"

"As you pointed out, you now have a much smaller house and therefore fewer servants. And this is very near the figure that Edmund was sending you when you lived here at the Park," Eleanor explained. "Of course, when Samantha makes her debut in a few years, there will be a much larger stipend to cover the expenses of a season, as well as a substantial clothing allowance. But here in the village, there are few expenses, and Samantha's clothes are rather inexpensive still. Of course, I will also be sending Samantha pin money every month for her personal purchases."

"Pin money?" Samantha repeated excitedly. "Really? All my own?"

"Yes, of course...for books and ribbons and whatever little things you might want to buy."

"But what about *my* clothes?" Honoria cried. "*My* expenses?"

"Lady Honoria, Sir Edmund bequeathed you a sum of money of your own, a rather substantial one," Eleanor pointed out. "He also told me that his father

had left you a healthy joinder. Your personal expenses would come out of those. I am talking here merely about household expenses for raising Samantha in the style in which she is accustomed."

"But it is simply not enough!" Honoria turned to her brother for support. "Anthony, say something. I know Edmund never intended to leave me penniless!"

"You are scarcely penniless, Honoria," Anthony replied somewhat impatiently. "I just read the will, and he provided amply for you."

"He cannot have wanted this," Honoria insisted, tears welling in her eyes. "Edmund loved me. He would have wanted me to have all his estate. I know it. After all, when I die, the money will go to Samantha."

Eleanor wanted to say that there would be little enough left for the girl after Honoria had run through it, but she kept a firm rein on her tongue. However hard it would be, she was going to have to deal with this woman until Samantha reached her majority. She said calmly, "Edmund wanted to make sure that his sister would have an independence. So that she would not have to marry where she did not want or—"

"It is you!" Honoria turned on Eleanor, flinging out her hand to point at her as if she were a witch calling down a curse. "You talked him into this. I know my Edmund would not have thought of this on his own. You convinced him. And oh, how you must

be reveling in this—doling out my money in little dribs and drabs, forcing me to cut corners. No doubt we shall have to go to tallow candles now, Samantha. Wax will be too dear."

Goaded, Eleanor opened her mouth to deliver a sharp set-down, but Lord Neale spoke first, cutting through his sister's histrionics. "Enough, Honoria. That is nonsense, and you know it. This is a reasonable sum for operating your household. More than fair, really. You will have plenty for wax candles and everything else you require."

His words shut Honoria up, though she cast him a fulminating glare that clearly labeled him a traitor in her eyes. Eleanor seized the opportunity to draw the meeting to an end, closing her ledger book and picking up the will.

"I think we are finished here," she said. "If you have any questions, please write to me, and I will answer them. And if there are any large purchases you need to make, please let me know, and I will adjust the allowance accordingly."

One look at Lady Honoria's mutinous face and Eleanor was certain that she would be receiving far more missives from the woman than she cared to deal with. She turned toward Samantha, who popped up from her seat and came forward impulsively, holding out her hands. Eleanor took them with a smile.

"I do hope that you will come to visit me in London sometime," she told the girl, adding politely

to Lady Honoria, "And you, too, of course, my lady. The season has started."

"And you hope that I will be your entrée into the *ton?*" Honoria asked acidly. "There is little hope of that, I assure you. If I wish to visit the City, I presume that I am still received at my brother's home." She turned toward Lord Neale a little questioningly.

"Mama!" Samantha gasped, shocked at her mother's rudeness.

"I think you have said enough, Honoria," Anthony told her brusquely.

Color flared in Eleanor's cheeks, and her hands curled into fists, but she kept a firm grip on her temper, saying, "I assure you, Lady Honoria, that was not my intent. Frankly, I care not whether I ever attend a party made up of a group of people who are invited only because of the happenstance of their birth. I am far more interested in people who have done something of value, or who have something intelligent to say. As for whether you visit me, you are right in assuming that I have little interest in your company. However, Edmund entrusted me with Samantha's care, and I intend to fulfill that trust. I will be a part of her life. If you do not care to allow her to visit me in London, then I will, of course, come to visit her here. You might consider whether you will enjoy my renting a house here and coming to stay in it periodically."

She paused, noting from the look of horror on the other woman's face that her words had sunk in.

"Now, if you will excuse me, I must be going. I wish to get back to London this afternoon."

Eleanor stood up, giving a smile to Samantha and bidding her farewell. Then she nodded to Lady Honoria and turned to give a quick nod to the two men. As her eyes fell on Anthony's face, it occurred to her that when she walked out the door, she might very well never see him again. A sharp pain shot through her at the thought, and she quickly turned away.

"Allow me to walk you to your carriage," Anthony said, rising and coming toward her.

Eleanor shook her head sharply as she picked up her materials. "I shall be perfectly all right. Mr. Paradella will help me."

Anthony stopped, his jaw tightening. "Of course."

Eleanor turned, not letting herself look at Anthony again. It was for the best, she told herself. The man held her in the utmost contempt; that had been clear from the start, and what he had done last night had only confirmed it. Being around him was dangerous, at least to her, and she was not the foolish sort of woman who rushed into danger.

She walked out the door and hurried down the hall, leaving him behind.

CHAPTER EIGHT

ANTHONY STOOD, looking after Eleanor's retreating figure until long after she had disappeared. He wanted to hurry after her, to catch up with her and explain.

But explain what? he asked himself sarcastically. Why he had acted like a cad the evening before? Why he had lost his head and kissed her and caressed her as he had sworn to himself he would not do? Or why, when he realized what he was doing, had he brought it to an end in the worst way possible, offending her and doubtless making her hate him?

Explaining, he knew, would be impossible. He could not even explain it to himself. For some reason, he seemed to lose all sense whenever he was around Eleanor. He was governed by some strange turmoil of desires and feelings that he scarcely realized were there until they burst out of him. He wanted her in a way he had never wanted any other woman, and no matter how foolish or wrong it was of him, he could not seem to make himself stop. As always after being with her, Anthony felt twisted into knots.

"Well!" Honoria exclaimed, coming up behind him. "I am sure she must enjoy holding the whip over her betters. If she thinks that she can make me foist her upon the *ton*..."

"Honoria, stop!" Anthony grated out. "Pray do not make a bigger fool of yourself than you already have."

His sister's mouth dropped open, and she stared at him in astonishment. "Anthony! How can you speak so to me?" Tears began to well in her blue eyes.

"Please, do not turn into a watering pot, either. I think it is clear that Lady Eleanor is not interested in rubbing shoulders with the *ton*."

"You think she meant what she said?" Honoria asked with a shrill little laugh. "Really, Anthony, men are so easily misled by a well-turned ankle and a pretty face."

"It has nothing to do with that. The fact is that as soon as she married Edmund, she could have gotten into the *ton*."

"Not among those who count," Honoria protested with a haughty sniff.

Her brother quirked a quizzical eyebrow. "Come, Honoria, you are not silly, however much you may like to appear so. The Scarbrough name would have gotten her far enough. But she did not go to parties. She did not even stay in London."

"Of course not. She wanted to get him away from me. She wanted to keep him from everyone he knew and loved."

"She took him there for his health. All the rest is nonsense that you have made up."

"She has worked her spell on you, as well!" Honoria exclaimed. "She has turned you against me."

She burst into tears. Anthony let out a sigh and cast a helpless look toward his niece. Samantha went to her mother and put her arm around her shoulders.

"Mama, I am sure that Uncle Anthony has not turned against you," Samantha told her soothingly.

"Of course not," Anthony snapped. "All I am saying is that I think you and I misjudged the woman. I don't think she will mishandle Samantha's money. Look at how well she did with Edmund's funds. She added to them. Clearly she did not take anything from him."

Sir Malcolm let out a bark of laughter, and Anthony and Honoria turned toward him, startled. He looked at them, then said, "Do you mean to say that you thought she was after Edmund's fortune?"

"Of course," Honoria replied indignantly. "A nobody from America maneuvers Edmund into marrying her—what else would she be after?"

"I have no idea about that," Sir Malcolm answered dryly. "But I doubt that it was for money." He sent Anthony a disbelieving look. "Really, Neale, did you not check into the woman's background when she married Edmund?"

Anthony stiffened. "I did not."

He did not add that he had been so certain that a woman of her beauty had married Edmund only for his money that he had not even made a move to investigate her. Indeed, he realized as he thought about it, he had been reluctant to learn anything more about her, a fact that had not struck him as odd until just this moment.

"Well, I haven't your gentlemanly reticence," Sir Malcolm told him with some sarcasm. "I did not relish the thought of losing any portion of my inheritance to an adventuress, so I set my solicitor on it. As it happens, she is an heiress. Her father made a fortune in the States, and when he died, she inherited it all. And increased it a good bit over the years, I might add. She is worth a great deal more than Edmund ever was. As much as you, I imagine."

He had completely misjudged her.

Anthony's mind reeled at the thought. It was no wonder that Eleanor hated him. She must have found him to be the very epitome of a British snob, judging her without knowing her at all. Thinking back on it, he could not but wonder at the way he had approached her. Why had he not asked her about herself? Why had he asked no one else about her? He had relied on his sister's judgment, which was something he never did. He had been hasty, and blind to the truth. None of that was like him—or so he would have said before this.

"Uncle Anthony?" Samantha's concerned voice

cut through his dazed thoughts. "Are you feeling ill?"

"What? Oh. No. That is, I am just thinking." He looked over at his sister, whose tears had dried and who was also looking at him in a puzzled fashion. "I must take my leave. Honoria. Sir Malcolm. There is—I have pressing business back at the Hall."

With an abrupt nod, he turned and strode out of the house, calling for his horse. There was no pressing business, of course. The truth was that he simply wanted to be alone. He had to think.

Anthony mounted his horse and turned him toward home, his mind galloping along at a much faster pace. If he was honest—and he usually was, even to a ruthless degree—he knew that it had been Eleanor's beauty that had sent him stumbling down the wrong path. He had assumed she was after Edmund's money because when he first saw her, his heart had dropped to his feet. She was the most beautiful woman he had ever seen, and he had wanted her fiercely.

And that beauty, he had told himself, meant that she was an adventuress, a woman like Viveca, who had taken his father's heart and turned his mind against Anthony…who had tried to seduce Anthony into betraying his father. He couldn't believe that this woman, whose beauty took his breath away, could truly love the quiet, gentle Edmund.

Or perhaps he simply had not wanted to believe that Eleanor was in love with Edmund.

The thought brought him up short. He had to wonder if what he had told himself for the past year was true. Had he simply been close minded? Had he actually been jealous? Or had it been something even deeper, more basic?

No, he would not follow that thought.

What he should be thinking of, he told himself, was not the past, but the problems at hand. The first problem, of course, was that Eleanor now hated him—and rightfully so. He doubted that she would even receive him. The second problem was that someone had broken into her room twice, looking for something. Assuming that she was an adventuress, Anthony had also assumed that these break-ins had had something to do with her undoubtedly nefarious past. He had also taken for granted that she knew who the culprit was and what he was after, that she just had not wanted to reveal the answers to him because they painted her in a bad light. She would eventually give the person what he wanted, and the matter would end.

But if she was not an adventuress but a woman of wealth, then in all probability her past had not involved anything nefarious at all. The thefts must be for some other reason altogether, which made them all the more alarming. She was probably telling the truth, that she had no idea what the intruder wanted…unless it was the simple locket containing Edmund's portrait, which seemed absurd.

This line of reasoning led him to the inescapable presumption that the intruder would return to Eleanor's house. And having been thwarted twice already, it seemed likely that he might take a more aggressive course of action. The next time, he might attack Eleanor herself.

Anthony kicked his horse into a gallop, his course of action determined. He had to return to London.

"I AM WORRIED about you, Eleanor," Dario said soon after they left Tedlow Park.

Eleanor, her thoughts elsewhere, turned toward him distractedly. "What?"

"This man, this intruder—I do not like this."

"Well, I did not care for it, either, I assure you."

"What could he have been after? A locket? It seems not valuable enough to break into a house to get. No?"

"No, it doesn't. You are right. It would have little value to anyone but me," Eleanor agreed.

"And to break into a house two times to get it?"

"We don't know that this was the same person," she pointed out.

Dario cast her a dubious look. She shrugged.

"All right, I admit it. It seems very unlikely that the two events are not connected. But it makes no sense."

"You have no idea what he wants?"

"None whatsoever." Eleanor shook her head in puzzlement. "I mean, I have some valuable jewelry, but I

don't keep it in my room. It is in the safe. And I would think any thief worth his salt would realize that."

"It is very puzzling." He paused, then went on. "I want you to come back to Italy with me."

"What?" Eleanor stared at him in surprise.

"These dangerous things have happened. It is not safe for you here. You should come back home."

"But Italy is not my home," Eleanor pointed out gently.

"It could be," he replied earnestly and reached out and took her hand. "Eleanor…"

Eleanor had the uneasy feeling that he was about to wax romantic. She pulled her hand away, saying firmly, "England is where I have to be. Edmund entrusted me with his sister's future. Not just the money. He wanted me to keep it safe for her, but I feel that he wanted me to help her, to guide her, as well. I cannot do that from afar. I have to be here in England. Besides, what is to say that whoever is doing this would not follow me to Italy?"

"I could protect you there," he answered. "You could live at my parents' villa. We would set up guards."

"No, Dario." Eleanor smiled, but shook her head. "I cannot do that."

"I feared you would say that. So…I must do what I can to protect you here."

"Thank you. That is most kind of you. But I doubt that I am in any danger."

"How can you say that? After what has happened?"

"I was not hurt either time," Eleanor reminded him. "I was not even in the house the first time. And last night, he offered me no harm. He was across the room, rummaging through my things."

"But you do not know what might have happened if you had not awakened and screamed. You were alone and vulnerable. And you are a very attractive woman."

"Dario…what are you saying? That he might have attacked me?"

"There was nothing to prevent it."

"Except me," Eleanor pointed out tartly.

Dario smiled in an indulgent way that spiked Eleanor's rising irritation. "My dear, I am sure you do not realize what could befall a beautiful woman like you." Seemingly oblivious of Eleanor's narrowed gaze, he went on. "And I cannot help but wonder—does it not seem a great coincidence that this person should enter your room on the very night that you are at Lord Neale's house?"

Eleanor stiffened. "Are you accusing Lord Neale of being the intruder in my room? That is absurd. He was in his room. He had obviously been in bed."

"You did not see where the intruder went," Dario reminded her in a reasonable tone. "He disappeared completely. We could find no trace of him. Think how quickly he could have escaped if he had only to run

down a door or two. A few seconds to whip off his shirt and shoes—or perhaps he had not even worn shoes. Bare feet make much less sound. Then, when you scream, Lord Neale comes rushing out of his room, looking startled and claiming to have just awakened."

"The exact same tale would apply to you, as well."

Dario nodded understandingly. "This is true. But, you see, I have the advantage over you in that I know that I was not the one who did it."

"Well, I cannot believe it was Anthony, either. He would have no reason." But Eleanor could not help remembering her thoughts after the first break-in, that Anthony might have orchestrated the whole thing to frighten her into leaving the country and giving up control of the trust. "No, it's absurd."

She shook her head. When she had suspected him before, she had not known that he was a man with great wealth of his own. He had no need to control Samantha's trust. Besides, he was too straightforward a man to devise such a roundabout plan. He was much more likely to confront her and demand that she leave.

"No more unlikely than the thought that someone might have followed us from London in order to look through your things. Without either of us or the coachman noticing."

"Sir Malcolm and Lady Honoria also knew that I was there."

"But why would they have done it?"

"Exactly the same question I would ask if it were Anthony. Or anyone else. I have no idea what the man is after."

"Eleanor, please…let me come stay at your house, where I can protect you."

"Dario, what would people say?" Eleanor responded, keeping her voice light. "An unmarried man under my roof? It would damage my reputation, and I know you would not want that."

"My darling Eleanor, I want only what is best for you. I am afraid of what may happen."

"I am sure I am in no danger."

"You cannot know that. It seems very likely to me that you were, or that you will be if this man did not find what he was searching for. What if he decides to make you give him whatever this thing is?"

"Then I will give it to him," Eleanor answered. "I would not value it above my life. And if I were to need protection, I already have it. Zachary and Bartwell are right there in the house, and since the 'robbery,' we have kept watch each night."

Dario spent a few more minutes futilely trying to get Eleanor to change her mind and allow him to protect her, but finally he lapsed into a sulky silence. Eleanor did not mind. She was frankly glad to have a chance to think in quiet.

But no matter how long and hard she thought, she could not come up with any explanation for anyone

looking through her things. What could anyone think he would find there?

When she got home, after she had greeted everyone and talked to the children for a while, she went to her bedroom and proceeded to look through all her things, going methodically through each and every drawer, and even through the chest at the end of her bed and the clothes in her wardrobe. She took out every piece of jewelry and laid them out on her dresser, since the intruder had concentrated both times on her jewelry.

She could find nothing that would rouse a thief's particular interest, especially since he had just looked through them, taking almost nothing. Except the locket. Why had he taken a brooch the first night and the second time the locket? Why not get them both?

Eleanor tried to remember if she had been wearing the locket that first night, in which case he would have been unable to find it. She was relatively certain that she had not. She had worn only jet earrings and the Italian brooch that Edmund had given her.

With a sigh, she returned all her jewelry to the jewelry box and stood for a moment, thinking, drumming her fingers upon the dresser. It occurred to her that the thief might have been looking for something that was among Edmund's things. He could, perhaps, have mistakenly thought that whatever it was lay in her room.

She walked down the hall to Edmund's room. She paused inside the door for a moment and looked around. Little of Edmund remained here. She had given away most of his clothes, and the things she had brought home were stored away in chests. One stood at the foot of the bed, and another was against the wall.

Eleanor had looked in here before, after the first theft. But that time she had merely looked to see if anything had been disturbed. She had not searched through everything to see if there was something here a thief might be after.

She pulled up a stool and sat down to go through the first chest. There was a small box containing a few cuff links and stickpins that Edmund had worn. He had not been a man given to much jewelry, and what few things he had were usually made of onyx or pearl, except for one bloodred ruby stickpin. The rest of the chest yielded nothing.

She went to the other chest and dug through it, as well. Finally, admitting defeat, she stood up and closed the lid. As she turned to leave, her eyes fell on the rosewood box that stood upon the dresser. She paused, feeling a pang of sorrow.

The box, about a foot and a half long and a foot wide, was Edmund's traveling writing kit, and he had taken it with him on any journey he made, even if it was only for a few hours. It carried music sheets, already lined, and pencils, as well as an inkhorn and

sharpened quills, which Edmund preferred to the new steel pens. With this portable writing desk, Edmund was able to jot down music wherever inspiration might strike him.

Eleanor reached out and ran a hand across the smooth top of the box. She opened the lid, looking down at the writing supplies inside. It was then that she remembered there was a secret compartment in the writing kit. Edmund had taken a childish pleasure in the secret drawer and had proudly shown Eleanor how it operated.

What if he had placed something of value in it?

Eleanor ran her fingers lightly over the wood, searching for the narrow lines that would indicate a compartment and trying to remember exactly what Edmund had shown her. She closed her eyes, thinking back.

It had been on one of the ends, a piece of inlaid wood that could be pushed aside if one did it exactly right. It took her a few tries at each end before she pressed down at the right spot at the same time that she pushed to the side, and a small square of wood slid aside to reveal a tiny keyhole.

Eleanor looked at it consideringly. She had no idea where the key was. There had been nothing like that in either of the chests she had just searched. She pondered the fact that it could have been on Edmund's person and been swept away in the ocean or burned up with his body. There was also the very

real possibility that, small as it was, it had been left behind, unnoticed in some drawer or other, in their house in Naples.

She sighed and slid the concealing piece of wood back into place. It would take tearing the writing box apart to find what was in the compartment—assuming anything was—and she did not want to do that. It had been quite dear to Edmund.

Besides, there seemed little real chance that there was something valuable concealed inside it. What would Edmund have put there? And why would anyone want it? It would be foolish to destroy the box on the off-chance that there was something of value inside it. She would wait, she decided, and see what transpired. Perhaps she might even be able to find the key somewhere.

Still… She picked up the box and carried it downstairs to her office, where she locked it away inside one of her cabinets. There was no point in taking unnecessary risks, after all.

That task accomplished, she went up to bed, still puzzled.

ELEANOR SPENT the next morning with Zachary, catching up on business matters, since she had been absent for two days. She had lunch with the children and looked over their recent schoolwork afterwards. She knew that she needed to bring in a tutor for Nathan. He had already outstripped Kerani's skills

OFFICIAL OPINION POLL

Dear Reader,

Since you are a book enthusiast, we would like to know what you think.

Inside you will find a short Opinion Poll. Please participate in our poll by sharing your opinion on 3 subjects that are very important to all of us.

To thank you for your participation, we would like to send you your choice of **2 FREE BOOKS** and **2 FREE GIFTS!**

Please enjoy them with our compliments.

Sincerely,

Pam Powers

Editor

P.S. Don't forget to indicate which books you prefer so we can send your FREE gifts today!

What's your pleasure...

Romance?

Enjoy 2 FREE BOOKS that will fuel your imagination with intensely moving stories about life, love and relationships.

(OR)

Suspense?

Enjoy 2 FREE BOOKS that will thrill you with a spine-tingling blend of suspense and mystery.

 Whichever category you select, your 2 FREE BOOKS have a combined cover price of $13.98 or more in the U.S. and $17.00 or more in Canada.

Simply place the sticker next to your preferred choice of books, complete the poll on the right page and you'll automatically receive 2 FREE BOOKS and a 2 FREE GIFTS with no obligation to purchase anything!

YOUR OPINION POLL
THANK-YOU FREE GIFTS INCLUDE

▶ **2 ROMANCE OR 2 SUSPENSE BOOKS**

▶ **2 LOVELY SURPRISE GIFTS**

OFFICIAL OPINION POLL

YOUR OPINION COUNTS!
Please check TRUE or FALSE below to express your opinion about the following statements:

Q1 Do you believe in "true love"?

"TRUE LOVE HAPPENS ONLY ONCE IN A LIFETIME."
○ TRUE
○ FALSE

Q2 Do you think marriage has any value in today's world?

"YOU CAN BE TOTALLY COMMITTED TO SOMEONE WITHOUT BEING MARRIED."
○ TRUE
○ FALSE

Q3 What kind of books do you enjoy?

"A GREAT NOVEL MUST HAVE A HAPPY ENDING."
○ TRUE
○ FALSE

Place the sticker next to one of the selections below to receive your 2 FREE BOOKS and 2 FREE GIFTS. I understand that I am under no obligation to purchase anything as explained on the back of this card.

Romance

193 MDL ELSZ

393 MDL ELVZ

Suspense

192 MDL ELRC

392 MDL ELUD

0074823 ||||||||||||| |||||||| |||||||| FREE GIFT CLAIM # **3622**

FIRST NAME

LAST NAME

ADDRESS

APT.#

CITY

STATE/PROV.

ZIP/POSTAL CODE

(TF-RS-07)

DETACH AND MAIL CARD TODAY!

The Reader Service — Here's How It Works:

in most of his subjects, and Eleanor and Zachary had been taking up the slack. Before long, Claire would be past Kerani's help, as well.

Kerani, of course, had been raised to be a woman of leisure in India, not a governess. It was only because she was so eager to earn her way in Eleanor's household after they had rescued her that Eleanor had given her the task of looking after the children. At first, of course, they had been young enough that a teacher was not required, and Kerani had studied hard to learn both English and a better grasp of numbers than she'd had before. She had been able to teach them the basics, and there had been the added benefit of her teaching both her charges to speak Hindi, Kerani's native tongue. It was not, perhaps, the most useful skill, but there was always a chance it might come in handy in the children's future.

However, it was clear that Eleanor now needed to hire a tutor for the children. The problem, of course, was how to do so without hurting Kerani's feelings or making her decide that she no longer had a place in the household. She could still look after the children when they were not in class, but even that position would grow less and less necessary as the years passed.

It would all work out, Eleanor thought, if only she could persuade Zachary to make a push with Kerani. But there were times when Eleanor despaired of ever getting the conservative Zachary to do so.

She was idly thinking about the problem later that afternoon when one of the footmen announced that a visitor had arrived to see her. Eleanor glanced at the card the man held out to her on a salver, and her eyes widened in surprise. Lord Neale.

Whatever was he doing here?

"Send him in," she told the servant, standing up, her heart pounding and her mouth suddenly dry. She straightened her skirts, then hurried to the small mirror on the wall for a last-minute look. She was not sure what she was feeling. A veritable storm of emotions was welling up inside her—excitement, embarrassment, uncertainty. But one thing she knew for sure was that she wanted to look her best when she faced him.

Just yesterday, Eleanor had thought that she would never see him again. And that, she had told herself, was for the best. The man was a boor. He had been rude and insulting to her the other night—and, truth be told, on every other occasion when she had seen him. He disliked her. She disliked him. Their lives would doubtless be much more pleasant if they never had to see one another.

In fact, it would probably have been much better if she had simply refused to see him. He should be made to realize that he could not just walk in and be received, given what he had done. But it was, of course, too late to follow that course.

Still, she could hide from him how much turmoil

his arrival had caused in her. He did not need to know that eagerness warred with indignation inside her. So she carefully schooled her expression into one of polite indifference and sat down again in her chair, folding her hands demurely in her lap.

Anthony strode into the room in his usual way, his steps rapid, his face alert, as though he were charging into battle. Eleanor looked up at him, her face faintly questioning, even a trifle annoyed.

"My lady."

"Lord Neale." She inclined her head but did not hold out her hand to him. She gestured toward a chair a few feet away and kept her voice cool as she said, "Pray sit down."

He did so, though he perched on the edge of it as though he might jump back up at any second. He looked, Eleanor thought, distinctly uncomfortable, and that fact allowed her to relax a little. At least he was not confident of his reception.

"I confess, I am somewhat surprised to see you here today," she began after a long moment of silence.

"I rode up yesterday afternoon after you left," he explained tersely. "I needed to talk to you."

"Indeed?" Eleanor raised her eyebrows. "I would have thought we said everything necessary yesterday."

"I did not." He popped up out of his seat and began to pace. "I discovered some things after you left."

Eleanor frowned, puzzled both by his words and his demeanor. "I'm sorry. I don't understand. What things? Something about Edmund? The money?"

He shook his head impatiently. "No. No. Nothing to do with that." He faced her squarely, looking a little as though he were facing a court about to sentence him. "The fact is…I came to apologize."

Nothing he could have said would have surprised Eleanor more. She just barely managed to keep her jaw from dropping open. "I beg your pardon?"

"I am offering my apologies," he said in a brusque way that did not sound terribly apologetic. He paused, then gritted his teeth and went on. "I must apologize for the way I have behaved to you from the moment I met you. I realize that I misjudged you. I leapt to conclusions. False conclusions. You were right. I should have thought more of Edmund's happiness and welfare. I made judgments about you based only on supposition."

"I must say, I am somewhat surprised."

Anthony's statement, honest and bald and obviously difficult for him to force out, spoke to Eleanor in a way that a smooth, flowery, compliment-strewn apology never could. She believed him. He had discovered that he had been wrong, and he regretted it.

"I am sure you *are* surprised," Anthony told her. "No doubt you think I am a hardheaded, misguided fool."

"Well, yes," Eleanor admitted, a small smile

creeping onto her lips. "But I must confess that I misjudged you, as well. I assumed that you were interested only in Edmund's money."

He cast her a rueful look. "I guess that makes us a rather suspicious pair, doesn't it?"

"Perhaps we have both had reason to be suspicious," Eleanor said, unbending a little bit more. "I have spent a good many years fending off fortune-hunting men."

"Yes, well, I have had a bit of experience with adventuresses, as well," he agreed. "But it doesn't excuse my behavior to you, especially the other night. I was rude and…and…"

"Boorish?" Eleanor offered.

"Yes." He came closer to her, looking down intently into her eyes. "I acted like a cad. I can only hope that you believe me when I tell you that I am not usually so."

"Perhaps it is something I bring out in you. I find that you seem to bring out the worst in me."

"You were a guest in my house. It was bad enough that I failed to protect you from an intruder. But then to…to force my attentions upon you…"

Eleanor did not point out that he had not had to use any force. She had been quite eager to accept his attentions. Indeed, it was that fact that had humiliated and angered her the most. She certainly was not about to remind him of the matter.

"I think the less said about it, the better," she replied. "I accept your apology."

He nodded, looking relieved. "Good. Thank you."

Anthony stood for another moment, silence stretching awkwardly. Then he said, "I have come upon another matter, as well."

Eleanor eyed him warily. Had the apology been only an excuse after all?

"I am here to offer you my protection."

Eleanor stared. Was he daring to ask her to be his mistress? "I beg your pardon?" The ice was back in her voice.

He looked at her, surprised; then his face cleared, and he said hastily, "No—I did not mean…bloody hell… I am making a regular hash of things. What I am saying is, I think you are in danger. I am offering you my help."

"You, too?" Eleanor murmured.

"What do you mean?" He scowled.

"Dario was preaching the same gospel to me all the way home," Eleanor said. Why was it that men were much more interested in a woman if they thought she needed protection? "I will tell you, as I told him, I am not a fragile flower in need of protection. I am well able to take care of myself."

"Don't be stubborn," Anthony shot back.

Eleanor stiffened, crossing her arms in front of her and arching an eyebrow. "I am not stubborn. I am simply not being hysterical. No harm has been offered me. And whatever the fellow was after, I would think that he has already gotten it by taking

the locket, or he has realized that I do not have it and he has given up."

"You cannot be sure," he argued.

"I have taken the necessary precautions," she assured him. "We have set up a guard at night. And I am keeping a pistol on my bedside table."

He grimaced. "I should not be surprised."

"No, you should not," she agreed. "I am accustomed to thinking and doing for myself."

"It is only sensible to accept help."

"Help generally comes with conditions attached, I have found…especially from men."

"I have no conditions," he grated out. "Blast it, woman, why won't you let me help you?"

"I think what you mean is, why won't I do as you say," Eleanor corrected.

He gazed at her for a long moment, then exclaimed, "Oh, the devil with it!" He turned and started to walk away, then stopped and looked back at her. He opened his mouth, then closed it, and finally said in a clipped tone, "Good day, my lady."

"Good day." Eleanor watched Anthony go, not sure whether to be more annoyed or amused.

He was not accustomed to not getting his way. That was clear. But then, she was just as unaccustomed to giving in to anyone. She ran her life as she pleased, and she was not about to start doing any differently now, no matter how easy it was to get lost in Anthony's gray eyes.

The rest of the day passed uneventfully, as did the one that followed it, enlivened only by a visit from Dario, who again pressed his invitation to return with him to Italy.

Eleanor politely refused, adding, "Are you planning to leave soon, then?"

Looking almost as irritated as Lord Neale had the day before, Dario replied darkly, "No. I cannot leave you like this. I will stay and see this thing through."

It was Eleanor's opinion that he was in for a long, boring wait, as once again that night there was no sign of any intruder. She was more and more certain that she was right in thinking that the thief had either found what he was looking for or realized that whatever he was searching for was not in her house.

The children went to fly kites in the park with Kerani the next afternoon, and Eleanor decided to go along. She had found the last few days that she seemed to have more difficulty than normal concentrating on business matters. Her mind kept going to the fact that Lord Neale had not called upon her again since his offer of an apology the day before yesterday. She wondered if she had offended him so by her refusal of his offer of protection that he had decided not to call upon her anymore.

Claire and Nathan ranged ahead of Eleanor and Kerani as they strolled along a path through the trees, heading toward a larger open area where they could

fly their kites. Claire's dark brown curls were warmed by the sunlight, and her face was animated as she chattered to Nathan.

Eleanor smiled as she watched her. She had found Claire two years earlier, begging on the streets of Paris, a thin little waif with eyes that were much too large in her hungry face. She had been set to begging on the streets by her uncle—her mother, a prostitute, had died two years earlier. Eleanor, touched by her plight, had taken her away from her uncle—his protests had been quickly stilled by the payment of fifty gold guineas she had offered. Claire had been quiet almost to the point of silence at first, shy and restrained, but it had not been long before she warmed up to Nathan, despite the difference in language. Over the last year, her true personality had begun to shine through.

Nathan, of course, Eleanor reflected with a smile, had never been anything but loquacious. It had been his talkativeness and his quick sense of humor that had brought him to Eleanor's attention in the first place. He had worked with his mother in a factory Eleanor had once visited in New England. She had been considering buying into the business but instead had come away with a healthy dislike of the owner. However, during her tour, she had been drawn to the boy, disturbed to see a child of that age working in such a place. His quick answers had amused her, despite the sadness she felt as she

looked at the mother and child, both far too thin, their fingers red and chilled as they worked at their jobs. The mother had paused now and then to cough, trying to hide it as best she could.

Eleanor had learned their address and taken them a basket of food, as well as the services of a physician. The doctor had confirmed Eleanor's suspicions about the mother's health. She was in the grip of pneumonia and not long for this world. Nathan's mother had taken Eleanor's hand in a viselike grip and pleaded with her to take care of her son. Eleanor had been reluctant, never having been around children much, and certainly not having anticipated taking one on, but she had been unable to resist the mother's pleas. She had made his mother as comfortable as possible, paying for coal to heat their rooms and providing them with blankets, food and medicine, but it was too late for her. And when she died a week later, Eleanor had taken Nathan into her house. She had never regretted it.

Nathan, almost ten years old, had been with her for four years now, and Eleanor was sure that she could not have loved him more if he had been her own son. Claire had crept into her heart in the same way.

They reached a large grassy area, and the children stopped. Nathan put down his kite and went to help Claire with hers. Eleanor walked toward them to help.

Suddenly a man moved quickly past Eleanor and straight toward the children. Eleanor watched, astonished, as the man bent and wrapped an arm around Claire's waist, picked her up and started to run away with her.

CHAPTER NINE

ELEANOR LET OUT a wordless shriek and ran forward, afraid that she would not be able to catch up with the man. Fortunately Nathan, who was much closer, was quick to react, and he threw himself at the ruffian, managing to grab the tails of his coat. Nathan clung to him, screaming, and the man had to stop to reach around and try to pull the tenacious child off him. Claire was squirming and kicking, screeching at the top of her lungs.

As the stranger struggled with the two children, Eleanor reached him. Raising her parasol, she brought it down as hard as she could on the man's head. He let out a bellow of pain and frustration, letting go of Nathan and raising his free hand to protect himself from Eleanor's blows. Nathan dropped down, wrapping his arms around the man's leg and hanging on. Then he sank his teeth into the man's calf.

The man squealed and dropped Claire as he reached down and pried Nathan off his leg. He looked up, saw a man running across the park toward them, yelling, and he quickly took off.

Eleanor knelt and took Claire into her arms, and the little girl wrapped herself around Eleanor as if she would never let go. "Are you all right? Oh, sweetheart, I was so scared! Nathan, you were superb."

"Are you all right?" the man who had come running to their rescue asked and when Eleanor nodded, he took off after their attacker, who was charging into the trees.

Eleanor watched him, and soon both men were gone from sight. She did not have much hope of the second man catching their assailant, who had gotten too much of a head start.

Nathan popped up, grinning. "I stopped him, didn't I?"

"You did indeed. I am so proud of you. And you, too, Claire. You were my little tigress." Eleanor hugged the girl even more tightly to her.

Kerani fluttered around them, babbling in a broken combination of English and her native tongue, and emitting little cries of distress, hugging Nathan, patting Claire's back, and brushing at the grass and twigs that had attached themselves to the bottom of Eleanor's skirts.

"Who was that man, Miss Elly?" Nathan asked. He was jiggling from foot to foot, unable to stand still. "Why'd he try to take Claire?"

"I don't know. But thank heavens he was not able to. Nathan, pick up your kites and let us go home."

Nathan did as she bade, and the four of them walked home in a tight little group. Eleanor carried

Claire almost half the way before the girl decided she was no longer afraid to let go of Eleanor's neck. But even then, she walked with one hand in Eleanor's and the other in Kerani's.

Eleanor's mind was racing as they walked. While she had no idea who the man had been who had tried to steal Claire, she had a pretty good idea as to why he had done it. She was sure that it was not some random act; the man had plainly targeted Claire. But it was Eleanor herself, she was sure, who was the ultimate target. And it had to do with the thing in her house that someone wanted and obviously had not yet found.

She was scared, more scared than she could ever remember being. This had been far worse than waking up to find the stranger in her room, for this was a threat to her loved ones. Eleanor had always been ready to stand and face danger. But the prospect of danger to either of the children filled her with terror.

When they reached the house, Eleanor went straight up to the nursery with Kerani and the children, where she checked the windows to make sure all were tightly closed and locked. Leaving Kerani with Claire and Nathan, she went downstairs and sent for Bartwell and Zachary.

Her terse explanation of what had happened in the park brought consternation to both men's features.

"Miss Elly!" Bartwell exclaimed. "What is going on?"

"I have no idea. But clearly I am going to have to

do something about it. I want a footman outside the nursery door at all times."

"It's done," he assured her gravely. "And I'll put two footmen on patrol at night. We may have to hire extra help."

Eleanor nodded. "Whatever is necessary."

"I am going up there myself," Zachary said tightly. "I will stay with them."

"Good." Eleanor nodded. "Bartwell, have the carriage brought round."

He looked at her, startled. "Where are you going, miss?"

"For help," Eleanor replied succinctly.

THE FOOTMAN at Lord Neale's door looked startled to see an unattended female standing there, seeking entrance. Eleanor suspected that his first instinct was to turn her away, but the haughty glance he sent her took in the quality of her clothes, and he hesitated, visibly torn.

"Tell Lord Neale that Lady Scarbrough is here," Eleanor said briskly, stepping forward so that the footman was forced to step back and allow her into the hall. "Lady Eleanor Scarbrough."

"Never mind, Burke, I will take care of this," Anthony said from the landing of the stairs. He came the rest of the way down the stairs, saying, "I was looking out the window and saw you step out of your carriage."

When he reached her, his eyes ran over her quickly, and he frowned, reaching out to take her hand. "Eleanor...what is it? You look...distressed."

He led her into the front drawing room and closed the door behind them, then turned to face her. "Now, tell me, what is the matter?"

"You must think me mad," she began, feeling suddenly shaky and on the verge of tears in the face of his concern. "I—I came without putting on my hat and gloves. I just ran out of the house."

"I see that." He came closer. "What happened?"

"I—someone tried to take Claire!" Eleanor blurted out.

"The little girl who lives with you?" he asked, startled.

She nodded. The terror that she had been trying to keep tamped down was rising in her, threatening to overcome her. "Oh, Anthony...you offered me your help the other day and I turned you down. I am here now asking for it. Will you help me?"

"Of course." Impulsively, he reached out and pulled her into his arms.

Eleanor, surprising even herself, leaned against him gratefully, tears welling in her eyes and spilling out. "I am so frightened!"

"Of course you are," he told her, his hand gently rubbing her back. He leaned his cheek against the top of her head. "Do not worry. We shall take care of it. I promise. Nothing will happen to the children."

A shaky little sob escaped Eleanor, and she clung to him. It felt so good to be able to be weak for once. She had always been the strong one, the one on whom everyone else relied, the one to whom they came for help. She would have said that she hated to appear weak, that she would have done anything to avoid it, but she found that here in Anthony's arms, it was a great relief, for once, to have someone else upon whom she could rely.

He wrapped his arms around her, cradling her to him. She felt the brush of his lips against her hair. "Eleanor," he murmured.

She trembled. She wanted to stay in his arms forever, she thought. She wanted to turn up her face to his and feel his lips upon hers again. She wanted to melt into him and let whatever would happen, happen.

Sternly, she straightened and pulled away. This was not the time for such weakness. She should be thinking only of the children, not herself. She wiped the tears from her cheeks and turned to face him.

"We went to Hyde Park. We were going to fly kites."

Anthony sighed inwardly. He missed the feel of her in his arms. He would have liked to pull her back and hold her again. But clearly Eleanor's moment of weakness had passed.

He crossed his arms and said matter-of-factly, "Who is 'we'?"

"The children's *amah*, Kerani, and myself. And the children, of course—Claire and Nathan. Kerani and

I were a few feet behind them. Suddenly a man rushed up and grabbed Claire. He started to run off with her, but Nathan had the presence of mind to latch onto him long enough that I was able to reach him."

"And what did you do?" The beginnings of a smile quirked at the corner of Anthony's mouth.

"I hit him, of course. Fortunately I was carrying my parasol. And then Nathan bit him."

The twitch had turned into a full grin now. "Naturally. So I take it that you vanquished the fellow?"

Eleanor nodded. "Yes, he dropped Claire and ran off. There was a man there who came to help us, and he ran after him. But I think there was little hope of catching him. I took the children straight home. But I'm frightened."

"You have every reason to be scared. But we will get to the bottom of this. Don't worry." He paused, then went on. "Did you get a good look at your attacker?"

Eleanor shrugged. "It happened so fast…. It was no one I knew. He was about medium height, not burly, but not slender, either. He was dressed roughly, like a workman, and he wore a cap. I could not see his hair."

"Was he dark? Pale?"

"He was not dark-skinned. He had a large nose. I could not see the color of his eyes. They were shadowed by the brim of his cap." She shrugged. "I'm sorry. I am afraid I am not very useful."

"I feel sure he did his best not to reveal much of himself," Anthony assured her.

There was a tap on the door, and Anthony turned to open it, saying, "Hopefully this is Rowlands."

He pulled the door open to reveal a young man, rather tired and sweaty. The man pulled his hat from his head, bowing a little toward Eleanor and saying, "Ma'am."

It was the man who had gone after their attacker.

Eleanor stared. "How did you—" She swung to face Anthony. "What is going on?"

"This is Rowlands. He does a bit of work for me sometimes. I set him to watching your house when you would not let me help you."

Eleanor bristled. "But that's—that's—"

"It was all I could do to protect you," Anthony pointed out.

"I'm sorry, sir," Rowlands put in apologetically. "I lagged too far behind in the park. I was afraid they would spot me, so I didn't want to stay close."

"Were you able to follow him?" Anthony asked.

The young man shook his head regretfully. "I chased him out of the park. Then he jumped on the back of a milk wagon, and I managed to catch a hansom to follow him. But then he got off, and I did, too, and I think he spotted me. He lost me in the East End. I spent some time asking around about him. Seeing if anyone knew him."

"So you got a good look at him?"

"Fairly good. But it wasn't much use, sir. One chap told me it might be a fellow called Smiley, on account of he has a scar, here by his mouth, makes it look like

he's grinning. Another one said it might be a fellow named Farnston, lives next door to him. But I think they were more interested in the money I offered than the truth, quite frankly. If it was one of those two, I couldn't find anyone who could take me to him."

"Probably just a hired thug, anyway. Though it would have been nice to have a chance to pry the name of his employer out of him."

Eleanor stood listening to the two men talk, trying to decide how she felt about the whole matter. Her independent nature was ruffled by Anthony setting someone to watch her without her knowledge or consent, but she also found that the concern that had prompted the action warmed her.

"Take another man or two and go back," Anthony told Rowlands. "See if you can find either this Smiley or Farnston. Hudgins will give you some money to spread about. I'd like to talk to the kidnapper, if you can find him."

Rowlands nodded and left. Anthony turned back to Eleanor. There was a wary look in his eyes that made her chuckle.

"You need not look at me like that," she told him. "I shan't bite you. I don't like your spying on me, but the fact of the matter is, I should have taken your words more seriously. If things had happened just a little bit differently today, your setting your man to follow us might have saved Claire from kidnapping."

"Then you believe the incident today is connected to your intruders?"

Eleanor shrugged. "It is hard to imagine all these things happening independently of each other. I can only think that whoever it is intended to take Claire and use her as a bargaining tool against me."

"That is what occurred to me. That he hoped to get whatever he has been looking for by trading the girl for it."

"But I still have absolutely no idea who he is or what he wants!" Eleanor exclaimed in frustration.

"If Rowlands has any luck, perhaps we can get a lead back to the culprit. And in the meantime, we ought to make a push to discover what it is the man is seeking."

Eleanor nodded. "Yes. But first I have to get the children out of danger. I cannot risk anything happening to them."

"I have an idea. I have a fishing lodge in Scotland. There's a caretaker there, a fierce Scot who's related to half the people around. No stranger could arrive there without his being alerted. We can send the children there with their governess."

"I'll send Bartwell with them. And Zachary. I am certain he will insist on going along to protect them." She chewed at her lip a little nervously; she hated the thought of letting the children out of her sight.

Anthony came over to her and took her hand in his, looking down into her face. "They will be safe there. I am certain."

Eleanor smiled faintly. "I know. I cannot help but worry, not having them right by my side, but I know you are right. I trust you."

The simple words, offered in her calm voice, warmed him. She was not, he knew, a woman for whom trust came easily, yet she was placing that which was most precious to her in his hands.

He raised her hand to his lips. "Thank you."

He kissed the backs of her fingers, then turned her hand over and pressed his lips against her palm. The velvet touch of his lips, the warm brush of his breath on her skin, sent a shiver through Eleanor. She looked up at him, her eyes darkening, and desire coiled in his loins.

He wanted to curl his arm around her and pull her close. He wanted to sink his lips into hers and take her in a slow, deep, leisurely kiss. But this, he knew regretfully, was neither the time nor the place.

With a sigh, he released her hand and stepped back. "If you will excuse me, I will set arrangements in place."

"I will go home and explain our plan to the children and the others. I am sure I can get them packed and ready to go by this evening."

He nodded. "I shall send them north in my carriage, with a couple of outriders. If anyone follows them, they'll catch him," he promised grimly. "Then," he went on, "as soon as they are gone, you and I are going to look for this mysterious object."

Eleanor returned home, looking around her carefully as she got out of the carriage. Had the would-be kidnapper kept watch on the house just as

Anthony's man had and then trailed them to the park? It seemed the most likely possibility. However, she would have expected Rowlands to have seen the man there, which meant, Eleanor concluded, that the kidnapper had been very adept at keeping hidden. She frowned, wondering if even now there was someone here, carefully hidden, watching her.

She shook off the shivery feelings such thoughts engendered in her and went inside. Calling for Bartwell, she trotted upstairs to the nursery, where she found Zachary, Kerani and the children. Kerani was trying to distract Claire and Nathan by reading a story aloud, but the effort was clearly in vain. There was a tight look on Claire's face that sent a pang through Eleanor's heart, and the girl had jumped when Eleanor opened the door.

Eleanor sat down, taking the girl onto her lap, and explained to them what she and Anthony had planned. Predictably, the children were loath to leave her, but she reassured them by pointing out that not only Kerani, but Zachary and Bartwell, would be there, as well, to make sure they were safe. Zachary chimed in with a description of the many pleasant activities that would doubtless await them in Scotland. Even though he had never been there, he made it sound like such a paradise that soon even Claire was asking eager questions.

"It will be a splendid vacation," Eleanor assured them, adding the clinching statement, "And you won't have to do any schoolwork for the next two

weeks, so you will have plenty of time to fish and ride and explore."

Eleanor set the maids to packing and the cook to preparing a basket of food to take with them for the ride. Soon everyone was bustling around, and by the time Anthony arrived in his spacious carriage, along with a second carriage for the travelers, everything was in order. Eleanor loaded the children into their carriage, kissing them goodbye and swallowing back the tears that threatened to rise in her throat. Zachary and Kerani climbed into the coach with the children, while Bartwell, a brace of dueling pistols tucked into his belt, took his place on the high seat beside the coachman.

From the trusting expression on Kerani's face when she looked at Zachary, Eleanor suspected that he might find his suit progressing during their stay in Scotland far faster and farther than he ever would have expected.

The coach clattered off, followed by the two horsemen Anthony had promised. Eleanor waved goodbye, then stood for a long moment, watching the dark street for any sign of movement in the shadows. Anthony, beside her, did the same.

"No one is following them," he said. "And if somehow they are, the outriders will spot them."

Eleanor nodded. "They are safe away."

The two of them turned and walked back into the house.

"Where shall we start?" Anthony asked.

She sighed. "I suppose with my jewelry. Obvi-

ously he must not have gotten what he wanted when he made off with my locket. But it seems to be the jewelry that interests him."

They checked on the expensive jewelry first, on the presumption that the intruder simply had not realized where to look for what he wanted. It was all there where it belonged, in the safe—a glittering parure of diamonds and rubies; a pendant necklace of deep blue sapphires; a brooch of pearls and another of rubies; two bracelets, one of heavy gold links and the other of emeralds; and several rings, including her mother's wedding ring and a large, mannish gold ring that had belonged to Eleanor's father.

"They're certainly valuable," Anthony commented, sifting through the glittering baubles.

"But not anything that one would have mistaken a locket for," Eleanor pointed out. "I cannot think that if he were searching for expensive jewelry, he would have taken the locket."

"Perhaps it just happened to be in his hand when you woke and he ran with it," Anthony suggested.

"I suppose that could be it." Eleanor inspected each piece of jewelry again. "Perhaps he might think I would keep good jewelry in my bedroom here, but why would he think I would take such pieces on a trip into the country for a few days?"

"If we assume that the intruder has any sense, then I think we must admit that he is not after these jewels," Anthony agreed.

Eleanor nodded and began to fold the jewelry

back into its soft velvet cases. She returned everything to its place in the safe, and she and Anthony went up the stairs to her bedroom.

When they stepped into the room, her eyes strayed immediately to the large bed. It seemed illicit to even be in a bedroom with Anthony. She remembered what had occurred the last time he had been in her bedchamber, and she could feel a flush rise up her cheeks.

"I have looked through everything here several times," she said quickly to cover her embarrassment, and led Anthony to the dresser where her jewelry box sat. "But on the basis that this is what the intruder concerned himself with both times, let us examine these again."

She pulled out all the necklaces, earrings and brooches from the box, and spread them out on the surface of her dresser. Carefully, one by one, she and Anthony picked up each piece and examined it.

"I was wearing this the night he broke in the first time," Eleanor commented, picking up the black inlaid brooch Edmund had given her before his death. "You know…Edmund gave me this, and he told me…"

Eleanor thought back, trying to remember his exact words. "He was rather odd about it. He said to wear it for his sake. Or to treasure it for his sake, something like that. Afterwards I wondered if he had had a premonition of his death. Or if he had…perhaps planned it."

"What?" Anthony looked startled. "You think that Edmund committed suicide?"

"I don't!" she protested, but even she could hear the desperate desire in her voice to believe her own words. "He did not seem unhappy. He was in the best health I had ever seen him, and his opera was being produced. He had every reason to live. Yet he said that to me, and he looked very solemn. When he died at sea, I could not help but remember how he had told me about Percy Shelley's death. He found Shelley's funeral pyre fascinating…somehow heroic. Sometimes I wondered if he meant to seek his death at sea so that he could leave this earth in the same grand fashion."

Eleanor looked up at Anthony, her blue eyes tortured. Quickly he reached out and took her hand.

"Do not think that. I do not believe that Edmund would have taken his own life. He had clung to it too hard for too many years. And why would he do it when he was at the very peak of his career and health?"

Eleanor gripped his hand, grateful for his reassurance. "Thank you. I want to think that, too. But why did he say what he said to me?"

"Perhaps it was just that he wanted to stress the importance of this brooch. Just in case something happened to him, he wanted you to take care of it. Is it somehow special?"

"It is of good quality. It is called *pietra dura,* an Italian method of inlaying tiny pieces of stone into a picture. It requires skill, of course, but it isn't as if it is made of precious stones."

Eleanor ran her fingers over the inlaid colored

stones that formed the picture of a flower, and the circle of gold that surrounded the black stone. She turned it over and looked at the back.

For the first time, she noticed a line running through the golden rim of the brooch. "Wait, what is this?"

She held the object closer to the candle. There, faint but distinct, was a line, no thicker than a hair. It ran all around the circular rim of the brooch, about a quarter of an inch from the back of the pin. "Do you see this?"

Anthony nodded, his head bent close to hers. Eleanor was vividly aware of his nearness, the brush of his hair against hers, the warmth of his breath upon her cheek, the faint scent of his masculine cologne. It was suddenly difficult to think of anything but his presence. She hoped he did not notice the faint trembling of her fingers.

"Can it be prised apart?" he asked.

Eleanor tried to insert her nail into the infinitesimal crack, but she could not. Holding it between her fingers on either side of the crack, she tried to pull, without any results, and then began to twist it.

She gasped as something moved beneath her fingers. "Look!"

She twisted again, and the back of the brooch rotated away from the front. She pushed it all the way apart.

There, nestled in a hollow in the back of the black stone, lay a tiny silver key.

CHAPTER TEN

"A KEY!" Anthony looked at Eleanor. "Do you know what it's for?"

"I have a suspicion," she told him, reaching in delicately and removing the small object. "Come. I will show you."

She turned and led him down the stairs to her office, where she unlocked a cabinet and pulled out the rosewood box that she had placed inside it a few days earlier. She pressed and pulled at the side of the box, so that the wood slid aside, revealing the small keyhole.

"It's a secret compartment," she told him.

"To what? What is this box? Was it Edmund's?"

Eleanor nodded. "It was his traveling writing desk. He took it with him almost everywhere he went."

She bent down and carefully fitted the small key into the hole. It slid in easily, and when she turned it, there was a soft click, and a slender drawer opened in the side of the box. Eleanor slid it out until it caught.

Inside the drawer lay several sheets of music, all

scored in Edmund's familiar hand. Across the top, in English, were the words *Neapolitan Sonata.*

"Are you familiar with this?" Anthony asked, looking at Eleanor.

She shook her head, feeling a little breathless. "No. I have never seen it. It must have been a new piece of music he was writing. But why would he have hidden it?"

She reached in carefully and pulled out the sheets of music, holding them reverently in her hands. "This could be what the intruder was after. He must have known that the key to this lay in a piece of my jewelry. He probably took the locket thinking that the key might be inside it."

"But why not just take the box?" Anthony asked. "Even though he didn't have the key, he could just smash the box open, couldn't he?"

"I suppose. But he may not have known all the details. He might not have known exactly what was hidden in the jewelry or that the key went to this box. I don't know. But that must have been why he was searching through my necklaces and things."

"For a piece of music?" Anthony said a little skeptically.

Eleanor's eyes flashed. "Edmund was a genius! This is his last work, found after his death. It is priceless."

"To you and other music lovers. But why would someone steal it? I find that theft is usually for the purpose of obtaining money."

"He could pass Edmund's work off as his own!" Eleanor exclaimed. "There are those who would do almost anything to receive the acclaim of the music world."

"I suppose."

Anthony was obviously not convinced, but Eleanor was too caught up in her elation to pay any attention to him. She swept out of the room and down the hallway, hurrying to the music room. There she lit the candelabra on the piano and sat down at the keys.

Setting the music on the piano before her, she began to pick out the notes. It was easy enough to follow…much too easy, she realized as she played. Edmund's work was usually much more complicated than this. This music was simple and pedestrian, even discordant at times.

Her fingers slowed to a halt, and she looked up at Anthony, confused. "I don't understand. This sounds nothing like Edmund's music."

Anthony frowned. "Perhaps it isn't his."

"I recognize his hand."

"Something that he copied?"

"But why would he copy this? And why keep it in a secret drawer? It is the least of anything he ever wrote."

"Perhaps that is why he hid it. It was an inferior work."

"But why not tear it up and throw it away? I have

seen him do that with work that dissatisfied him. And it was never as bad as this."

She picked up the sheets of paper and stared down at them for a long moment. "Perhaps he…what if he thought that he was losing his talent?"

"Is that possible?"

"I'm not sure. This is so far below what he usually wrote that I cannot imagine him even putting the notes to paper." Eleanor set the pages down on the piano. "If he was having trouble writing music, if this was the best that he was able to accomplish…"

Eleanor looked at Anthony, sorrow welling in her eyes. "If he thought that his talent had deserted him, I can imagine him ending his life."

"No. That's absurd. He couldn't have believed that his talent would have left him so suddenly. Did he ever talk of it?"

"No, never. But it would have been a tragedy of such proportions that he might not have been able to speak of it to anyone, even to me. Music was what Edmund lived for. His improved health, the acclaim that would come to him when his opera was mounted, none of those things would have mattered to him if he thought that he had lost his ability."

"Why are you so insistent on his suicide?" Anthony asked roughly. "It isn't true."

"Because of what he said to me about that brooch, the odd way he said it. It bothered me. And because he went sailing that day alone. He never went out

alone. He always went with Dario or one of the others. I think one of the things he enjoyed the most about sailing was the companionship. But that day he told me that he was going alone. I offered to go with him, but he said no, that he had things to think about. He seemed...looking back on it, I thought that he had seemed troubled."

"That is only because you are afraid that he took his own life. You are tingeing his words, his actions, with meanings that were not there."

"But why did he have an accident? The sea was not rough. It was a calm, cloudless day. His boat was sound, and he was quite competent, even though he had not been sailing long. All those things bothered me. But I could not believe that he would choose to leave his life like that, not when he was doing so well. But this! If he thought his talent was gone, then life would have held no meaning for him."

"None of this means that he killed himself. It is all supposition. Even though this is his hand, you cannot be certain that it is Edmund's composition. Or perhaps he was trying some experiment. It seems absurd that he could lose his talent so abruptly, or even mistakenly think his talent was gone in an instant. Talent fades away, it doesn't fly."

Eleanor started to speak, but he held up a forefinger to silence her. "No, wait. Ask yourself this: why would Edmund have put this worthless piece of music into a secret drawer, then given you the key

in the brooch and told you to treasure it for his sake? He wouldn't want anyone, including you, to know that he had written this. As you said earlier, he would have torn it up and thrown it away."

Eleanor paused. "That *is* odd."

"It occurs to me that there is another explanation for the oddities surrounding Edmund's boating accident besides suicide." He paused, then added, "Murder."

Eleanor stared at him. Her cheeks flamed with color. "You still suspect me of killing Edmund? How can you—"

"No. No. Don't fly into a temper," he said, smiling down at her. "I do not think that. I know you much better now."

He lifted his hand, and with a forefinger brushed back a stray curl that had come loose from her hair and fallen beside her face. It was a tender gesture, but the gentleness of his touch did not disguise the desire that lay beneath it. And where his finger brushed against Eleanor's cheek, her skin warmed, hunger sparking down through her body.

Everything about her felt suddenly looser, softer, warmer, and she was aware of a strong desire to move closer to him, to press her body into his and feel the strength of his flesh and bone.

Rattled and uncertain, Eleanor turned away. "Oh. Um…then, what did you mean about murder?"

Anthony moved up behind her, wrapping his arms around her and gently pulling her back against him.

"Nay. No more talk of murder. Let us just have this moment. You and me."

He nuzzled her neck, sending bright shivers of desire shooting through her. Eleanor melted against him, giving herself up momentarily to the feelings coursing through her. She was exquisitely aware of his long, hard body against her back, his arms wrapped around her, the velvety heat of his lips upon the tender flesh of her neck. Her breasts felt full and heavy, curiously aching. She remembered the touch of his hands on her breasts that night at his house, the taut response of her nipples. Just the thought of it made her breasts tighten again.

His teeth nipped lightly at the side of her neck, moving up the skin to tease at her jawline. He nibbled delicately at the lobe of her ear, taking the flesh lightly between his teeth and teasing it until a deep, throbbing ache started up in her loins.

Eleanor let out a soft sigh of desire and moved her hips against him. His hand smoothed down her front and spread out across her abdomen, pressing her hips back into the cup of his pelvis. She could feel the rigid length of him against her, even through their clothes, and somehow that mere touch made her flesh tingle all over her body.

He kissed her ear, his tongue gently circling and exploring, as his other hand moved languorously over her breasts, cupping and caressing them, stirring the nipples into hot, hard points. He slipped

his fingers beneath the neckline of her dress, stroking her satin-smooth skin, delighting in the contrast of the pebbled flesh of her nipples. His body was like flame against her back, enveloping her in his heat.

His hand slipped lower down her stomach, sliding between her legs, seeking the center of her heat. Eleanor moaned softly, moving restlessly against him. His fingers moved over her through the cloth of her dress, the silk caressing her flesh. The ache grew in her, flowing between her legs, washing all through her body.

She moved her hips against him, anticipating the shudder that ran through him at her movement, her own hunger rising at this indication of her effect on him. Eleanor yearned to feel him against her, within her. She wanted to wrap her arms around him and encompass him, wanted to fill the ache inside her.

"Anthony…" She murmured his name in a dreamy haze, for a moment allowing herself to drift in the pleasure of his touch, his mouth.

Yet even as she floated, eager and humming with an unfulfilled hunger, deep down she knew that she could not allow herself to give in to the desires that washed through her. She was stronger than the sum of her needs, and gradually, steadily, her mind exerted its power, pulling her back from the brink of passion with a slow, inexorable motion.

"No," she murmured at last, sighing as she said it. "No. We cannot."

With an effort of will, Eleanor pulled away from Anthony's embrace. She opened her eyes, taking in the room at a glance. It was Edmund's place, the music room, with traces of him everywhere. And though she had never felt for him what she felt for this man, it seemed a violation of their marriage to be here this way with Anthony.

"Eleanor…" he grated out, taking a step after her.

"No." She took a hasty step away, holding out a hand in a stopping gesture. "We must not."

"Why not?" he argued. "Don't deny that you feel the same desire that I do."

"I do not deny it," she retorted somewhat shakily.

The very unsteadiness of her voice betrayed her passion, and he knotted his fists at the sound of it, a low growl forming in his throat.

"But it's not right. Not here. Not now. I am not the sort of woman who—"

"Do you think I do not know that?" he responded quickly. "I promise you, I do not regard you lightly."

"Don't." She shook her head and uttered the one word that would have the most effect on him. "Please."

He stopped, setting his jaw, and turned away from her, struggling to bring his raging desire under control.

"I think it would be best if we removed ourselves to my office," she said after a long moment, during which she wrestled with her own strong emotions.

She swept from the room, leading the way down

the hall to her plainly furnished, more comfortable office. "Would you like a drink?" she asked as she made her way to the liquor cabinet, pouring a liberal splash of whiskey into a glass for him even before he responded.

She poured a glass of sherry for herself, handed him his drink and sat down in the chair across from him. After taking a sip from her own glass, she looked at Anthony and asked evenly, "Why would anyone try to murder Edmund?"

"That I don't know," he acknowledged. He was having some difficulty sitting here calmly talking to Eleanor when his body was still thrumming from the desire that had raged through it only minutes before, and his mind was still filled with memories of how she had looked and felt beneath his hands.

"His death brought monetary benefit only to Sir Malcolm and Samantha," Eleanor mused out loud. She, too, was highly aware of every feeling in every part of her body, but she spoke with all the calm she could muster, doing her best to drive away the feelings with a flood of words. "I think we can both agree that Samantha can be ruled out. I don't know Sir Malcolm, but as far as I know, he was in England at the time of Edmund's death, was he not? And I don't think anyone doubted that he would be receiving Edmund's estate before very long, in any case. Edmund's health had improved, but Sir Malcolm did not know that, and even with the improvement,

I think it unlikely that Edmund could have conquered his consumption."

"I agree." Anthony took a quick gulp of his drink and tried to keep his mind on the matter at hand. "It seems unlikely that Sir Malcolm did it. And I have no real reason to think that Edmund was killed, other than the oddities you mentioned earlier. But just because the reason is not obvious to us, it does not mean that it is not there. I would say that it's absurd to think that his death was anything but an accident. But the things that have been happening here lately cannot but make me wonder. A sudden and violent death, even though it was seemingly an accident, looks more suspicious when it is followed by people burglarizing your house and trying to kidnap your children."

"But what do they want?" Eleanor asked. "This key?" She held up the small silver-colored key. "Those pages of music? I cannot imagine why anyone would want either of those things, let alone kill for them."

"I don't know that anyone did kill for them. But he has obviously broken in here, and he has tried to steal Claire from you. And all the evidence points to the thing they want being in your jewelry. Do you think there could be another mysterious object in your jewel case?"

"Coincidence rears its ugly head again," Eleanor murmured. She sighed. "What shall we do? I must

find some way out of this. I cannot leave the children at your fishing lodge forever."

Anthony rose and began to pace restlessly about the room as he spoke.

"Since we appear to have found what he is after, and it makes no sense, it seems to me that our best course of action is to try to lay our hands on the fellow who is after it. I want to hire a Bow Street Runner and install him secretly in your household. He can pretend to be a new servant. Then you need to go about your daily life as normally as possible and wait for him to make a move. Give him opportunities to enter the house again. Attend parties or the opera or plays. Whatever you choose. But let him have plenty of chances to try again."

"But this time the Bow Street Runner will be waiting for him?" Eleanor interjected.

"Precisely." He turned and looked at her. "I don't like the idea of your staying here alone."

Eleanor stood up, facing him. The glass of sherry had warmed her stomach, but she found that it had calmed her nerves only a little. She was still tinglingly aware of Anthony, even though he stood several feet from her. "I will scarcely be alone," she told him. "There are the servants."

"None of them are even on the same floor with you at night," he pointed out.

"There will be a Bow Street Runner, as you said,

and I will have a footman on guard on the first floor. No one will be able to get in."

"It's not enough," Anthony said flatly. "I think I should stay here until we catch whoever is doing this."

Eleanor's skin warmed, her pulse suddenly picking up. She imagined him sleeping only a few doors away from her, and the thought made her feel both hot and cold all at once.

"Anthony, you cannot," she said quickly, aware of the curious breathless quality to her voice. "It—it wouldn't do. What would people say?"

"I thought you didn't care what people say," he retorted.

"In general, I do not. But a bachelor staying here beneath my roof, alone with me? Especially with the children and Kerani gone? My reputation would be ruined. You know it."

What she did not mention, though it was uppermost in her mind, was the fact that his staying there would be far too dangerous for her. Her body still tingled from his touch; she remembered vividly the pleasure of his kisses, the deep yearning she had felt. If Anthony was so near to her each night, she was not sure that she would be able to retain her control. She was unaccustomed to the sort of effect he had upon her, and Eleanor did not like feeling so vulnerable, so out of control.

Anthony ground his teeth, obviously aware of the

truth of her words. "Dammit! It is too dangerous. Without even your butler and man of business here, you are too easy a target."

"I will be fine. I sleep with a pistol by my bed," she reminded him.

He scowled, swinging about and beginning to pace again. Finally he stopped, his face clearing, and exclaimed, "I have it! I shall send for Honoria and Samantha. They can come stay with you."

"What?" Eleanor stared at him. "Believe me, I would far rather brave the dangers of an intruder than have your sister living with me. Besides, what good would it do to have them here? It isn't as if they can protect me."

"The point is that if they are here, I will have a ready excuse for being here a great deal of the time. It will not harm your reputation. No one would question the chaperonage of my own sister and niece."

Eleanor dug her fists into her skirts. She found herself longing to agree, which was rather frightening in itself. Unpleasant as was the thought of Edmund's mother in her home, she found the prospect of Anthony hanging about the house even more alluring.

"But what about the danger to them?" she pointed out a little desperately. "You cannot bring your sister and your niece into the path of harm."

"I will be here to watch over them," he told her. "Just as I can make sure that you are not hurt."

He walked over to her, reaching out to take her hands, and looked earnestly into her eyes. "Please, Eleanor…let me do this. I cannot stand idly by and worry about you alone and vulnerable in this house. I want to be here, to protect you, and this is the only way."

Eleanor's hands trembled a little in his. Her heart was pounding in her chest. "All right," she murmured.

He smiled, sweeping her into his arms and kissing her. His kiss was brief and hard, full of promise, and when he pulled back, Eleanor was left breathless, her cheeks flushed.

"Now lock your door and windows," he told her.

"I will." She smiled back at him, though she set her hands on her hips in a combative pose. "But don't think that because I agreed on this that you can come in and start issuing orders."

A long deep dimple popped into his cheek, making his grin difficult to resist. "My dear Eleanor, I would not think of issuing orders to you."

She made a noise of disbelief. He looked at her for an instant longer, reaching up to run his finger down her cheek in a tender gesture; then he turned abruptly and walked away. Eleanor watched him leave the room. She felt foolish, standing there smiling at nothing, but she could not seem to stop

smiling any more than she could halt the joy swelling in her chest.

It was ridiculous to feel this way, she told herself. Absurd, really. Anthony's overprotectiveness should annoy her, not amuse and warm her. Yet somehow it did all three.

She picked up her candlestick and left the room, making her way upstairs to her bedchamber. She felt restless, not yet ready to go to bed, but uninterested in doing anything else, either. Strolling to the window, she moved aside the heavy drape and looked out into the quiet night street. Anthony was still standing there, his eyes slowly searching her yard.

Eleanor watched him as he turned away, apparently satisfied, spoke to his coachman, then climbed into his carriage. She continued to watch, but the carriage did not pull away. The side curtain was pulled back, and she caught a glimpse of Anthony's face in the dim light. The coachman climbed down from his high seat and fussed about with the horses before he climbed back up and settled himself in his seat. It was then that she realized the carriage was not going anywhere.

Anthony was clearly settling in for the night, intending to keep watch on her house from outside. That, too, she thought, should have stirred up irritation. Instead, amazingly, it made her feel warm and safe.

She took out the silver key and looked at it. It looked so small and delicate, lying there in her hand. Could this really be the item that had caused someone to invade her bedchamber on two occasions? Could anyone really want those pages of music so much? Or did he think this key opened something much more valuable?

Eleanor shook her head. None of this made sense. There seemed no logic to it. What, she wondered, had Edmund done that had brought about this mess? And how was she to get out of it?

Most of all, she wondered, how was she to keep her heart whole and free, when every moment she spent with Anthony was sending her sliding closer and closer to loving him?

CHAPTER ELEVEN

THE BOW STREET RUNNER arrived late the next morning. He was a short, square, taciturn man whose presence was soon barely even noticed. Unfortunately, Eleanor thought, the same could not be said of Lady Honoria, who arrived with her daughter two days later.

From the moment Honoria stepped down from her carriage, she kept up a ceaseless barrage of complaints, beginning with the length of the journey, the travel sickness that had plagued her, as it always did, the lack of consideration on her brother's part in hauling her up to London on such short notice, and continuing through her narrow-eyed inspection of Eleanor's house, her questions about the size of the house and the number of rooms, as well as her gloomy regret over the fact that she had never been to visit the house—as though, Eleanor thought, she had never been asked to visit rather than consistently refusing to step foot in any abode occupied by "that creature Edmund married."

Samantha looked embarrassed at her mother's

lack of manners and gamely sought to make her look less rude by earnestly explaining to Eleanor that her mother "traveled poorly." Eleanor smiled at the girl and assured her that she understood, then sent a maid to bring Honoria lavender water for her headache and a cup of tea to revive her.

"Samantha, perhaps you will take tea with me," she suggested as she steered Lady Honoria into her room, then whisked Samantha out before Lady Honoria, busy giving the maid instructions, even noticed that her daughter was no longer there.

"I would love to," Samantha agreed gratefully.

As disagreeable as Edmund's mother was—and she proved to be so at almost every opportunity—his sister was just as pleasant and winning a companion. Eleanor was glad of her company and even more grateful to her for the many times the girl swooped in to take her mother away just when Eleanor thought that she could not stand the woman's presence any longer.

Anthony, true to his word, spent most of his time at Eleanor's house after Honoria's arrival, a fact that Eleanor heard Honoria marveling at to Samantha. Eleanor was not sure exactly how Anthony had managed to persuade his reluctant sister to come stay with the woman she detested most in the world. There were times when she suspected that he must have simply paid her. She could not imagine any sort of reasoning that would have worked. Or perhaps he had merely pointed out how much she

could plague Eleanor if she were in the same house with her.

Two days passed in which nothing happened. When she mentioned this fact to Anthony, he responded that they needed to get out of the house.

"We are not giving him any opportunity to get in. Guards posted, people here all hours of the day and night. We need to leave for the evening. Haven't you any invitations to parties?"

"I haven't been attending parties," Eleanor told him. "I am still in half-mourning."

"Really, Anthony," Lady Honoria put in admonishingly, having arrived in time to hear the last bit of the conversation. "You should not encourage a widow to be frivolous."

"It's hardly riotous living to attend a party," Anthony rejoined. "One can go out in half-mourning."

"Not every night. I would like to save my evenings out for something I enjoy," Eleanor told him.

"Where are your invitations?" he asked.

"Anthony, really, you are being rude," Honoria scolded. "No doubt she doesn't have a wealth of invitations."

With perverse pleasure, Eleanor went to her mahogany secretary and opened the door, pulling out a thick stack of envelopes. Honoria's eyes widened as she looked at the bundle.

"Nonsense, Honoria," Anthony told her. "Lady

Eleanor is both wealthy and the widow of a baronet. That makes her prime marriage material." He flipped through the stack of white squares, shaking his head over most of them, muttering. "Boring…even worse… Good Gad, not Lady Montrose. Ah, here is one that might not prove completely stultifying. The consul from Naples is having a ball tonight. In honor of some count or other."

"Probably the Conte di Graffeo." Eleanor made a face. "I am not overly fond of the count. I find him…disagreeable."

"That would doubtless be true of any number of the guests," Anthony retorted.

"Why do you want to go to this party?" Eleanor asked curiously.

He answered quietly, for her ears only. "Because, my dear, it seems to me that there might be something to be found out there—or perhaps people who might be stirred to action at the sight of you out of your house." When Eleanor just looked at him, one eyebrow raised, he went on. "Hasn't it occurred to you that there is a great possibility of some sort of connection with Naples or some resident of Naples? Your house there was broken into, as well, don't forget. If this has to do with that key, which Edmund gave you in Naples…"

"Key?" Honoria, who had walked over to eavesdrop, asked, looking blank. "What key? What are you talking about, Anthony?"

"Just a bit of a puzzle, Honoria. A sort of game that Eleanor and I have been playing."

"Oh. A puzzle." Honoria made a face and returned her attention to the ribbon she was adding to the hem of one of her dresses.

Anthony took Eleanor's arm and led her over to the window seat that overlooked the street. They sat down and watched the nearly empty street, talking in low tones.

"You think that it is someone from Naples who is doing this?" Eleanor asked.

"It must be someone who knew about that key and that brooch, if that is what they have been looking for. You have been in Naples for the past year."

"Yes, but…" She sighed. "It just seems so absurd that someone would follow me from Naples in search of that key."

"Nevertheless, it seems to me more likely than that someone in England would even know about it." He paused, then said carefully, "If you will notice, your Italian friend turned up conveniently around the time of the break-ins."

"Dario?" Eleanor exclaimed. "You think it was Dario?"

"Dario?" Honoria's blond head came up. "Do you mean that nice gentleman who accompanied you to Tedlow Park? Will he be at the ball?"

"Yes, that 'nice' gentleman," her brother replied,

giving a sardonic twist to his words. "And I would not be at all surprised if he is there, given that he is Italian."

"Well, that will be very pleasant," Honoria decided, her eyes sparkling. "Such a polite young man. I wonder what dress would suit." She stood up, calling, "Samantha! Come up to my room. Mummy needs you to help her."

"I am sure you are wrong about Dario," Eleanor told Anthony, getting up from the window seat and moving away.

"Why? He seems a most suspicious character to me," Anthony remarked, following her. "He turns up at the same time as the intruder. And he was just down the hall from you the night the locket was stolen."

"Amazing," Eleanor said dryly. "As I recall, Dario said precisely the same thing about you."

"He intimated that *I* had stolen your locket?" Anthony exclaimed, looking thunderous.

"I believe it was more than an intimation," Eleanor corrected, the corner of her mouth lifting in amusement.

"Of course. What better way to deflect suspicion off oneself than to cast it on another?"

Eleanor quirked an eyebrow at him.

"Don't be absurd. That is not what I am doing." He stopped, his expression changing to one of concern. "You don't actually still think that I—"

"No, of course not. I am simply saying that

everything you are saying about Dario would apply just as well to you. It is no reason to assume that he is the culprit."

"I'm not. I am keeping an open mind. Still, I think we cannot ignore the Italian connection."

"No." Eleanor sighed. "You are probably right."

Anthony looked at her, putting his hand to his heart dramatically. "I am shocked. You are agreeing that I am right?"

"Pray, do not let it go to your head. I am sure it will not happen often."

"I know." He looked into her eyes, smiling. "You are a most contrary female." His hand circled her wrist, his thumb softly rubbing over the thin skin covering the inside.

Eleanor tried to ignore the shiver that the touch of his finger sent through her. After all, his sister and niece were in the house and could come in at any minute. "Um…I, yes, I agree that we should attend the consul's ball."

"Very well. You must promise to save me two waltzes."

"Two?" Eleanor teased, her eyes dancing. "Careful, you will shock the *ton*."

"Two is perfectly acceptable," he reminded her, his smile slow and seductive, emphasizing the sensual movement of his hand as it slid lightly up her arm.

Eleanor's breath caught in her throat, and she glanced away. "Anthony…"

"Yes."

"Lady Honoria and Samantha are here."

"Not in this room," he pointed out.

"But nearby. And there are the servants."

"We are doing nothing untoward. Only talking."

She shot him a look that was meant to be quelling, but she feared that it came out warm and inviting. "At the moment."

"Shall I close the door?" he asked.

"That would be even worse."

He gazed down into her eyes, his own gray eyes heavy-lidded and sensual. "At the moment, I could wish them all at the devil."

Frankly, so did she, Eleanor thought, but she called up all her willpower and stepped away from him, saying, "So Lady Honoria will come with us?"

He sighed but did not pursue her. "Yes. I think we should leave the house as empty as possible."

"But what about Samantha?" Eleanor asked, realizing suddenly that the girl would be left alone in the house. "She cannot attend a ball. She's only fifteen. But neither can we leave her here if the intruder should come."

He nodded. "I will have Rowlands take her and her governess over to my house for the evening."

Eleanor nodded. "Very well."

Reluctantly, Anthony walked to the door, where he paused. "I shall return to escort you around, what, nine o'clock?"

Again Eleanor nodded. It seemed safer than speech. She was afraid that if she opened her mouth she would blurt out a request to him to stay a few minutes longer.

"Remember the waltzes," he said, and with a smile he was gone.

Eleanor sank down onto the couch with a sigh. Working with Anthony on this was proving to be more difficult than she had imagined.

She spent extra care on her toilette that night, though she tried to tell herself that she was doing only what she would normally do. She wore her finest half-mourning ball dress, an underslip of white satin with an open robe of white lace over it, draped and caught on the side. The lace was edged with a row of jet beads, with small black satin roses sewn on at each of the three places where it was caught and bunched. A row of black jet beads was sewn around the bottom of the underslip. The neckline was low and round, revealing much of Eleanor's white shoulders and the soft upswell of her bosom, and the sleeves were short and puffed, the white lace slashed in the Spanish style to reveal satin sleeves beneath. Jet earrings and necklace completed the ensemble. The only adornment in her hair was a few small white flowers pinned into her dark curls.

She looked, she thought, both elegant and attractive. The look in Anthony's eyes when he arrived to escort them to the ball confirmed her opinion.

Samantha oohed and ahhed over her, and even Lady Honoria seemed unable to come up with a critical statement, other than a general observation that ladies were certainly wearing their necklines low this year.

Samantha and her governess were sent in Anthony's carriage over to his house, and Anthony, Honoria and Eleanor got into her coach for the short drive to the home of the consul from the Kingdom of Naples.

The consul, a short, rotund, voluble man, greeted Eleanor with delight, introducing her to his wife, a vague woman as slender as he was round, and explaining that Lady Scarbrough was the widow of the English genius of the opera, Sir Edmund Scarbrough. His wife's expression lost some of its vacuity at that statement, and she talked quite animatedly for a few minutes about opera. Both of them greeted Anthony and Honoria with a good deal less interest.

Eleanor knew that Honoria was looking at her now with a newfound...not respect, she would not go that far, but at least a certain surprise, even wariness. Honoria, she thought, was seeing her for the first time in a far different light.

The consul's wife handed her down the line, introducing her to their guest of honor, the Conte di Graffeo.

"No need to introduce us, Sofia," di Graffeo said, with a thin smile. "Lady Scarbrough and I are already acquainted."

"Conte, it is a pleasure to see you again," Eleanor lied, smiling. She really had no reason to dislike the slender, silver-haired count, she knew, aside from Dario's evident distaste for him, but Eleanor was one who relied on her instincts.

Lady Honoria, however, clearly had no such instincts, for she beamed at the man when Eleanor introduced him, bridling and blushing at his slick, indifferent compliments.

"I am most desirous of a dance with you this evening, Lady Eleanor," di Graffeo told her, holding her hand a moment longer than was strictly polite, then releasing it with a slight squeeze.

"Of course," Eleanor replied smoothly. She had little desire to dance with the man, but their purpose here tonight was to stir up whatever they could. The count seemed to her a much likelier prospect as the villain of the piece. She had some trouble imagining him actually sneaking into her bedchamber, but she could well believe that he had hired someone to do it...if, of course, she could only come up with a reason for him to have done so.

But first she had a waltz with Anthony penciled in on her dance card. Eleanor pushed aside all thought of their purpose here and gave herself over to the pleasure of dancing with him. He was not the best dancer she had ever taken the floor with, being more methodical and correct than inspired, but no one else's arms around her had ever made her pulse

race or her flesh tingle with pleasure. She looked up into his face as they danced, trying to decide what it was about him that made him so different from other men. In the end, she gave up the effort and simply enjoyed the moment.

All too soon, the dance ended. As they walked off the floor, Conte di Graffeo intercepted them.

"Ah, Lady Scarbrough," he said, smiling and bowing to her. "I believe that you have promised me a dance."

"Yes, of course." Eleanor swallowed her irritation and let the man lead her back onto the dance floor.

The dance was a slow-moving one of intricate pattern, requiring some degree of concentration, but which unfortunately, in Eleanor's view, kept a couple close enough and moving slowly enough for ample talking.

"I am a great admirer of your late husband," the count began by saying. "I believe I told you that."

"Yes. I am so glad that you enjoyed his music," Eleanor replied politely.

"I regret that I never spoke with Sir Edmund at any length," he went on.

Eleanor had no idea what to reply to this, so she said nothing. She could scarcely imagine Edmund and this man conversing about anything.

"Of course, I am sure he was interested in many subjects outside the area of music," di Graffeo continued.

Eleanor glanced at him, wondering what he was talking about. Edmund's pursuit of his music had been single-minded. "He liked to sail," she offered.

"Ah, yes. Sailing." He cast a sideways glance at her, his dark eyes unreadable. "An unfortunate hobby, as it turned out. But young Englishmen seem to have a fondness for the ocean. A national trait, I suppose. Shelley. Lord Byron, I am told, is quite fond of swimming."

"So I have heard." Eleanor was quite lost. The count's words seemed the most bland chitchat, and yet there was an ironic undertone to his voice that lent emphasis to what he said, as if it were particularly meaningful. She could not imagine why he was talking about poetic Englishmen.

"I admire the English," di Graffeo continued. "So determined in their beliefs. So sure that they know what is right."

Again Eleanor had the strong feeling that the man's words expressed the opposite of what he was saying. "I have found, sir, that the same can be said for people of most any nation. My own countrymen, for example, are often regarded as bullheaded. In my experience, Italians are equally passionate in their beliefs, though, of course, they express them quite elegantly."

He gave a careful smile at Eleanor's small witticism. "Indeed, Lady Scarbrough, you are right about that. Romans, Neapolitans, Venetians…we are all

quite devoted to our beliefs. It is sad to see, however, when such devotion leads one down the wrong path."

Eleanor looked at him. "Conte, why is it that I think that you are trying to tell me something?"

His eyes remained on hers for a long moment. Then he looked away as they began the steps that took them away from each other down the line of dancers, until they finally circled all the way back around and were once again partners.

The steps now took them in a long promenade, side by side, their hands joined across each other in front. As they walked in a slow, dignified cadence to the music, the count said, "Your husband's sympathies, Lady Scarbrough, were doubtless heartfelt. That does not mean, however, that they were right. There are many complications, which the young do not always see."

"His sympathies?" Eleanor asked. She turned to look at her partner and found him watching her, a knowing look in his eyes. "I am an American, sir, and I prefer plain talk. What do you mean, his 'sympathies'?"

"Come, Lady Scarbrough, surely you do not expect me to believe that you were not aware of what your husband did or thought. With some wives, that is possible. With a woman like you? I think not."

"I have told you—"

"Lady Scarbrough, I want to help you. Your

husband is no longer here. You are no longer in Naples. There is no reason for you to—" he gave a slight shrug "—to follow in Sir Edmund's path. You should think about your own future, your own well-being. I beg you, do not make the mistake of clinging to a dead man's preferences."

Eleanor swung her head around to stare at him, shocked. "Are you threatening me?"

At that moment the music ended, and the count stopped, dropping her hands. He bowed to her formally. "My lady, thank you for the dance."

The count walked off, leaving Eleanor standing on the dance floor, staring after him in amazement.

CHAPTER TWELVE

SHE TURNED to see Anthony striding toward her, frowning.

"What happened?" he asked, coming up beside her. "What did he say to you?"

He glanced toward Conte di Graffeo, walking away from them.

"I'm not entirely sure. It was most peculiar."

"You looked upset." Anthony took her arm and led her away from the dance floor to a secluded spot between the wall and a potted palm. "Tell me what happened."

"He kept making vague statements, things that sounded like small talk—a trifle odd, perhaps, but still only the sorts of things strangers might converse about. Lord Byron and Englishmen's fondness for the sea."

"What?" Anthony's brow quirked. "He talked to you about Lord Byron?"

"Yes. I told you, it was odd. But he said everything with a certain undertone. You would have had to hear it to understand. It was a trifle sardonic and...

knowing, as if he was talking about something else and thought that I knew what he was talking about."

"There must have been more."

Eleanor nodded. "He mentioned Edmund several times, and then, toward the end of the dance, he told me that Edmund's 'sympathies' were wrong, and that I should not make the mistake of following Edmund's 'path.' I think he was threatening me. He told me I should think of my future and my well-being."

Anthony stiffened, his eyes suddenly hard as flint. "He threatened you?"

He turned, searching the room for Conte di Graffeo. Eleanor quickly tucked her hand into his arm. The muscle beneath her hand was taut, and she pressed her fingers into it, holding on to him.

"No, do not go over there and confront him," she said in a low, urgent voice.

He glanced at her. "I will not stand by and allow him to threaten you. You cannot expect me to."

"I *expect* you not to make a scene here at the consul's ball," Eleanor countered. "We came here tonight to try to stir something up. You cannot get into a fight just because we did."

The muscle in his jaw tightened, and he cast another look at the count's back, where he stood talking to a group of people.

"Please," Eleanor went on, moving closer to Anthony. "A fight with him will accomplish nothing,

other than insulting the consul. We need to figure out what is going on and why someone keeps trying to steal something from me. Engaging in a duel will not help."

He relaxed, casting a small smile in her direction. "I was not actually planning on engaging in a duel."

"Then you don't know Italian men," Eleanor retorted acidly. "If you go over there and start dressing him down for what he said to me, his honor will be bruised, and the next thing you know, he will be talking about seconds. It will be a great scene and not at all helpful. What we need to do is figure out what he was talking about."

Anthony turned back to her. "Very well. What *was* he talking about?"

"I'm not sure," she admitted. "But when Dario saw him at the opera the other day, he—" She stopped abruptly and glanced around. "Do you know, I have not seen Dario here tonight?"

Anthony glanced around in a disinterested way. "Nor have I."

"Doesn't that seem peculiar? That he was not invited or did not accept the invitation to his own consul's party?" She paused, looking thoughtful. "He seemed to distinctly dislike the count."

Anthony shrugged. "No doubt that is why he is not here."

Eleanor nodded. "But his absence indicates a great deal of dislike, I think. Which only increases the impression I received that night at the opera.

Dario was very stiff when the Colton-Smythes brought Conte di Graffeo to my box to introduce him to me. The two of them barely spoke to each other. After they left, he told me not to let the count worry me. He said that di Graffeo was despicable."

"Strong words," Anthony commented. "What did he mean about not letting him 'worry' you?"

"I'm not sure. I suppose he simply noticed the fact that the count...bothered me. Di Graffeo was speaking as he did tonight, in that oblique way, as if he was talking on more than one level."

"Why does Paradella dislike the chap?"

"I did not ask him, but I assumed it was because they were on opposite sides of a political issue in Naples. Di Graffeo is a well-known supporter of the king and his government, and Dario, I think, is one of those who supported the *Carbonari* movement."

"*Carbonari?* What is that?"

"Well, literally it means charcoal makers or coalmen. But it is the name given to a liberal, even revolutionary, movement in Italy. I am not sure exactly why they chose that name—I think to identify with the common man, the workers, even though I think most of the followers are members of the educated classes. They advocate political freedom, as well as unifying the various small Italian states into a single country. It started in Naples. I'm not sure how much you know about Naples."

Anthony shrugged. "I know that it is a kingdom,

that it is ruled by King Ferdinand, who is married to one of the princesses of the Austrian Empire. And that Napoleon conquered it and put one of his followers in power."

Eleanor nodded. "Murat. He was married to Napoleon's sister. But, little as the people of Naples liked being ruled by a foreigner, Murat did institute some reforms in the government, and he had his followers."

"But after Napoleon was defeated, Naples was given back to King Ferdinand, correct?"

"Yes. But there was a great deal of ill will against the king. There was a strong movement in favor of a constitutional monarchy. It was this cause that the *Carbonari* favored, and only two years ago there was an uprising, led by the *Carbonari*, and they forced King Ferdinand to accept a constitution. However, the Austrians then sent in troops, and they routed the revolutionaries and reinstated absolute rule."

"What happened to the *Carbonari* after the defeat?"

"They were crushed. Their leaders were largely thrown into prison. As far as I know, that was the end of them."

"Do you think that Dario was a *Carbonari?*"

"I'm not sure. He could have been. It was a secret society. But it was favored by young men such as Dario—students, intellectuals, the more liberal

element of Neapolitan society. I don't know that he or anyone is still active in the movement. But certainly Conte di Graffeo would have been opposed to the *Carbonari*."

Anthony frowned thoughtfully. "Was Edmund involved in it? Is that what the count meant by his 'sympathies'?"

Eleanor sighed. "I'm not sure. He did sympathize with their ideals, I know. I often heard him and his friends talking about political freedom and the rights of the people. He hated oppression in any form. But, on the other hand, I never knew Edmund to be particularly political. His main interest was his music, as you know."

Anthony nodded.

"But if he was involved, why would he never have said anything to me about it?" Eleanor went on, frowning.

"It was, as you said, a secret society. Perhaps he did not want to involve you in it." Anthony cast her a wry look. "No doubt you will consider it absurd, but husbands often try to protect their wives."

Eleanor sent him a flashing glance. "I cannot believe that Edmund would get involved in something dangerous!"

"No?" He regarded her skeptically. "Why? Because he had been sickly all his life?"

"Yes. He had struggled so with his health."

"Perhaps when one has been facing death for so

many years, it does not seem so fearsome," Anthony said quietly. "You know how he hated his ill health."

Eleanor sighed. "He regarded it as a weakness."

"As did others," Anthony pointed out. "He knew that, and he despised that fact."

Eleanor looked at him. "You think he would have gotten involved in something dangerous just to prove that he was not weak?"

"Not only for that," Anthony said. "He would have had to believe in it strongly. But I do not think he would have allowed himself to hold back from it just because it might prove dangerous."

Eleanor half turned away from him, gazing out at the dancers. She was silent for a long moment, then said quietly, "Lord Byron favors the movement against absolutism. He is a proponent of nationalism and freedom."

"Was he involved with the *Carbonari?*"

"I don't know. But he is not reluctant about expressing his belief in their ideals."

"Do you think that is why the count referred to him?"

"Again, I have no idea. But it does make some sense. If the count thought I knew about Edmund's involvement in the movement, then I would have understood what he was hinting at, I suppose."

"But why is di Graffeo threatening you? It seems as though he, or some underling, is the one who

stole your locket and ransacked your room. But why? What is he seeking?"

"I don't know. But I fear he is mistaken. He apparently believes I was much more in Edmund's confidence than I was. He may believe that Edmund entrusted something to me. I don't know how he would know about that key, but if he does, he might believe that the secret compartment it opens contained something important rather than just some music."

"But what could that be?"

Eleanor shook her head. "I am woefully ignorant. Obviously, if Edmund was involved in any of this, he did not confide in me." Eleanor could not keep a note of bitterness from her voice.

Anthony hesitated, then said, "Eleanor...I am sure that if Edmund hid something from you, it was only to protect you. He would not have wanted you placed in harm's way. It is perfectly understandable. When a man loves someone, he wants to keep her safe."

She cast him an ironic look. "Ignorance is not the same as safety. Don't you think I would have been safer if I had known what he was doing? I could have been prepared for the things that have happened."

"Love blinds a person to what is wise, I find."

Eleanor smiled at him. Obviously Anthony understood how learning of Edmund's apparent secrecy had hurt her. "Thank you," she told him softly.

He smiled back at her, and Eleanor felt a little flutter in her chest. She wished, briefly, that she could ignore the things that had happened and just enjoy being at a dance with Anthony, that she could smile and tease and cast flirtatious glances over the top of her fan. It would be so nice to have nothing on her mind other than anticipation of how it would feel the next time he swept her out onto the floor in a waltz.

He bent a little closer to her, his eyes darkening, almost as if he had read her thoughts. Eleanor wondered if they were so plain on her face, if he had only to look at her to know how much he affected her. She wished she had as much knowledge of him. She would have liked very much to know whether at this moment he was thinking of kissing her as much as she was thinking of kissing him.

She turned aside a little, a flush rising in her cheeks. "I should talk to Dario," she said, seizing on the first thing that came to her mind. "Perhaps he can tell us what Edmund was doing in Naples."

Anthony grimaced. "I'm not sure you can trust the man."

Eleanor rolled her eyes. "You are entirely unreasonable about Dario."

That, Anthony knew, was true. He disliked the fellow, but he had some difficulty telling whether the feeling came from an instinctive recognition of something wrong or just from the prick of jealousy.

The man was altogether too free and easy around Eleanor. She might think he hung about her only because he had been good friends with Edmund, but Anthony had seen the way the man looked at her. Paradella was not interested in a merely platonic relationship.

"I want to go with you when you talk to him," he told her, regretting as soon as he spoke the demanding tone of his voice. Nothing was more likely to make Eleanor contrary than acting as if she should obey him.

But, to his relief, she did no more than nod.

"Lady Scarbrough!" a high-pitched woman's voice called from behind them. "There you are! I knew you would come. Mr. Colton-Smythe tried to tell me that I was wrong, but I felt sure that you would wish to join us all in honoring the count tonight."

Suppressing a sigh, Eleanor turned to greet Mrs. Colton-Smythe. "How do you do? Mrs. Colton-Smythe. Mr. Colton-Smythe. Have you met Lord Neale?"

If she hoped to divert the woman's attention onto Lord Neale, she was doomed to disappointment. While Mrs. Colton-Smythe did flutter and smirk a bit over meeting an earl, she was distracted for only a moment before returning her attention to Eleanor.

"Lady Scarbrough, I beg you will allow me to introduce a friend of ours from Naples." She turned

and pulled a petite dark-haired woman forward. "Signora Malducci has come from Naples to visit us. Isn't that wonderful? I told her that she should have come earlier, so we could have traveled together."

Eleanor smiled at the woman beside Mrs. Colton-Smythe. "How do you do, Signora? I hope you are enjoying your visit to England."

"Oh, yes, thank you, Lady Scarbrough," Mrs. Malducci answered in heavily-accented English. "I want very much to see you. When Mrs. Colton-Smythe tell me she know you, I told her, I must talk to you."

"Really?"

"Yes. I admire so your husband. His music..." She held her hands to her breast, as if about to swoon.

"Thank you."

"He was a genius. So sad. So sad."

"Yes. We all miss him very much."

"I want to talk with you," the Italian woman said earnestly, taking Eleanor's hand. "I saw him that day, you know. So sad, such a young man."

"Sir Edmund?" Eleanor asked.

"Yes. I, how you say, think back. I wish I told him not to go out."

"You must not let it worry you," Eleanor said, trying with some difficulty to extricate her hand from the woman's tight grasp. "You could not have known what would happen."

"So you will come see me, yes?" Signora Malducci went on hopefully. "We can talk. I will tell you about him. Please come; I am at Signore Colton-Smythe's house."

She looked hopefully into Eleanor's face, still clutching her hand. Eleanor did her best to smile. She did not want to call on the woman and have her describe exactly where she had seen Edmund and how he had looked. It had been this way immediately after the funeral, with everyone calling on her and offering their sympathy, often merely as a mask to hear all the gruesome details about his death and the funeral pyre. Mrs. Malducci, Eleanor feared, was one of those people. There was an undertone of eagerness in her voice that bothered Eleanor.

"Oh, yes, please do call on us, Lady Scarbrough," Mrs. Colton-Smythe put in. "Our humble home is nothing like what you are used to, I will warrant, but it would be such an honor to have you visit."

Mrs. Colton-Smythe, Eleanor decided, was an expert at trapping one. Her deprecating statement had made it almost impossible to refuse to call on her without seeming snobbish.

Eleanor's smile was more a result of tightly-clenched teeth than any real expression of friendliness as she said, "Yes, of course. I should be happy to call on you."

"Soon," Mrs. Malducci pressed, squeezing Eleanor's hand. "You will come soon, yes?"

"Yes, of course."

It was actually a relief when Lady Honoria wedged her way into the group, more or less ignoring Mrs. Colton-Smythe and Mrs. Malducci as she launched into a long list of complaints regarding the heat, the crush of people, the quality of the refreshments and the state of her feet.

Eleanor watched, unexpectedly amused, as Lady Honoria's conversation managed to bore even Mrs. Colton-Smythe, who after a moment took her leave, steering her friend like a prize before her.

"Where is that young friend of yours?" Honoria asked somewhat petulantly, turning toward Eleanor. "You said that he would be at the party."

"Yes, I thought he would, but I have not seen him all evening," Eleanor responded calmly. She was acquiring a knack for dealing with Honoria as the days passed. One had to simply avoid taking the woman seriously, just nod and let her comments slide past, only half listening to what she said. "The next time he comes to call, we shall have to scold him."

Honoria looked slightly cheered at the thought of Dario paying a call on them. "Yes, you are right. We shall."

"You know, Lady Honoria, *you* are right," Eleanor went on cheerfully. "The party is much too much of a crush. Perhaps we should leave. What do you think, Anthony?"

"I think we have gotten as much out of this thing

as we can," Anthony said, quick to agree. "Let us take our leave. Honoria…" He offered his sister his arm.

Honoria looked somewhat disconcerted. Eleanor suspected that she had not been as discontented with the ball as she had sounded—Honoria's main form of communication was in the way of complaints—and was not especially happy at the thought of leaving. However, given what she had said, she could offer little opposition to the decision to go. So they made their way out of the party, stopping to thank their hosts, and into the evening air, blessedly cooler than the crowded ballroom had been.

Anthony escorted them back to Eleanor's house, which was dark and quiet, leading Eleanor to suspect that nothing had happened in their absence. A quick talk with the Bow Street Runner confirmed that impression. The house, he told them, had been as quiet as the grave all evening. He had made his rounds of the building and the outside every hour, but had found nothing out of the ordinary.

"I fear that he feels we are sadly mistaken in thinking that anyone is going to try to enter the house," Eleanor said after the Runner had left her office.

"I only wish he were right," Anthony replied with a shrug. "Something will transpire, I think. The problem is what it will be, and when."

"Well, tonight was not a complete loss," Eleanor

said encouragingly. "We found out a few things—or at least created some more suspicions to work on."

Anthony nodded, looking grim. "The count is someone to watch." He went over to her. "After what he said to you tonight, I wonder…perhaps I should stay the night here."

Eleanor thought of him sleeping just down the hall from her, and her pulse sped up. "I—I don't think that would be wise."

"Not wise?" He looked at her quizzically. "It seems very reasonable to me."

"There is no need," she went on a little breathlessly. "The Runner is here. Your sister. Two of the footmen will be on guard."

"I do not think that Honoria would be a great deal of help if someone tried to harm you," he remarked. "And the footmen and the Runner might not be close enough to hear you if you called for help."

"Neither might you hear me," Eleanor pointed out. "It isn't as if you would be in the same room with me."

As she heard her own words, a blush spread over her cheeks. She sounded, she thought with horror, as if she were hinting. "That is…I mean…" She whirled and moved a few feet away. "What I am saying is that the safest thing for me is to lock my bedroom door and windows. You need not stay. You should not."

"If you are going to go on about your reputation again, the presence of my sister would obviate anyone's objections."

"It isn't that," Eleanor replied quickly.

"Then what is it?"

She looked at him. She did not know what to say. She was filled with emotions and sensations that were not clear, even to herself. All she knew was that she wanted him to stay, but she dared not let him. Her desires were too strong, her thoughts too confused. Never had a man had so strong a hold over her; never had she felt so little in command of a situation...or even of herself.

All her life, Eleanor had run things. She had been certain of her decisions, her abilities, her ideas. Whatever emotions she had felt—happiness, pain, hurt, excitement, loneliness—had been subordinate to her mind. She had used her head no matter how distraught anyone around her might be; she had been the one to whom people turned in an emergency.

Even during the worst time of her life, when her father, with whom she had been so close until then, had remarried and acceded to his wife's wishes, sending Eleanor across the sea to school for three long years, she had not let pain swamp her. She had pushed the bitterness and hurt aside. She had told herself that parents and children always parted at some point, that it was only natural that his wife would become a larger part of his life and Eleanor herself would take on a lesser role. It was simply a matter of setting out a little early on her adult life, and she was more capable than most of doing so. She

had made friends, had come to appreciate England and its people, its beauty, the cultural advantages of London.

When others of her age fell in love and married, she had not fretted. She had told herself it was simply the way she was, a woman whose head ruled her heart. Instead, she had filled her life with other people to help and love—the children and Edmund, good friends in England and Naples. There were many things to enjoy, from great art to the satisfaction of her business dealings, and if the sort of passion poets wrote about did not enter her life, so be it. Her life was good.

And when Edmund had died, she had carried on, sad but filled with determination to bring his work to completion. She had buried her sorrow in work, making certain that everything came out perfectly in the production of his opera.

She was used to knowing what to do and doing it.

Now, for the first time in her life, she felt at sea. The passion she had never experienced before simmered beneath the surface, bubbling up at unexpected moments—when she danced in Anthony's arms, certainly, but also when she glanced at him across the room or heard his voice in the hallway when he arrived, or when she came down the stairs and caught sight of him standing with his back to her. It struck her like a blow at times, and at other moments slid through her like a silken ribbon.

She was never quite sure what to do or how to deal with this unexpected desire. It was clear that she was not the cool creature she had always envisioned herself being. With some amazement, she realized that she wanted to fling herself into this new and startling experience. She wanted to embrace the hunger that swelled in her, to give herself over to the sensations that swept through her at his kiss, his touch. She wanted to know the delight that she sensed waited for her in Anthony's arms.

But what then? What would come after the pleasure? For the first time in her life, Eleanor knew that her heart was in danger. She was not sure that she could separate the passion that welled in her from deeper, stronger emotions. Could she let him into her bed and not open her heart to him, as well?

She feared it would be impossible. Sometimes, when her heart rose inside her with happiness just at the sound of his voice, she suspected that she was halfway to loving him already.

However, the result of loving Anthony would be, in the end, heartbreak for her. She was certain of that. He had not even wanted her to marry his nephew. Even though he had admitted his mistake in assuming her to be a fortune hunter, she was not naïve enough to think it had been only that suspicion he had held against her. She was an American, and no matter her wealth or the importance of her family in the United States, to a British aristocrat, she was

a woman of no name, no background. She was as common, as unacceptable, as the mate for an earl as the daughter of a wealthy London merchant.

She had learned much of the British nobility in the time she had lived in the country, and as a general rule, the nobility married the nobility, and the higher one moved in the ranks of that system, the less and less likely one was to marry below one's station. Their passion they would indulge with a woman of inferior birth, but they would not give her their precious name.

Anthony might want her, might respect her, might even come to love her. But, she knew, he would never marry her. A woman whose grandfather had been the son of a cobbler who had moved to the colonies was not proper material for the wife of an earl. The most she could ever hope to be to him was a mistress.

And however unconventional Eleanor might be, she knew that she could not accept such a life. She could not imagine giving her love to a man who could not fully love her back, could not acknowledge their love to the world.

So now she looked back at Anthony, unable to answer his simple question because it called for such deeper, harder answers on her part. She shook her head.

"It is not my reputation," she said quietly. "It is the reality of it."

He moved even closer, his hand coming up to rest on her arm. "I would not take advantage of you."

Her smile was a trifle wobbly. "The problem is that it would not be taking advantage."

His eyes darkened, his hand suddenly searing against her skin, and she knew that her words had awakened the hunger that dwelled in him, as well. "Eleanor…"

The word was scarcely a breath. It sent desire shivering through her.

"Nay." She pulled away from him, turning aside. "We must not. I cannot." She looked back at him, her eyes bright, her body rigid. "You must not ask it of me."

He hesitated for a long moment, looking at her in a way that made her blood heat in her veins. Then, finally, he gave a short nod.

"Of course." He turned away, saying, "I will see you tomorrow."

Anthony walked to the door, then stopped, his hand on the doorjamb, not looking back at her. "We cannot run from it."

He turned then and gazed at her, his eyes boring into hers. Eleanor nodded, not trusting herself to speak.

Then he was gone.

She stood for a long moment, waiting for her heart to slow and her nerves to settle back to normal. He was right, she knew. There was no escape from

the decision that was thundering down upon her. She had only delayed it. But before long there would come a moment when passion would overtake her. And she would have to give in to it...or turn away from him completely.

CHAPTER THIRTEEN

ELEANOR WROTE A NOTE to Dario the next morning, asking him to call on her. When he arrived, she was in the morning room, chatting desultorily with Anthony while she held a skein of yarn for Samantha as the girl rolled it into a ball. Honoria was dozing by the window.

Dario paused in the doorway, taking in the cozy scene. "Lady Eleanor, I beg your pardon. Have I come at an awkward time?"

"Not at all, Dario. Do come in. I was just about to ring for some tea. Samantha, dear, perhaps we should finish this project later."

"Of course." Samantha took the yarn. "I'll just go up and read, if I may be excused." She had been listening to Anthony and Eleanor talk for the past few minutes and had already picked up more of what had been happening lately than Honoria had in the whole time they had been there.

"You are excused." Eleanor smiled at her. She got up to go over to the bell pull, unobtrusively touching the dozing Honoria's arm as she passed her,

saying brightly, "Lady Honoria, isn't it nice that Dario has decided to visit us?"

The older woman awoke with a start, blinking. Her eyes widened when she saw Dario shaking Anthony's hand, and her hands flew to her hair, patting it to make sure that the fetching little white lace cap she had donned that morning had not become tip-tilted. "Mr. Paradella, what a pleasant surprise."

"Lady Scarbrough."

Dario bowed over Honoria's hand, spouting his usual compliments before he turned to greet Eleanor, who gestured toward the chair beside hers, saying, "Do sit down, Dario. It seems ages since we saw you last."

"Yes," Honoria added with a girlish simper. "I was quite disappointed not to find you at the consul's ball last night."

"The consul's ball? Did you go?" He looked toward Eleanor even though Honoria jumped in with a lengthy description of the event.

"Yes. I, too, thought I might see you there," Eleanor put in when Honoria finally paused for a breath.

"It was in honor of a man whom, well, I hold in very low regard. I could not attend in good conscience," he replied.

"Conte di Graffeo talked to me at some length," Eleanor said, watching Dario's expression carefully. "He hinted at Edmund's sympathies and warned me against following his path."

Dario uttered a short, obviously uncomplimentary, phrase in Italian.

Eleanor went on to ask, "Do you know to what he referred?"

Dario gave an eloquent shrug. "My dear Eleanor, who knows what is in that man's mind?"

"Dario, pray do not play games with me."

"But I—"

"Blast it, man, don't you see that Eleanor's ignorance in this matter is endangering her?" Anthony burst out, jumping to his feet. "Or have you no concern for her?"

Dario leapt to his feet to face Anthony. "How dare you imply that I am not concerned about Eleanor? I would die for her!"

"Danger? What are you talking about, Anthony? Mr. Paradella?" Honoria asked, looking from one man to the other, confused.

"Dario, I have no interest in your laying down your life for me," Eleanor put in impatiently. "Just sit down and tell me what Edmund got himself involved in."

Dario hesitated, looking from Eleanor to Anthony and back; then, with a sigh, he sat back down in his chair. "Yes, you are right. It is not fair. I had not realized that you did not know, but I am sure that Edmund did not want you involved in something dangerous."

"Edmund was involved in something danger-

ous?" Honoria asked, her voice rising in a shriek. She raised a hand to her forehead dramatically. "Anthony, my hartshorn. I feel faint."

"Blast it, Honoria, I don't know where it is," her brother answered with a notable lack of sympathy. "Ring for a servant."

Honoria, with a grimace, dropped her hand and returned her gaze to Dario.

"I must ask all of you to swear yourselves to silence on this matter," Dario told them. "Many lives could be ruined if these secrets came out. Edmund believed in our cause. As you know, Eleanor, we talked many, many nights about the things we believed in. He wanted justice for the people, freedom. He saw our vision of a free and united people of Italy, and he wanted to help."

"He joined the *Carbonari?*" Eleanor asked.

"Not the *Carbonari,*" Dario replied. "It was in tatters after the Austrians slaughtered them. But the cause cannot be denied. Other groups have arisen, new names, but with the same principles, the same beliefs. We call ourselves *L'unione.* We desire unity and freedom for our people, but we must work in secret. We are in even more danger than the *Carbonari* were. At every turn we run the risk of betrayal. But our enemy is not just the government, not only the king. There are groups, secret societies, formed to track down and kill us. You know, my lady, of the *Calderai? The Sanfedisti?* They are mortal enemies

of *L'unione*, sworn to do away with us all and crush their dreams into dust. There is another group, even more secret, and its head is di Graffeo."

He said the count's name as if it were a curse, his mouth twisting with bitterness.

"They are a cruel and violent group of men. It is said that the count recruited murderers from the prisons, the dregs of our society. Their sworn mission is to hunt down the members of *L'unione* and kill us."

The others stared at him in silence; even Honoria was too shocked to emote. Finally, in a quiet voice, Eleanor asked, "Is that what happened to Edmund? Was he killed by di Graffeo's group?"

Dario's face crumpled. "I do not know. None of us are certain. However, we have wondered why he went out that day alone. As you know, I had planned to go out with him, but I could not. You cannot imagine how many times I have wished that I had not been delayed that day. Why did he go out by himself? Was he lured to his boat by some false message to meet one of us? Did someone purposely cause my horse to pull up lame so I would not be with him? Was he kidnapped and murdered, then taken out to sea and dropped overboard to hide the evidence?"

A gasp escaped Honoria at his words, and her face paled.

"Paradella…" Anthony said warningly. "Remember, the man's mother is here."

"My lady, I am so sorry!" Dario cried, jumping up and going to her. He took her hand and stroked it, murmuring his apologies and sorrow.

Anthony looked at Eleanor meaningfully, and she nodded and went to the bell pull, summoning her own maid, Janet. The girl arrived promptly, and Eleanor coaxed Honoria, for once too upset even for sobs, to let the maid help her upstairs and fetch Samantha to be with her.

When Honoria and Janet were out of the room and the door closed behind them, Anthony turned again to face Dario. "Tell us all of it. What did Edmund do for your group?"

"He wanted to help us. And we—we hoped that, as an Englishman, he would not be suspected of joining us. Even if he were, we thought none would dare touch an Englishman, especially a titled one. He was entrusted with our names."

"Your names? I don't understand."

"You see, because the society is so secret, because we are under such a threat, it is safest if we do not know the names of the others in the group. We meet only in very small groups, two or three at a time. Word is passed from group to group. This is the way the *Carbonari* worked, as well. But it proved quite a problem for them, for none knew who all their members were, who they could rely on and who they could not. It made it hard to grow and to reach people. So we wanted to have a roster, a list of all

our members that would be kept someplace safe. It was this that Edmund did for us."

"He knew all your names?" Eleanor asked. "And he held this list for you somewhere in our house?"

Dario nodded. "Yes. When he died, we were afraid that if it had not been an accident, if the other side had gotten him, perhaps they had forced him to reveal the names. We waited, in fear for our lives. But as we were not all dragged out and put in jail or killed, we realized that his death probably *had* been an accident, and that di Graffeo and the others did not know about Edmund." He paused, then went on. "Still, we worry about that list. Edmund must have hidden it somewhere. What if it should fall into the count's hands? We would be ruined."

"Is that why you came to England?" Eleanor asked.

"Is that why you broke into this house?" Anthony barked, striding over to loom above Dario. "To steal the list?"

"What?" Dario jumped to his feet, his eyes blazing. "How dare you? You accuse me? Of—of frightening Eleanor? Of trying to harm her?"

Anthony quirked one eyebrow. "You have not exactly been honest with her."

"No! I did not tell her about the list or what Edmund was doing, that is true. We do not talk about *L'unione.* It could mean our death. But I would never hurt Eleanor!" He turned to her, his eyes pleading,

then reached out and took her hand between both of his. "You must believe me. I honor and respect you. I would not do anything that would frighten you. Yes, I wanted the list. That is why I came to England." Dario looked abashed. "But when I talked to you, I soon realized that you knew nothing about Edmund's activities. That you would know nothing of any list."

"I don't think it exists, Dario," Eleanor told him gently. "After what happened, I looked high and low all over the house. I searched all Edmund's possessions, and mine, as well. But I found no list. I promise you that. Either Edmund hid it far too well, or he destroyed it before he died. If—" her voice caught, but she swallowed and continued "—if in fact the count's men did kill Edmund, perhaps he realized what was going to happen and got rid of it."

"That will not stop di Graffeo from searching for it," Dario said. "He must be the one who has broken into your house. Oh, not the man himself. He would not dirty his hands with such work. But I am sure he paid someone to do it. He wants that list. He would stop at nothing to get it."

"He will not have it," Eleanor assured him. "I promise you, it is not here."

"That is why I wanted you to return with me to Italy," Dario went on. "You must be protected from the count."

Anthony let out an inelegant snort. "Then why

take her back to Naples? That's bringing the hen to the fox's den, don't you think? You need not worry. I will make sure that Lady Scarbrough is protected."

Dario faced Anthony, his chin rising pugnaciously. Eleanor quickly stepped between them. "*I* will make sure that I am protected," she said firmly. "Neither of you need worry about it."

She gave first Dario, then Anthony, a long, warning look. After a moment, Dario stepped back and swept her an elegant bow. "Of course, my lady. I would not presume. Still, I hope you will not object if I stay in London. I want you to know that I am here to do any service you wish."

"Thank you." Eleanor smiled. "I will keep that in mind."

With a final defiant look in Anthony's direction, Dario turned on his heel and left.

"I do not trust that man," Anthony commented darkly.

"I had no idea," Eleanor said, smiling faintly.

Anthony turned his scowl on her. "And you, doubtless, find him a charming, dashing rapscallion. The man has lied to you from the moment he set foot here. Does that not make you suspicious of him?"

Eleanor shrugged. "If a woman distrusted every man who was silent about something because he wanted to 'protect' her, then I fear she would be able to rely on no man."

He grimaced. "Blast it, don't try to turn this

around on me. I have not lied to you or kept silent about anything. I asked only that you let me help keep you safe."

Eleanor smiled at him. "You are right. I'm sorry."

He relaxed and smiled back at her, crossing the floor to her. He put his hands on her arms and looked down into her face. "Perhaps I am too hard on the man. I do not like how he looks at you."

"He is Italian. He would think it was an insult not to pay me flowery compliments and send me meaningful glances."

Anthony slid his hands up her arms and back down, his eyes darkening, as he gazed at her. His voice was husky when he spoke. "And is that what is necessary to win you? Flowery compliments? Meaningful glances? Should I tell you that my heart beats faster every time I see you? Or that last night I found myself looking for you across the room whenever I was not with you?"

Eleanor found herself aware suddenly of every physical sensation in her body—the pumping of her blood, the prickling of her skin, the shallow breaths that passed through her lips.

"It matters only if it is true," she replied softly, her eyes not moving from his.

"Oh, it is true," he told her, his mouth softening as he raised his hand to touch the side of her face, gently pushing a stray strand of hair back from her cheek. "It is all too true. There were times these past

few days when I hardly knew myself. All I can think about anymore is how it felt to kiss you. All I want to do is take you in my arms again."

He bent and brushed his lips lightly against hers. Eleanor felt herself warming, weakening, all over.

"Anthony…the servants."

"Damn the servants." He kissed her again, his lips searching, and when he pulled back, she was breathless.

"But Honoria…Samantha…"

"And them, as well," he went on ruthlessly as he kissed his way across her cheek to her ear.

His breath brushed her ear, sending shivers through her, and he nibbled gently at the tender lobe. Eleanor's hands came up and curled into the lapels of his coat, holding on; she felt as if her knees might give way at any moment, so shaky were they. She knew they should stop; this was foolhardy. But she could not force herself to move away from him or even to protest. Everything he was doing was precisely what she craved, she realized, even before she knew she wanted it.

He moved back to take her lips once again, kissing her long and deeply. At last he raised his head, staring down into her face. He looked predatory, fierce. Desire flooded her.

With a low growl of frustration, Anthony released her and turned away, balling his hands into fists and shoving them into his pockets. "Bloody hell! I cannot think when I am around you!"

Eleanor stood where she was, torn with indecision. Every muscle, every nerve, every drop of blood in her body, cried to her to go to him, certain that if she put her arms around him, even touched him, the taut reins of his control would snap. Then there would be no holding back, no stopping. The passion between them would rage like a fire until at last it was spent.

But if that happened, there would be no return. Their lives would have changed irrevocably.

Eleanor let out a long sigh and also turned away, walking over to the window and staring out sightlessly at the garden.

"Forgive me," Anthony said at last, his voice tight. "I should go now."

Eleanor turned, her eyes flying to his face. He looked as cold and hard as when she had first met him. She could not quite keep the anxiety from her voice as she said, "You will come back?"

His face softened a little. "Yes, of course. I will return this evening. I would not leave you to deal with this alone."

She did not tell him that she had not feared his leaving because she would have to face whatever danger lurked, but simply because she hated to be away from him. Better to let him think she was afraid than to let him know how completely she was falling under his spell.

"I have a few things to do first," he went on grimly.

"Of course. I have kept you too much from your own concerns."

Anthony took his leave of her without admitting that it was not his own business that took him away. The fact was that he had decided to pay a visit to the Conte di Graffeo. He could not stay with Eleanor or he was all too likely to forget his good intentions, as well as his duty as a gentleman, and carry her off to her bedroom upstairs. Passion was thrumming in him, and he was as taut as a pulled bowstring.

The only thing to do was to take himself out of this house for the next few hours. Paying a call on the count seemed the perfect distraction. He had intended to do so since Eleanor told him what the man had said to her last night. Now, as he strode out of her house and down the street, his purpose grew and hardened in him. All the pent-up hunger and emotion that boiled within him were channeled into his dislike of the count.

He had set his butler, Hudgins, to finding out where the man was living while in London. Hudgins, while affecting an aloof and tight-lipped manner that implied he was above such mundane things as gossip, in fact kept his ears open and had tentacles of influence that spread throughout the servant world, enabling him to be the prime source of any information one wanted about the habits of anyone in the *ton*. A notable visitor's leasing of a house and hiring

servants for it would be something Hudgins could find out with little problem.

Anthony felt sure that Hudgins would have come up with an answer by now, and he was not disappointed. The butler directed him toward one of the most fashionable streets in Mayfair, a small crescent with a sliver of park between it and a major thoroughfare. The count from Naples, Hudgins informed him, had leased a narrow charcoal-gray house set cheek-by-jowl among larger abodes, a perfect spot for a man of position, wealth and taste to stay temporarily.

The house was, in fact, not far from where Anthony himself lived, and he walked the few blocks to it. After trotting up the steps to the red door, the only splash of color against the dark, white-shuttered house, Anthony brought down the knocker firmly. When the liveried footman opened the door, Anthony stepped inside without waiting for an invitation. He had no intention of being denied a talk with Conte di Graffeo.

The servant appeared somewhat startled, but automatically took the hat and gloves that Anthony removed and handed to him. "I am here to speak to the count," he told the man, taking out his silver card case from an inside pocket of his jacket and handing the man his card.

The footman bowed. "Right this way, my lord. I will tell the count you are here."

He showed Anthony into a small drawing room off the entryway. It was several minutes before Conte di Graffeo appeared. Anthony suspected that he had left him cooling his heels in order to demonstrate that he was in control of the visit, but, in fact, the wait only gave Anthony's anger time to cool into a hard, unyielding block.

"Lord Neale," di Graffeo said, bowing slightly. His expression was polite, but faintly supercilious. "An unexpected pleasure. Please, sit down."

"I prefer to stand," Anthony answered tersely.

"Indeed? Well…to what do I owe the pleasure of this visit?"

"You made certain threats to Lady Eleanor Scarbrough last night," Anthony told him, his face like stone. "I came to inform you that I will deal personally with anyone who harms, or attempts to harm, Lady Scarbrough."

"Threats?" The other man raised his eyebrows, looking faintly amused. "My dear sir, I fear the lady misunderstood what I said to her. Women are, after all, rather excitable."

"Not this woman," Anthony retorted flatly.

The count shrugged. "I merely pointed out that her husband had been involved in some rather foolish activities. I would not like to see such a lovely lady get drawn into the same activities. That is all."

"Did you kill Edmund?"

Anthony was somewhat pleased to note that his abrupt question had startled the other man out of his sophisticated calm. Di Graffeo stared at him for a moment before his features relaxed once more into their usual smooth state.

"I would not stain my hands with such as him," the count said, making a dismissive gesture. "Scarbrough was a boy playing at adult games. He was weak—an impressionable idealist. Precisely the sort who falls prey to the thugs and criminals who masquerade as revolutionaries. He came to Naples and fell in with the wrong crowd. He became a member of *L'unione*. They are the remnants of a ragtag group that tried to overthrow the king. Most of them are now resting in prison. But there are always foolish young men ready to take their place. They want to unify Italy under a democratic government. It is absurd, of course. It will never work. But the men are persuasive, especially when they work on the minds of the young or ignorant."

"Sir Edmund was my nephew," Anthony told him coldly. "And he was neither foolish nor ignorant. He was, in fact, a man of enormous talent, as well as ideals. But you, I am sure, would have trouble understanding such a man."

"His music was exquisite. I have no argument with that. But he would have been better served to work on his operas, not dabble in politics."

"Why? Because you killed him for it?"

"I told you. I did not kill him. Nor order him killed. I did not really care about him. Englishmen like him come to Italy every year. They develop their little enthusiasms, spread their English ideas around, and then, after a year or two, they return to England. It would have been the same with him."

"Then why did you make such a point of talking to Lady Eleanor? Why are you so concerned about what she does or what she gets involved in?"

"Sir Edmund had information I want," the count told him bluntly. "Now Lady Scarbrough is in possession of it. That is all I care about—a list of names that was entrusted to him. The lady would be well-advised to give the list to me."

"Another threat?" Anthony asked.

"You may take it as you will," the count replied, gazing back at him blandly.

"I take it that you have broken into Lady Scarbrough's home and tried to steal this information, but you could not find it, so now you intend to make her give it to you."

"I have not broken into Lady Scarbrough's house or any other house. I am not a thief," di Graffeo told him scornfully.

"Of course not. You paid someone else to do it for you."

"You are sadly misinformed. I have no need to try to steal anything. I have always found that money works much better. I am quite prepared to pay Lady

Scarbrough for the list of names. You may tell her so."

"Let me assure you that an offer of money will have no effect on Lady Scarbrough," Anthony said flatly. "I can also tell you that you are wasting your time. Eleanor knows nothing about any papers relating to *L'unione* or anything else. Edmund told her nothing about his involvement with the group. He wanted to protect her. He gave her no papers. She has searched the house thoroughly, because of the attempted thefts, and she has found nothing."

"Or so she says."

"You are questioning the lady's honesty?" Anthony's voice was low and silkily dangerous.

"People lie, even beautiful women. Especially beautiful women."

Anthony took a long step forward, so that he was standing only a foot away from the man, looming over him. His eyes were as hard and emotionless as flint.

"Lady Scarbrough does not lie. Nor do I. And I am telling you this for a fact: if any harm comes to Eleanor Scarbrough or any of the people about whom she cares, I will hunt you down, wherever you may hide, and I will see to it that you pay."

For a moment the men's gazes remained locked. The count was the first to move, turning away as he said, "As I told you, I mean no harm to Lady Scarbrough. I simply want the list."

"Then I suggest you return to Italy and look for it there." Anthony turned and strode out of the room.

He lingered in the entryway for a moment and was pleased to hear something hit the wall in the room behind him with a crash, followed by a string of Italian curses. A frosty smile touched Anthony's lips as he reclaimed his possessions and walked out the door.

AFTER ANTHONY LEFT HER, Eleanor went upstairs to Honoria's room. She found the lady stretched out on her bed, a lavender-scented cloth laid across her eyes, both her daughter and Eleanor's own maid hovering over her.

For the first time, it seemed to Eleanor that the woman was genuinely grieving for Edmund.

"Why would he do such a thing?" she asked Eleanor plaintively, taking off the cold compress and looking at Eleanor with red-rimmed eyes. "Why would he endanger himself like that? All his life, I was so careful with him."

"I know you were," Eleanor answered. "I don't know. I think he must have felt very deeply about it."

"Was he—did someone kill him?" Honoria asked, her voice tinged with horror.

"There is nothing to say that anyone did," Eleanor replied carefully. Certainly the things that Dario had told her had raised her suspicions about the manner of his death, but she feared that voicing

those suspicions would only make his mother feel even worse. "Try not to think about it. Why don't you sleep now? I will tell the kitchen to send you up a nice cup of hot chocolate, and then maybe you can nap."

Eleanor left the room and, after ordering the chocolate, went straight to her own to change into a dress suitable for an afternoon call. While she had been talking to Lady Honoria, she had remembered Mrs. Malducci from the night before. She had promised to pay a call on the woman, and though she had not particularly wanted to do so, now she was eager to follow through with her promise. Signora Malducci had acted in an odd fashion. Eleanor remembered feeling that the woman was eager to talk to her about Edmund and his death. She had assumed that Mrs. Malducci was simply a ghoulish sort who wanted to rehash the details of his death and his funeral pyre.

But when she thought about Edmund's death in the light of the things they had learned from Dario, she had to wonder. What if Signora Malducci had something important to tell her? What if she knew something about Edmund's death? She said that she had seen Edmund "that day." Perhaps her odd manner was because she had seen something untoward, something that might indicate whether Edmund had been murderered...and by whom.

As the Colton-Smythes' house was at some

distance from hers, on the edge of Mayfair, Eleanor took her carriage. When she arrived at their door, she mounted the steps quickly and knocked, then waited. After a long wait, when no one answered the door, she raised the brass knocker and tried again.

Finally the door was opened by a harried-looking maid. "I'm sorry, miss, no one's receiving today. Everything's all at sixes and sevens."

"Oh." Eleanor was taken aback. "I—I'm sorry. I was asked by Signora Malducci to call on her. Could you take her my ca—"

She stopped as the maid let out a squeak and quickly covered her mouth. "Oh, miss, I'm ever so sorry," the maid said in a rush. "But that Italian woman…" She hesitated, then continued in a rush. "She was in an accident this morning."

"What?" Eleanor's stomach went cold. "No."

The maid nodded. "Yes, miss, she was. It was 'orrible," the girl went on, her careful accent slipping in her distress. "She went for a walk this morning— not more than an hour ago, it was. Right out there on this street. And a carriage come down the road and hit her! I'm sorry, miss, but Mrs. Malducci's dead."

CHAPTER FOURTEEN

ELEANOR SUCKED IN her breath sharply and took an unconscious step backward, her hand coming up to her throat. "She died?"

"Yes, miss. It was 'orrible. And the missus, she took to her bed, and she can't see anyone."

"I—I see. This is so awful. Please, tell Mrs. Colton-Smythe that I called, and give her my most sincere sympathy." She pulled out the calling card she had been about to give the maid earlier and handed it to her.

The maid took it, nodding, and shut the door. Eleanor turned and slowly retraced her steps to the carriage. Numbly, she let the coachman hand her up onto the seat, then sat back as the carriage rolled away.

Signora Malducci dead! It seemed impossible. She had just seen the woman last night.

Eleanor rode home, her head whirling with suspicions. She wanted to see Anthony, to talk to him about what she had just learned, and she considered

for a moment telling the coachman to take her to Anthony's house. However, she was not sure that he would be there, and shaken as she had been by the news, she was uncharacteristically indecisive, so she did nothing. She would write him a note when she got home, she thought, and then scolded herself for feeling she had to have Anthony's help. Surely she could handle this on her own, could do whatever had to be done. But, she realized, she had no idea what to do. Signora Malducci's death had just closed her last avenue of inquiry. She feared that she would never find out what had really happened to Edmund.

When they arrived at her house, she hurried inside. A footman met her at the door to take her hat and gloves.

"Lord Neale is waiting for you, my lady," he told her.

"He is?" Eleanor turned to the man, her chest feeling suddenly lighter. "Where?"

"I put him in the front drawing room, my lady."

Eleanor smiled at the man, unaware of the way her face had lit up, and hurried toward the drawing room. "Anthony!"

He was standing at the mantel, and he whipped around at the sound of her voice. "What is it? What's the matter?"

"Oh, Anthony!" Suddenly, seeing him, everything she had heard today seemed too much. Tears welled in her eyes, and she ran to him.

"Eleanor!" He moved to meet her, his arms opening to take her in.

Then she was against his chest, hearing the reassuring thud of his heart, wrapped in his warmth, his arms tightly around her. "Oh, Anthony, it was awful."

"What? What was awful? Did something happen to you?"

He moved back a little and lifted her chin to look down at her, his forehead creased with concern.

"Not to me. To Mrs. Malducci!"

"Who?"

"The woman from last night. Mrs. Colton-Smythe's guest from Naples."

"Oh, yes, the one who wanted you to call on her."

Eleanor nodded. "Yes. I went to see her, and when I got there, the maid told me she was dead. She was killed this morning in a carriage accident."

"What?" He stared at her. "What happened?"

"The maid said she went for a walk and a carriage hit her."

"My God."

"Yes!" Eleanor turned away and began to pace agitatedly. "I cannot help but think that it is connected to Edmund and everything that has been happening."

"But why? What would she have to do with Edmund?"

"She told me last night that she wanted to talk to me about him. She said that she had seen him the day he died."

"She had? I didn't hear that. She saw him?"

"I am sure that is what she said. And she seemed…I don't know, a little excited. I didn't want to call on her. I thought she was just morbidly interested in his death. But it occurred to me that perhaps she wanted to talk to me because she had seen something suspicious. If she saw Edmund right before he died, she might have noticed that he was scared or… or sad, or even, perhaps, that someone was dragging him along with them."

"Surely she would have reported that earlier."

"Well, perhaps it was not something that clear. It could have been that only after she thought about it, she began to realize there was something wrong about what she saw. So that is why I decided to call on her this afternoon. Then, when I got there, the maid told me a carriage had run her down this morning. That cannot be a coincidence."

"Slow down. You cannot assume that she knew anything. She may simply have wanted to hear the gruesome details, as you said," Anthony argued.

"No. I know it, Anthony. I know it! She had something to tell me, and now she is dead. I didn't want to talk to her. I held back. I could have gone over there this morning and I did not. I think she had information we could have used, and I didn't pay enough attention. I should have asked her right then what she saw. I should have gone over there this morning. But I didn't. She is dead now, and it's my fault!"

Eleanor's voice caught on a sob. Anthony let out an oath and swung her back into his arms.

"Hush. Don't talk like that. You are not responsible for Mrs. Malducci's death."

Tears clogged her voice. "I failed her," Eleanor said thickly. "Just as I failed Edmund. Oh, God, why didn't I see what was happening? I should have talked to him. I should have known what he was doing and stopped him!"

She broke into tears, crying into Anthony's shirt-front. He wrapped his arms around her tenderly, cradling her against him and stroking her back.

"Shh…no…do not blame yourself for that. For either of them," Anthony told her. "Eleanor, the whole world is not your responsibility. You could not have known that Signora Malducci would be killed. In truth, you do not even know that she had anything important to tell you. Accidents do happen. It may have been nothing more than that. And even if it was not, there is nothing to say you could have saved her. And you did not control Edmund. He was a grown man. He was free to do what he liked. He believed in this group's ideals. He knew the dangers, and he took the risk because he believed so strongly. It was not your decision to make, it was his."

He was right, she knew, yet still she cried, the remnants of her grief for Edmund pouring out. But Anthony's words soothed her, and gradually her tears slowed and then stopped. Still, she continued

to lean against him, enjoying the comfort of his strength.

Anthony pulled out his handkerchief and gently wiped the tears from her face. "There." He kissed her forehead. "I hate to see tears on you."

"I hate to cry," she responded, letting out a little sigh. The bout of tears had left her weary somehow, and it was so pleasant to lean against him. The truth was, she wished she never had to leave the comfort of his arms. It was the place she wished to be. It felt like home.

It occurred to her that they were standing in a compromising position, that she should probably step away from him, but somehow she could not at the moment find it in herself to care. It felt too good to be there.

His hand stroked rhythmically up and down her back, soothing and warming her. Eleanor nestled a little closer, breathing in his masculine scent, and when she moved, she heard the steady thump of his heart suddenly flare into a faster beat, and his hand on her back was hot and a trifle unsteady. She realized in that instant that her movement against him had aroused him, and somehow that knowledge set spark to her own desire.

In a flash, the stroking of his hand became no longer soothing but sensual, a long, slow caress that caused her skin to tingle even through the material of her dress. Eleanor's breath came faster in her

throat, her blood heating in her veins. She arched back against his hand, raising her head and looking up at him through heavy-lidded eyes.

His eyes were the color of molten iron, boring down into her, melting her. "I want you," he told her bluntly, his voice taut. "I've wanted you since the first moment I saw you. You were Edmund's wife, but still I wanted you."

He bent closer to her, his mouth hovering only inches from hers. "Beyond all reason." His lips brushed hers, then tantalizingly moved away. "Beyond all decency." He kissed her upper lip, then her lower, each kiss lingering just a little more than the one before. "I want you in my bed. Beneath me. I want to hear you moan my name."

His words stirred her unbearably, igniting a fire low in her abdomen. She trembled, hovering on the brink, stretching up to him. And then his mouth settled on hers at last, and he kissed her deeply. Eleanor clung to him, beyond words or thought, aware only of the hunger pounding through her.

At last he raised his head, breaking off the kiss. He gazed down at her for a long beat, then bent and swept her up into his arms and started out the door.

"Anthony!" Eleanor protested in a low shriek, laughter bubbling up in her. "Someone will see!"

"I don't care," he replied as he walked into the hallway and up the stairs.

Eleanor buried her face in his shoulder. She knew

she should be embarrassed, but all she really wanted to do was to laugh with sheer delight.

As it happened, they passed no one on their way up the stairs and into her bedroom. He set her down inside the door and closed it behind them, turning the key in the lock with a decisive click. They stood for a moment, looking at each other. Eleanor knew that even at this last moment, she could turn away from him, could ask him to leave. There was still a chance to avoid taking this final step.

She looked into his eyes; then, slowly, not taking her eyes from his, she reached behind herself and began to undo her buttons. He watched her, his eyes feverishly bright. He peeled off his own coat and tossed it toward a chair, not looking to see where it landed. He unbuttoned his waistcoat and shrugged out of it, never taking his gaze from Eleanor.

The buttons down her back were small and legion, but gradually, as she worked her way down, the sides of her dress began to part and sag, sliding down from her shoulders, inch by inch revealing more of the tops of her milky breasts. Anthony's eyes remained glued to that slowly lowering neckline, his chest rising and falling as his breath came ever faster.

It was still not completely unbuttoned, but finally the dress was loose enough that Eleanor was able to slip out of it, letting it pool at her feet. She stood, clad in her petticoats and chemise, blushing a little with

embarrassment, yet at the same time filled with excitement as Anthony's eyes roamed over her.

He had unbuttoned his shirt, but he seemed to forget what he was doing as he stared at her, his hands falling to his sides. Slowly he came forward until he was standing in front of her. He reached out and softly skimmed his fingers over the tops of her breasts.

"You are so beautiful," he breathed. "You make a man forget everything else but you."

He took hold of the ribbon that bound the top of her chemise and pulled. The bow slid undone, and the chemise parted, revealing the inner curve of her cleavage. He traced the line of her breast, skimming around it and down the middle, then moving back up, following the curve of the opposite orb. The soft flesh trembled beneath his light touch.

Her nipples tightened, her breasts full and aching for his touch. He slipped his hands beneath the sides of the soft cotton garment, pushing the fabric farther apart and down, revealing the full, white mounds. His hands curved around them, filling his grasp. He bent and laid his lips gently to the top of one breast, then the other.

Eleanor trembled, the hot moisture of desire flooding between her legs. She sucked in her breath, closing her eyes, as arousal swept through her, startling her with its intensity.

His thumbs moved across her nipples, circling

and caressing them, teasing until Eleanor let out a soft moan of hunger and frustration. She wanted more, though she was not certain what that was. She knew only that she ached and yearned, her body softening and opening, eager for more.

At last he bent and touched the tip of his tongue to one nipple, and a hot frisson of pleasure shot through her. Softly, slowly, his tongue teased at her, until finally he took the hard button of flesh into his mouth. Desire shook her, and her knees threatened to buckle, but he looped his arm around her back and held her up as his mouth continued to feast upon her breasts.

She moved restlessly, and he slid his knee between hers, opening her legs to him. Instinctively Eleanor moved against him, pressing the hot, yearning center of her desire against his thigh. He let out a low, guttural noise, and suddenly his hand was there between her legs, pressing into her through the cloth of her petticoats.

Eleanor shuddered. She had never felt anything like the sensations that were flooding her now. She was all fire and hunger. She dug her fingers into his hair, almost sobbing with the intensity of her desire.

He released her to tear at his clothes, ripping off his shirt and flinging it away, then starting on the buttons of his breeches. Eleanor slipped out of her chemise, and her eager fingers slipped on the ties of her petticoats, turning the bows into knots.

Anthony, having divested himself of the rest of his clothes, turned back to her. Slipping his hand inside the recalcitrant tie, he jerked once, snapping the ribbon from its mooring, and the soft cotton petticoats tumbled to the floor.

He picked her up and laid her on the bed, then pulled off her slippers and slid her stockings down her legs, his hands caressing each inch of flesh as it was revealed.

Eleanor watched him as he rolled down her stockings. She had never seen a man's naked form before, and she drank it in now. He was so lean and powerful, so wonderfully different from her own body. She wanted to touch him, to caress him as he caressed her, to taste his flesh with her mouth as he had tasted hers.

And so, when he finished and crawled onto the bed beside her, Eleanor turned to him, her hands going out to his chest and traveling slowly, deliciously down him. He drew in a sharp breath, closing his eyes.

"I'm sorry," she whispered. "Is that wrong?"

"No," he responded tightly. "It is right. It is very right."

She continued her exploration, smoothing her hands down over the thickly padded muscles of his chest, sliding over the dips and curves, then down onto the smooth, satiny skin of his abdomen and the sharp outthrust of his pelvic bones. Her hands glided

back and around to the softer curve of his buttocks, and her fingers dug in, squeezing and massaging.

A groan escaped him, and he pulled her to him, his mouth sinking into hers. He kissed her wildly, deeply, as if he could not have enough of her, and his hands ran down her body eagerly. Eleanor kissed him back, matching his hunger, and she dug her fingers into his back, urging him closer.

His hand slipped between her legs, his fingers separating and stroking, exciting her beyond anything she had ever imagined. She moved against his palm, her whole body aching for completion.

"Please," she moaned, pulling her mouth away. "Anthony, now. I want…"

"I know," he said thickly, moving between her legs. "I know."

She felt him then, gently probing the tender flesh between her legs, sliding into her. There was a flash of pain, and she tensed. Anthony flung up his head, startled, and looked into her face.

"Eleanor! Why—"

She shook her head, wrapping her legs around him and taking him inside her. He sank deep into her, filling her, and Eleanor bit back a moan at the pleasure. Her fingers dug into his back, urging him on, and he began to move within her. With each stroke he drove her pleasure higher, carrying her deeper and deeper into the hot, dark maelstrom of passion. Eleanor rocked against him, the knot of

hunger deep inside her tightening and tightening until she was shaking.

And then, at last, the pleasure burst inside her, washing out from her center in great waves. She wrapped her arms around Anthony, holding on as the desire took her, and she felt him shudder against her and cry out as the two of them gave themselves up to their passion.

ELEANOR DRIFTED, stunned, awash in the sweet aftermath of their lovemaking. She had never dreamed that anything could feel like this, that she could be so replete, so satisfied, or that she could feel joined this way to anyone. Anthony was part of her now in a way she had never imagined, and she could not keep from smiling to herself.

"Eleanor, I'm sorry," he murmured, stroking her hair. "I did not know…why didn't you tell me you had never—that you were untouched. I thought…"

"It made no difference," she told him, snuggling closer. "This was what I wanted."

He kissed the top of her head, then, wrapping his arm around her, pulled her over on top of him. Eleanor looked down into his face, smiling, her hair falling like a curtain around them.

"It is what I wanted, too," he said softly, reaching up to stroke her cheek.

Eleanor laid her head on his chest, listening to the steady thump of his heart, content simply to lie there

as he stroked her hair, twining it around his fingers, then setting it free. She thought she could lie there forever, basking in the shared warmth. There were no worries, no problems, no thoughts of the future. She closed her eyes, her mind drifting.

Suddenly her eyes flew open. She drew in a sharp breath and sat up.

"Eleanor?" Anthony blinked at her, startled. "What is it?"

"I just thought of it!" she exclaimed and jumped out of bed.

"Thought of what?" he asked, confused, as he watched her scurry about the room, grabbing up her clothes and pulling them back on.

"The names!" she cried, sweeping up his clothes and handing them to him. "Here, get dressed. We have to go look."

"The names?" he repeated, struggling into his breeches and shirt. "Are you talking about Edmund's list? The one the count is looking for?"

"Yes. The members of *L'unione*. I know where Edmund hid the names!"

CHAPTER FIFTEEN

ANTHONY THREW ON his clothes in haste as Eleanor wound her hair up in a careless knot atop her head and pinned it. She started fastening the buttons up her back, and Anthony came over to help her finish. He was putting on his jacket over his unbuttoned waistcoat as she opened the door and popped her head out, then waved him into the hall.

"How do you know where it is?" he asked as he followed her down the stairs.

"Well, I *think* I know," she answered. "It suddenly popped into my head. I don't know why I didn't think of it before. I realized suddenly that Edmund would have hidden it in the thing he knew best. His music."

"You mean you think the list is hidden among the sheets of music?"

"No." Eleanor swept into the music room and grabbed the sheaf of papers from the top of the piano. Flourishing them, she said, "I mean, I think he hid them *in* the music!"

He stared at her for a moment; then his face cleared. "The notes are a code?"

Eleanor nodded. "Yes. That has to be the answer. He carefully hid this pedestrian, even bad, sonata in a secret drawer, the key to which he also hid in a piece of jewelry that he told me I should keep for his sake. I couldn't understand why he would so protect a piece of music that doesn't even begin to approach his standard."

Anthony nodded. "That makes sense. More so than his suddenly losing his talent. He wouldn't go from a wonderful piece of work like his opera straight to something like this. A lesser work, perhaps, but not this."

"Exactly. And the real beauty of it is that even if someone did take the key and did discover the secret drawer, he would find only music. He would not realize what it was, just as we didn't. So the count, or whoever it was, would probably just leave the music or throw it away."

"All right. Now…" Anthony looked down over her shoulder at the top sheet. "All we have to do is decipher the code."

Eleanor tossed him a dazzling smile. "We can do it. At this moment, I feel as if I can conquer the world."

His smile in return was slow and sensual, lighting his eyes even before it touched his lips. He reached up and curled his finger around one of the stray curls that had escaped from her hastily-knotted hair. "I agree."

The way he looked at her made Eleanor want to stretch up on tiptoe and kiss him. He must have seen her thought in her face, for his eyes darkened, and he reached out, pulling her into his arms.

"Nay," Eleanor told him, her voice a trifle shaky, as she slipped out of his hold. "If we start that, we may never get back to deciphering this code."

He grinned. "Frankly, at the moment, the code is not uppermost in my mind."

"Your mind?" Eleanor repeated wryly, grinning. "Why, I would have said it was another part ruling you now."

"Saucy wench," he retorted without heat, then heaved a dramatic sigh. "Very well. Let us look at this."

They removed to her office, where they laid the sheet music out on her desk and pulled up an extra chair. Eleanor took out a piece of foolscap and the nub of a pencil she had been using for totting up numbers the day before.

"Let's see… I suppose the simplest thing is that the notes represent letters."

She drew a quick series of lines and jotted down the notes of a musical scale, below them putting the corresponding letter. They looked at it for a moment.

"But that leaves us with far too few letters," Anthony pointed out. "There would have to be more than seven letters to spell out a number of names."

"Perhaps the next octave up is the next set of

seven," Eleanor offered. She wrote out that scale and added the next seven letters, then repeated it.

"Then the third one up?" Anthony looked at her, and she shrugged.

"It's worth a try. But what about the bass clef?"

"I'm not sure. Let us try the first few bars with the letters we have," Anthony suggested.

Eleanor read the music, jotting down the letters they had agreed upon for the treble clef. The result was a jumble of nonsense.

"That cannot be right," Anthony mused. He studied the music again. "How do you suppose he divided the names? How do you tell where one stops and the next one starts?"

"A bar for a name?" Eleanor proffered, then immediately answered her own suggestion. "No, that would be too regular. It would accommodate only a certain number of notes."

She set her chin on her hand, and they gazed silently at the music. Finally Anthony tapped a notation. "What about the rest sign? I notice that there are a number of them on the pages."

Eleanor perked up. "You might be right. There are eleven notes here before this rest. Then…" She counted quickly to the next rest sign. "Thirteen notes. Those sound right for the length of names, don't they? Fifteen here. There are entirely too many rests to be proper."

"Now if only we could figure out the letters."

"Wait…wait…" Eleanor said, excitement rising in her. "There are really twelve tones in an octave. You have to add in the flats and sharps. There are seven white keys and five black keys. What if we assigned the letters of the alphabet to the twelve tones? You would need only two sets to make 24 letters."

"And the last two? Start again?"

Eleanor wrinkled her nose. "You don't really need all the letters."

"The last two could be left out."

"Not z. There are a number of zs in Italian names. But w, x, and y likely would not appear."

"Then which two octaves do we choose? The first on treble and the first on bass? The first two on treble?"

"I don't know." Eleanor frowned down at the music. "Let's try it both ways."

They jotted down several permutations of the eleven notes before the first rest, but again the result had little meaning.

"Look at the repetition of As," Anthony pointed out, tapping at the series of notes before the end. "A, blank, blank, A. That seems a likely part of a name."

"So do the double Cs. That's very Italian. But taken together, they're a mess. There are not enough higher notes for it to be the two right-hand octaves. This tune is very simple, very basic. It does not really wander out of the first octave. But if you use the bass as the other twelve, it is simply gibberish."

Eleanor sighed and sat back in her chair. "Perhaps I was wrong. Maybe this is not what Edmund did at all."

"No, don't give up. I think you must be right about this music being the key to the names. Otherwise, why would Edmund have hidden it so carefully? Indeed, why would he even have written it?"

They were silent for a moment, contemplating the page of music. Finally Anthony suggested, "Perhaps if you played it on the piano it would make more sense."

Eleanor shrugged. "I suppose I could try picking it out again. It is so odd—look at the variation of quarter and half notes. Quarter, quarter, half, half, quarter, half, quarter, and then a rest. Then quarter, half, quarter, quarter, half, half, qua…" Her words trailed off.

She turned to Anthony, excitement rising in her voice. "What if it's not different octaves but different lengths. Look—not a single whole note, at least in the treble clef. All quarters and halves. What if the quarter notes are the first half of the alphabet and the halves the second half? Or vice versa."

"And forget the bass altogether?"

"I think it may serve only as a way to further disguise the truth."

Eleanor began to scribble down a new set of letters. She stopped, sucking in her breath. "Look…pietrocannata. Pietro Cannata. I know him. He was one of Edmund's friends."

"And the next one?"

She scribbled away, glancing from the sheet of music to her lines of code. "Angelo Fasso. Raffaele Savaglia. Anthony!" She turned to him, her eyes glowing. "This is it! This is the list of names!"

She let out a laugh as Anthony jumped to his feet, pulling her up and into his arms, exclaiming, "You did it! Eleanor, you are incomparable!"

He picked her up and whirled her around, both of them laughing. Then he set her down and planted a quick, hard kiss on her lips.

There was a sound at the doorway, and they turned toward it. One of the maids stood there, wide-eyed. She quickly bobbed a curtsey and fled.

"Oh dear," Eleanor murmured.

She was aware suddenly of the careless state of her hair, which had been twisted up quickly and pinned haphazardly, clearly not the work of her skillful personal maid. Her clothes, as well, were not in their usual neat order, having been flung on in a rush. Her somewhat ramshackle appearance would, of course, be no cause for gossip if it weren't for the fact that she had just been caught kissing Anthony.

She glanced at Anthony, who was scowling at the doorway where the maid had stood. "Eleanor…"

"No," she said lightly. The last thing she wanted to hear was any statement of regret over what had happened between them. "Do not worry. My staff knows better than to gossip. If she starts to jabber

about this in the kitchen, she will be set straight." Or, at least, she would be normally, when Bartwell was here. "It is no problem."

She gave him a glittering smile, and his face softened in response. Eleanor took advantage of the moment to turn away, saying briskly, "Well, I guess this leaves us with the question of what to do with the list."

"Yes. I am sure you do not want it to fall into di Graffeo's hands," he said.

"Absolutely not," she agreed.

"I suppose the safest thing might be to destroy it, so that the count cannot possibly get it."

"Yes, and yet, I would hate for all Edmund's effort to go for naught. He could have destroyed it himself, but it was important enough for him to go to some lengths to hide it. I think he would like for *L'unione* to have it back. I can't help but feel that perhaps I should give it to Dario."

Anthony grimaced.

"I know you do not like him," she continued.

"Yes, I know, I know, it is just my jealousy," he finished for her. "All right, I do not like the way he hangs about you, oozing compliments and charm."

Eleanor had to smile. "Yes, it is terribly wicked of him."

"But just because I am jealous, that does not mean he is a good man," Anthony pointed out.

"No. And I will admit that I do not know much

about him. But I do know that he was Edmund's friend. Edmund liked and trusted him."

"Not enough to entrust the papers to him."

"It was expedient to leave them in my care. And Edmund knew that I—"

"Would make sure everything worked as it should. He was right, God knows, to trust you, but, blast it, I could have wished he had not been so ready to put you into the middle of danger."

Eleanor smiled at him, warmed by his concern. She placed her hand upon his arm. "Do not worry so. I shall wait a little before I decide what to do. We can decode the rest of the names and see if Dario's is among them. If it is not, then we must suspect that he is lying. If it is, then it would seem that he is our best choice to give them to, since he is a member of *L'unione*. In the meantime, I will put the original music, as well as our decoded list, in the safe beside the butler's pantry. That should keep it away from any thieves."

"That sounds like a reasonable solution," Anthony agreed, and they sat down again at the desk, side by side, and began to work their way through the sheet of music.

It was not difficult, now that they had the secret of it, and they worked quickly. It was pleasant, Eleanor thought, to sit thus, enjoying one another's company as they completed the task. Her happiness was marred only by the knowledge that she could not

lean against him or touch his hand or brush her lips
across his cheek, as she would have liked to do now
and then as they worked. But it was too likely that
someone might come by and see.

She had not lied when she told him that her
servants were loyal to her and disinclined to gossip.
But with Bartwell gone, she knew that the reins of
the household were not held as tightly, and because
the footmen had to take up extra duties guarding the
household at night, they had had to take on extra
maids to keep the household running smoothly.
Eleanor had not recognized the maid who had seen
them, and she felt a little more doubtful of a new
maid than one of her own. Of course, if the girl
wished to keep her job, then she would find out
quickly enough that she needed to mind her tongue.
But still, Eleanor realized that she must be especially circumspect.

Even more important, she had no idea whether
Samantha or Honoria might walk in on them. She
certainly did not want to give Honoria a weapon to
use against her, and Samantha was too young and
impressionable for Eleanor to be flouting convention
around her.

Eleanor suppressed a sigh. The sooner she did
something with these papers, she thought, the sooner
she could dispense with Honoria's chaperonage. Of
course, then the children and Bartwell and the others
would be returning. She thought of the few precious

days of a relatively empty house that lay between those two events. Then she would do exactly as she liked.

She looked at Anthony and wondered what he was thinking, whether he, like she, chafed at the restrictions around them, if he wished that they could spend the whole long night together, sleeping twined in each other's arms and waking to make love again.

"If you keep looking at me like that, I shall be compelled to kiss you right here, and the servants be damned," he said, leaning closer to her.

"What?" Startled, Eleanor came out of her daze and looked at him. She flushed as she realized how her thoughts must have been written on her face. She covered her burning cheeks with the palms of her hands. "Oh, I'm sorry."

She started to turn away, but he grasped her arms. "No. Don't be sorry. I'm not. I like to think that you—" he stroked his finger along her hand, tracing a line down the back and to the end of each finger, bringing her skin to life along each sensual path "—enjoyed what we did. That there is a possibility of it happening again."

A smile flickered across her face. "I think there is a definite possibility."

"And how soon would you see this occurring?" he asked.

"Well…" Eleanor tilted her head a little to one side, pretending to consider the question. This was

flirtation, she thought. It was something she had never done much of, but she was finding it quite enjoyable.

"Lady Eleanor?" At that moment Samantha's voice sounded in the hall.

Anthony let out a groan and sank his head onto his hands.

"Lady Eleanor?"

Eleanor sighed softly, then called, "In here, Samantha."

"There you are!" The young girl entered the room with boundless energy. "And Uncle Anthony. I'm so glad I found you both. There is something ever so special happening the day after tomorrow. May we go? It's a balloon ascension in the park. It sounds terribly exciting."

"Indeed, that does sound intriguing," Eleanor agreed, looking at Anthony. "What do you say, Lord Neale? Shall we take Samantha to see the balloons?"

"Of course," he answered easily, turning his attention to his niece. "Where did you hear about this?"

"Mama's friend, Lady Bricknell. She was here visiting Mama just a few minutes ago, and she said that Mama and I must come. But Mama does not wish to. So you are my only hope."

"Well, then, clearly we must take you. We cannot have you beyond hope," Eleanor said lightly, smiling at the girl.

Samantha stayed, chatting about this and that, for

several minutes before she finally left to get ready for supper. Eleanor and Anthony finished up their work on the list. She pointed out to him that Dario Paradella's name was indeed present.

"Very well. I suppose it might be best to give him the names," Anthony agreed reluctantly. "We should at least talk to him."

Eleanor nodded. "I shall send him a note asking him to call on me tomorrow afternoon. When shall we say? Around two o'clock?"

"All right. I will join you." He paused, then added, "If I may."

"Of course you may." Eleanor smiled at him. At the moment, quite frankly, she preferred to have Anthony here with her at all times.

She carried the list to the safe room, a small locked room beside the butler's pantry. Only she and the butler had the keys to this room, as its shelves contained all the expensive silverware, and silver and gold serving dishes, epergnes and so on. Also in the room was the squat heavy iron safe in which she kept important documents and her expensive jewelry. Eleanor stashed the list of names, as well as the original sheet music, inside the safe and relocked the outer door. The list was now as secure as she could make it.

It was time to get ready for dinner, and Anthony had to return to his own house to put on his more formal clothes. Eleanor found herself surprisingly

reluctant to let him go. She strolled with him to the door. In front of the waiting footman, there was no possibility of any exchange of kisses or tender words, so she simply smiled and offered him her hand, as she would any gentleman of her acquaintance. But the look in his eyes as he bent over her hand warmed her.

She bathed and dressed for dinner, choosing, in a burst of happiness, to wear a deep blue dress that was one of her favorites. It was not really suitable for half-mourning, but she decided to ignore that fact. The dress was one in which she looked her best, its vivid color emphasizing her blue eyes and its wide scooped neckline showing her white shoulders to advantage. Pearls adorned her ears and throat, and dotted her black upswept hair.

Lady Honoria's lips set in a disapproving line when she saw Eleanor's gown, but Eleanor scarcely noticed. She was too busy looking at Anthony, whose eyes had widened appreciatively when she entered the room.

He came to her, taking her hand and bowing over it in a courtly manner. His back was to his sister and niece, blocking the fact that his lips lingered softly on Eleanor's hand. He looked into her eyes, and she smiled up at him, her mouth softening in a way that was unconsciously sensual.

Dinner was an agonizingly slow affair. Eleanor could think of little except Anthony and their love-making that afternoon, and whether there was any

possible way for them to sneak away from the others. She kept glancing at him, only to find him watching her in a way that made her blood hum. He seemed as unable as she to contribute to the dinner conversation, so it was dominated by Lady Honoria and her usual litany of complaints and melodramatic statements.

The meal finally ground to a halt, and they rose to leave the room. Samantha was usually sent up to bed after they ate, and Honoria generally retired, also, but tonight she perversely decided to join Eleanor and Anthony in the drawing room, allowing Samantha to stay, as well.

Eleanor gritted her teeth and resigned herself to another hour of Honoria's company. She played draughts with Samantha, taking turns with Anthony. Then, much to her surprise, Honoria decided that they should play whist.

"What?" Eleanor stared at her in consternation. She had absolutely no desire to while away the rest of her evening playing cards.

"There are four of us," Honoria pointed out.

"But Samantha doesn't play whist," Anthony countered, shooting Eleanor a flickering glance that told her he was as little interested in an evening of cards with his sister and niece as she was.

"We shall teach her," Honoria replied brightly. "It's time she learned. Please, Anthony, I am so dreadfully bored here." She turned her limpid blue

gaze on her brother, looking pitiful. "At home I am accustomed to playing quite often. Here I have nothing to do except knit and read." She sighed.

"Well, perhaps you can return home soon," Anthony told her, his voice revealing a little of his impatience.

"Oh, no, please…" Samantha pleaded. "Not until after the balloon ascension."

"No." He smiled at his niece. "Definitely not until after we see the balloons."

"Let us play cards," Samantha went on, looking from Anthony to Eleanor. "Please? It would be ever so much fun. I've never done so."

Finally Eleanor gave in, and they repaired to the card room. Eleanor sat across from Samantha, being her partner, and Anthony and Honoria took their places opposite each other. They sat down and began to play, explaining it to Samantha as they went along.

Eleanor felt something brush her leg. Startled, she looked up from her cards and turned her head toward Anthony. He was studiously examining his own cards, but he shot her a little sideways glance from beneath his lids. Again she felt the brush against her leg, longer and slower this time. It was, she realized, his knee touching her.

Heat blossomed between her legs as he slowly, rhythmically moved his leg against hers. Eleanor swallowed, her mind wandering far from her cards.

"Eleanor…"

She looked up to find Honoria staring at her in irritation.

"I'm sorry. What?" she asked a little breathlessly.

"It is your turn," Honoria told her as if she were a trifle dim-witted.

Quickly Eleanor apologized and made her play. She shot Anthony a fulminating look, but he only smiled, keeping his gaze on his cards. Her mouth tightened. Two, she thought, could play at this game.

She folded her cards together and held them against her, the tops of the cards slightly above the neckline of her dress. The cards rested against the swell of her breasts. She trailed the fingers of her other hand slowly down her throat and over the smooth, white expanse of her chest. Gently her finger skimmed across the soft curve of her breast till it reached the neckline of her dress. She paused for a moment there, then drew her finger back up the same path.

She cast a sideways glance at Anthony and was pleased to see that he looked a trifle slack-jawed, his eyes glazing over. He straightened, clearing his throat, and shifted a little in his chair. He studied his cards, his forefinger at his lips. His finger tapped against his full lip, then moved slowly one way, then the other. Eleanor found herself watching his finger trail across the soft, sensitive flesh. She could almost feel his touch upon her.

Her breasts were full and heavy, the centers tight-

ening, and her loins melted still more. Anthony looked up from his cards, his eyes raking her hotly. Eleanor watched as his eyes fell to her breasts, and she knew he must see the hard buttons of her nipples thrusting against the cloth of her dress. His nostrils flared, color tinting the high line of his cheekbones.

Pleased that he was no more immune than she to the teasing play between them, she crossed her legs beneath the table. Her foot found the side of his calf and slid insinuatingly up it. The look he shot her was fierce, a promise and a challenge all in one.

They continued to tease one another throughout the evening with looks and touches, flirting and arousing without a word spoken between them. By the time Lady Honoria delicately covered a yawn with her cards and declared herself done for the night, Eleanor was so warm she had to ply her fan, her blood singing through her veins and her loins pulsing with longing.

"I suppose it is time for you to leave us, Anthony," Lady Honoria said. "Will you be calling on us again tomorrow? You have been unusually attentive, I must say. It is quite a pleasant change." His sister looked at him a little quizzically.

Anthony cleared his throat. "Um, well, yes, I will be here tomorrow afternoon, in fact. I am glad that you have, uh, noticed the difference in me. I, ah…" He cast a glance around as though seeking inspiration.

Honoria let out a little tinkling laugh and waggled her fan at her brother. "You cannot fool me, you know. I am aware of what you are doing."

"You are?" he asked, startled.

"Oh, yes." Honoria nodded sagely. "I suspect there is some woman behind this behavior."

"Really?" Anthony's gaze flickered almost imperceptibly to Eleanor and back.

"Oh, yes. There must be a young woman fresh to the marriage mart, whom you are doing your utmost to avoid." Honoria cast him an arch glance.

"Honoria, you astonish me," he said with a smile.

His sister smiled. "Of course. Now, good night, my dear. Shall I walk you to the door?"

She stood up, and Anthony rose, as well, saying, "No. That is…there is, um, something in Lady Eleanor's office. Something she said she would give me." As his sister continued to gaze at him blankly, he finished, "Isn't that right, my lady?" He turned and looked at Eleanor.

"Yes, of course," she responded brightly, getting to her feet. "I had almost forgotten about it. Of course, it is rather late, and I am not sure where I put it," she added, sending Anthony a teasing glance. "Perhaps we should wait until tomorrow."

"Yes, Anthony, that sounds much better," Honoria added.

Anthony glared at Eleanor. "Lady Eleanor, I am sure it will not be much trouble. And my need is

rather…urgent. I would appreciate it if you would take the time for it now."

Eleanor smiled, her eyes twinkling at him mischievously. "Very well. Why don't we go to my study and look for it? I am sure it will not take us too long to find, um, what we want."

"I am certain of it," he responded in a heartfelt tone.

Eleanor turned and bade good night to a somewhat puzzled-looking Honoria and her daughter, then swept out of the room. Anthony followed on her heels, their steps growing quicker and quicker, until at last they reached Eleanor's office. They slipped into the room, and Anthony closed and locked the door behind him.

"Vixen," he told her huskily, reaching out and laying his hands around the column of her throat. "You delighted in torturing me this evening."

He slid his hands slowly downward, spreading his fingers as they moved over her chest. His eyes followed the movement of his hands, feasting on the white expanse of her skin, the swelling fullness of her breasts.

"No more than you," Eleanor responded saucily. "And you deserved every moment. You began it."

"And I shall end it," he said thickly, sliding his hands inside the low, wide neckline and cupping her breasts, lifting them up and out of her dress. "God, you are beautiful. I could barely sit still all night, I wanted so much to hold you. Kiss you."

He bent and kissed each breast, tasting and teasing with his tongue and lips until he felt as near to bursting as she, aching for fulfillment. He clutched her skirts, bunching them up with his hands, until at last he could reach under her petticoats. Splayed, his hands moved up the sides of her thighs and cupped the round fullness of her buttocks.

Eleanor's head lolled back, a long, shaky sigh of pleasure escaping her, as his fingers dug into her flesh, squeezing and stroking. Slipping his fingers beneath the waistband of her pantalets, he shoved them down in one swift movement, exposing her to his intimate touch.

His mouth came up to take hers in a long, deep kiss as his fingers slid between her legs, caressing and arousing her, sending the heat already there flaming into an inferno. Eleanor moaned, wrapping her arms around him and pressing into him. She ached to take him inside her once again, to feel him fill her in a way so complete that she could want nothing else.

"Anthony, please," she murmured against his lips.

He let out a low growl, his hand going to the buttons of his breeches. He pulled her up and set her down on the edge of her desk. His face, only inches from her, was fierce with hunger as he thrust her skirts up roughly and opened her to him. Eleanor wrapped her legs around him eagerly, urging him to her.

He sank deep within her, his eyes closed, his breath

ragged in his throat, his face stark with a pleasure that was almost pain. She buried her face in his neck as he thrust into her again and again. They teetered on the edge of dark oblivion, desire lashing them further and further beyond where they had gone before.

Eleanor let out a cry, stifling it against his skin, her teeth sinking into his flesh. Anthony groaned, holding on to her desperately, as they tumbled blindly over the edge.

CHAPTER SIXTEEN

THE MORNING DRAGGED for Eleanor. It had taken her some time to fall asleep after Anthony left. She had lain in the darkness in her bed, all too aware of the vast emptiness beside her. Her body was soft and faintly sore, her flesh still awash with pleasure. Yet at the same time, she was aware, in a way she had never been before, of how very alone she was.

She awoke late and therefore found herself alone at the breakfast table, a state she welcomed after a week of breakfasts spent listening to Lady Honoria's litany of complaints.

Accounts awaited her in her office, but she found it difficult to concentrate on them. She kept thinking about the list in the safe down the hallway. It would be a relief when Dario came and she was able to hand the thing over to him. Then her duty to Edmund would be done, and she would, she hoped, be free of the men who wanted it.

She endured a light lunch with Honoria, then returned to her office to work until Anthony arrived

for their appointment with Dario. Her head was bent over her work when she sensed that someone was at her door. She looked up, and her heart rose into her throat when she saw the man standing there.

"Conte di Graffeo."

Eleanor rose to her feet. *How had he gotten in here?* No servant had announced him. She had not even heard his footsteps in the hall.

"I am sorry," she said, admirably quelling any tremor in her voice. "I did not realize you were here."

"I told the maid I would show myself in," he said easily, coming into the middle of the room. "I hope I am not disturbing you, but I had some matters of importance I wished to discuss with you."

"Of course." Eleanor mustered a faint smile and stepped around her desk to sit in one of the chairs, gesturing toward the chair across from hers. "Please, sit down."

She could not help but wonder if the count had somehow found out about their discovery of the coded list. It seemed bizarre that he should show up the very morning after they had found it, yet she did not see how he could know what they had done. She and Anthony had told no one about it.

Di Graffeo sat down across from her, flashing her his urbane smile. "I am a straightforward man, Lady Scarbrough. I do not wish to engage in a round of accusations and lies. Let me begin by saying that I

know you are in possession of the list of the members of *L'unione*."

"Conte, really, I have told you before—"

"Please, my lady, no more subterfuges." The count held up a hand as if to stop her. "You think that I do not know what goes on in this household? I have had an employee among your servants for some time now. I know everything that happens here. I know that you and Lord Neale were celebrating, jubilant, last night. That you were talking about the list and how you decoded it from Sir Edmund's music. A clever ploy on Sir Edmund's part, I must say."

Eleanor's mind flashed to the maid she had seen standing in the doorway last night. At the time, her only concern had been embarrassment that the girl had seen her and Anthony kissing. But now she wondered exactly how long the maid had been there and how much she had heard, as well as seen.

She stood up, eyes flashing. "You dare to bribe my servants to spy on me? I think it is time you left now."

"Don't be so hasty, my lady," he said, also rising. "You should hear me out."

"There is nothing you could say that I wish to hear."

"I am prepared to pay quite handsomely for that list," he went on.

"I would not dishonor my name nor my husband's memory by selling it to you," Eleanor told him flatly.

"Your husband was wrong. It is no dishonor to admit that someone behaved foolishly."

"Acting on one's convictions is not 'behaving foolishly'," she retorted. "Edmund believed in what he did, and I would not in any way undermine his actions."

"Not even to save your good name?" he asked. His voice was a lazy drawl, but his eyes were sharp and bright as he gazed at her. "I know a great deal about you, you see. I am aware that you and Lord Neale are engaged in an affair." He tsk-tsked in an exaggerated way. "I do not think English society would approve, do you?"

"I don't give one bloody damn what English society would approve or not approve," Eleanor retorted, her hands curling into fists and her eyes blazing with fury. "You can spread your dirty little secrets all over London, and it will not make me give you those names. Now, get out of my house, or I will call a servant to throw you out."

She started toward the bell pull to summon one of the footmen, but the count reached out and grabbed her arm, stopping her. She swung around, furious, to face him, and saw that he held a pistol in his hand, leveled at her heart.

"I am not fool enough to come unprepared, my lady," he said quietly. "I did not expect you to immediately see the sense of my suggestion. Now...I suggest that you give me the list."

Eleanor's mind was racing. Anthony was sup-

posed to join her, and they were going to talk to Dario about the list. She had sent Dario a note asking him to call upon her at two o'clock. Anthony, she thought, would arrive before that time. If only she could keep the count occupied, Anthony might arrive before di Graffeo could take the list and leave.

"I suppose I have little choice," she said, wishing that she could see the clock. It was not in her line of sight, and she feared that turning her head to look at it would make the count immediately suspicious. "Unfortunately, however, I do not have the list. I gave it to Lord Neale."

Di Graffeo's lip curled up in a sneer. "A nice little fabrication, Lady Scarbrough. But, you see, I know that you and Lord Neale put those papers in your safe last night." He motioned impatiently with the gun. "Now, please, let us go retrieve them."

Eleanor turned and walked to the door. She thought about what she could do. There was certainly a possibility that there would be servants about as she walked to the safe. Would the count hesitate to shoot her in front of a witness? Or would she only be putting the servant in danger, as well?

As she stepped out into the hall, she heard her name called. "Eleanor."

It was Anthony's voice. He had arrived at the worst possible moment. He could not see di Graffeo or his gun, because the count was still behind her in the room. But the count had heard his voice and

would know that Anthony was there. He would be prepared, whereas Anthony, unaware, would be walking straight into danger.

She had hoped that Anthony would arrive in time to help her, but her only thought now was to warn him away. She whirled, crying, "Anthony, no!"

Before she could say anything else, however, the count stepped out into the hall, grabbing her arm to hold her where she was and bringing the pistol up to her head.

"Stop right there, Lord Neale," di Graffeo commanded.

Anthony came to a halt, staring at the scene in front of him. "What the devil is going on here?" he exclaimed, his voice reverberating with fury. "Unhand her, di Graffeo, or I promise you, you will regret it."

"You will regret it much more, sir, if you try to stop me."

"I see only one pistol," Anthony retorted. "You cannot shoot both of us."

"No. But I can promise you that Lady Scarbrough will be dead before you ever reach me. Is it worth it?"

"You know it is not," Anthony replied.

"Very well, then. Now, walk toward us...slowly."

Anthony did so, his eyes intent upon the count and the pistol he held to Eleanor's head. "I don't know how the devil you think you are going to get away with this," he told the count. "You will have

the list, but I think you will have a hard time getting out of the country before I catch up with you."

"Ah. Well, then, you give me a very good reason to incapacitate you," di Graffeo replied, his voice amused. "Now, walk past Lady Scarbrough. My lady, step back a little, please."

The count wrapped his arm around Eleanor, effectively pinning her arms to her sides, and pulled her back against him, taking a step back into the room so that she would be out of Anthony's reach as he walked by. Anthony strode past them and paused. Count di Graffeo released his hold on Eleanor's waist and once again grasped her arm, guiding her into the hallway in front of him.

They started down the hallway toward the butler's room, Anthony walking with a slow, measured pace. Eleanor waited, alert, for whatever opportunity might arise. It had occurred to her that Anthony had spoken rather loudly, and she wondered if he had known of the presence of a servant outside their range of vision, if he had perhaps been informing a footman or someone of what was going on. With luck, the footman might have enough sense to arm himself. She wished, quite fervently, that Bartwell was there. But she knew that whatever happened with the footman or anyone else, Anthony was biding his time, waiting for the best chance to attack di Graffeo. Eleanor needed to be ready to jump aside so she would no longer be leverage for the count to hold over Anthony.

"Conte!" a man's voice called from behind them.

Di Graffeo turned his head. "Paradella!"

Eleanor felt, more than saw, the count's gun hand relax, moving a little from her head as di Graffeo turned toward the new threat. She dropped to the floor just as Anthony let out a roar and threw himself at the count.

Di Graffeo turned back, bringing up the gun, but Anthony wrapped both hands around the count's arm, jerking it upward as he crashed into the man, sending them both tumbling to the floor. Eleanor scrambled to her feet and looked down at the two men thrashing and wrestling across the floor. She glanced up. Dario stood a few feet away from them, a pistol in his hand and leveled at the men on the floor. He watched, his face stamped with frustration, clearly unable to get off a clear shot.

Eleanor ran to the table against one wall of the hallway and grabbed a vase, intending to smash it down on di Graffeo's gun hand and separate him from his weapon. Once that was done, she was certain, the two men could restrain the count. But even as she turned, vase in hand, di Graffeo managed to land a blow on Anthony's chin with his free hand, stunning him enough to allow the count to roll out from under Anthony and start to rise.

In that instant Dario fired. The ball hit the count in the chest, and he went sprawling, blood welling from the wound.

Anthony pulled the gun from the count's hand

and stood up. Eleanor dropped the vase back on the table and ran to him, throwing her arms around him. Anthony hugged her tightly to him, and they both turned to look down at their enemy.

The count was sprawled on his back, blood staining his shirtfront. He looked faintly surprised. "Paradella," he said, contempt in his voice. Blood trickled from the corner of his mouth. *"Traditore!"*

"No, di Graffeo," Dario replied, his face as hard as his tone. "I am not a traitor. Just a man who loves freedom."

The light faded from di Graffeo's face, and he settled into the stillness of death.

Eleanor shuddered and turned her face into Anthony's shoulder. He rubbed his hand down her back soothingly. "Perhaps you should go lie down. I'll send for a magistrate."

"No. I am all right." She straightened. "I intend to get this over with right now." She looked at Anthony. "I think we should give it to Dario."

He nodded. "Agreed." He cast a half smile at the other man. "It is little enough thanks for saving our lives."

Dario shrugged. "I am just happy that I was far enough behind you that di Graffeo did not see me, too. I apologize for taking so long. I had to return to my coat to get the pistol."

"Do you always carry a pistol with you?" Eleanor asked in astonishment.

"Only since I found out that he was in town." He jerked his head toward the body at their feet. "Even though he could not prove it, the count was certain that I was among *L'unione*. I could not help but wonder if he would decide to get rid of me here, where there would be no one to retaliate." He turned toward Eleanor. "But what do you mean? What are you giving—"

They were interrupted by a loud scream from above, followed by running footsteps and a man's voice shouting, "No, my lady, no, you don't understand!"

"Eleanor! Anthony! The footman has a gun!" Honoria came flying down the staircase and into the hall at a faster pace than Eleanor would have thought possible. Right on her heels came one of the footmen, carrying a dueling pistol.

Honoria came to a sudden halt when she saw the group gathered beside the body on the floor and stared, for once rendered speechless. The footman, unable to stop, slid into her back, sending her tumbling to the floor.

Honoria began to shriek, over and over, while the footman babbled apologies and asides to Eleanor to the effect that he meant no harm, but had only run to fetch Eleanor's pistol when he heard Lord Neale's words.

At the commotion, everyone in the household came running, including Samantha and all the servants. Eleanor groaned and looked at Anthony.

The babble rose all around them until, finally, Anthony put his fingers to his lips and gave a loud, piercing whistle.

Silence fell immediately.

"Thank you," Eleanor said, then turned to the housekeeper. "Mrs. Jasper, in Bartwell's absence, I expect you to take charge of the servants. Keep them in the kitchen until such time as the magistrate decides whether he needs to talk to them. Everson, fetch the magistrate. Harmon, stand guard over the body. And Janet…" She turned to address her maid. "If you will take Samantha and Lady Honoria upstairs…"

"Of course, miss." Janet, efficient as ever and now used to dealing with Edmund's mother, took the older woman's arm and gently led her upstairs, murmuring sympathies at the fright she had endured. Samantha, wide-eyed, followed her.

Last, Eleanor turned to the maid who had walked in on her and Anthony the night before, fixing her with a gimlet gaze. "I will deal with you later," Eleanor promised.

The girl paled visibly. "I'm sorry, my lady," the maid began to wail. "I didn't know he was a wicked man. I only—"

"You only betrayed me, and I will not stand for that," Eleanor told her crisply.

"Yes, my lady," the girl answered in a subdued voice as the other servants turned to stare at her in shock.

Eleanor, Anthony and Dario turned and went into the small sitting room on the other side of the hall from where the count's body lay. It was a less formal room than the front drawing room and was used primarily as the anteroom to the dining room.

"I need a drink," Anthony said flatly, crossing to the liquor cabinet against the far wall. "Paradella? Eleanor?"

Eleanor nodded.

"Please," Dario said in a strained voice.

Anthony poured their drinks and handed them to Eleanor and Dario, then downed his own quickly. "Now…what the devil happened here?"

"You know most of it. Di Graffeo found out about the list. It seems he had paid one of the maids to spy on me for him."

"Ah…" Anthony's brow cleared. "That explains the maid whom you laid low with that look."

"You found the list?" Dario asked, astonished. "But how—where—"

Eleanor told him, though she was careful to leave out where and when she had thought of Edmund using his music as a code.

Dario's face brightened. "Of course! That sounds exactly like something Edmund would have done. How clever of him."

Eleanor nodded. "Yes. Anthony and I worked out the code and translated it. But one of the maids was at the door. I don't know how long she had been lis-

tening, but she heard enough to bring the count here. First he offered to buy it, and when I would not sell it, he tried to blackmail me."

"Blackmail you," Paradella repeated. "But how could he—with what?"

Eleanor shook her head. "It does not matter." She cast a quick glance at Anthony. "I would not have given him the list, in any case. That was when he pulled out the gun and demanded that I give it to him. But then, thank heavens, you arrived."

"I am simply grateful Paradella came to the door right after me," Anthony interjected. "Without his help, I am not sure what I would have done."

"We are all very fortunate," Dario said, smiling. He looked at Eleanor. "Dare I hope that the list is why you wished to speak with me this afternoon?"

Eleanor nodded. "You had said that *L'unione* needed it."

"Yes, it would be of great help to us," Dario told her.

"Then I will give it to you. I think that is what Edmund would have wanted."

"Thank you." Dario's dark eyes shone. "You have done a great service for my country."

At that moment the magistrate arrived, and they had to spend some time explaining to him what had happened. After he finished interviewing them, Anthony went with him to talk to the servants and arrange for the body to be taken away.

Eleanor retrieved the list and its musical code from the safe. She handed it to Dario, who read it over eagerly.

"I can scarce believe it," he told her, grinning. "I had all but given up hope of finding this. Our mission has been thwarted greatly by the secrecy in which we have had to dwell. It will go much more easily now. And now we know that the list will not be found by di Graffeo and his men."

"It puzzles me that the count did not make an attempt to find the list of names earlier. I was there for months, yet there was only that one time, right before I left, that the house was searched."

"Perhaps he did not know of its existence until recently. Even I was unaware that Edmund had been given the responsibility of keeping the list. As I told you, we must operate in great secrecy. But one of our number was captured by di Graffeo's men. He was the only one who knew about Edmund, you see, and about the list, besides the leader of our group. Though he did not know exactly how Edmund had hidden the list, he was aware that Edmund had entrusted it to you. When our leader realized what he might have revealed, I was dispatched here to keep you safe."

"And to get the list."

Dario gave her a roguish smile. "And to get the list." He bowed, brushing his lips over the back of her hand. "I am eternally grateful to you, my dear Eleanor. I promise you that I will safeguard it with my life."

"Then you will be returning to Italy?"

"Yes. Straightaway. I will pack and leave as soon as I can. Hopefully tomorrow." He paused, then added, "I still hope that you will return to Italy, as well."

Eleanor smiled and shook her head. "No. My place is here."

"With him?" He cast a glance toward the door through which Anthony had gone.

Eleanor followed his gaze, unaware of the wistful look that had stolen over her face. "I do not know." She straightened and forced a smile. "Well, then, this is goodbye. Godspeed, Dario."

"Goodbye, Eleanor." He bowed again and left.

Eleanor walked back to the kitchen, where she found that the magistrate had finished with the servants and left the house, after arranging to have the count's body removed. Anthony, she was informed, had gone with the magistrate.

Eleanor went up the back stairs to her bedroom, not eager to have to walk past the spot where the body had lain in order to get to the front stairs. She had always loved this house, but now she was not certain that she could bear to continue to live here.

She heard no word from Anthony, a fact that made her feel increasingly unhappy. Moreover, the fact that she felt unhappy because she might not see him that evening made her feel all the more displeased. Had she reached such a point that she could not be

content if a man was not there? It was absurd, she told herself.

She occupied herself for a while by writing to Zachary to tell him that he and Bartwell could return with Kerani and the children. But then she was once again at a loss.

Supper was a lonely affair, just herself and Samantha at the long table, clumped together at one end, as Honoria had declined to come down to dinner, claiming that her nerves were far too shattered for company. Even Samantha was uncharacteristically quiet. It was no wonder, Eleanor knew, since the girl had just seen a dead body. She wished that she could somehow take away Samantha's distress. She tried a time or two to talk about it, but Samantha seemed unwilling, so she gave up the effort. When the girl was ready, she would come to her, Eleanor hoped.

After dinner, Eleanor passed most of the evening up in her bedchamber again. She felt all at sixes and sevens. It was due, she told herself, to the events of the afternoon. But she knew, deep down, that Anthony's absence nagged at her.

Shortly before midnight, after she had already undressed and gotten into her nightrobe, there was a rattle at her window. She flew to the window and peered outside. There stood Anthony in the street, looking up at her window. Smiling, she waved to him, then turned and hurried quickly down the stairs. She unlocked the door and opened it, stepping aside to let him in.

He enfolded her in his embrace. "I am sorry. I thought I would get away sooner, or I would have sent you a note."

There was the sound of footsteps hurrying, and they turned their heads as a footman rushed into the room. He came to a dead stop upon seeing them. Eleanor and Anthony parted quickly. Eleanor blushed, very aware of the fact that she was wearing only her nightshift and dressing gown.

"It is all right, Everson," she told him with as much dignity as she could muster. "I saw Lord Neale arrive, so I opened the door myself."

"Yes, my lady, of course," he said quickly, backing up. "I was just…I heard the door close, and with all that's been going on, I was afraid…"

"Yes. Thank you. You were quite right to check on it. You may go to bed now, however."

"Yes, my lady." He bowed again and was gone.

Eleanor turned a little self-consciously back to Anthony. "Have you been all this while with the magistrate?"

He shook his head. "No. I have been back and forth from our government to the consul's house and back again. The count's ties to the king of Naples made it a somewhat delicate issue. They called in Paradella, too, even though the magistrate took my word for his shooting the count to save my life."

"Is it over now?"

He nodded. "I believe so. The consul seemed

somewhat suspicious, I thought, but he could not bring himself to call me a liar."

"I am sorry for the trouble."

He shrugged. "'Tis little enough." He looked at her, reaching out to take her hands. "When I think what might have happened to you…"

"It did not."

"No, thank God." He pulled her into his arms. She felt his lips press against her hair. Eleanor wrapped her arms around him and held on tightly.

"I must leave soon," he told her. "I do not want to cause gossip among the servants."

"Of course." She wanted to tell him that she did not care about the servants or what they said. She wanted him to stay. She wanted to have his arms around her, to go to sleep with him by her side. But she would not let herself say the words. It mattered to Anthony if the servants gossiped. This was his world, and their gossip would blacken him.

"I just wanted to see you again before I went home," Anthony said.

"I am glad you came."

He bent his head and kissed her, and Eleanor melted against him. When at last he raised his head, she was breathless and shaky, and it was all she could do not to cling to him and ask him not to leave.

"Tomorrow…" he said in a low voice. "I will come to call on you tomorrow, if that is all right."

"Yes. Of course." She smiled, stepping back from

him and adding lightly, "We have promised Samantha that we will take her to the balloon ascension."

He grimaced. "I had forgotten about that. Do you still want to go?"

"Yes, I do," she replied firmly. "I don't want to disappoint her. It was bad enough that she had to see the count's body. Perhaps the festivities will help her to forget it."

He sighed. "No doubt you are right." He kissed her again, hard and quick, then stepped back, his face set. "I must go now, or I shan't leave at all."

She closed the door behind him and hurried up the stairs to her room. Pulling aside the curtain, she watched him until he was out of sight in the darkness.

Eleanor turned away, surveying her room with a sigh. Was this, she wondered, to be her life from now on? Was she to spend her nights alone, aching for Anthony's touch, his presence, his smile? She would never have thought that she would want—nay, need—to be with a man so much, but she could not deny the feelings inside her.

She loved him. She knew it now, knew it deep in her soul, in the very marrow of her bones. She loved him as she had never dreamed of loving any man, and she knew that she would never stop.

But could she endure the life to which her love would condemn her? She knew Anthony would not marry her. Could not, really. A peer of the realm did

not marry an American, a woman whose name held no importance, no history. And Anthony, whatever desire he might feel for her, valued his name and his heritage. She was well aware of that; she had known it from the beginning. All she could ever be to him was a mistress.

She quailed at the thought of living always on the fringes of Anthony's life, seeing him when she could, watching him leave every night because of the talk it would cause if he stayed. Surely she had too much pride for that.

Yet how could she give up whatever chance of love she had with him? It seemed foolish to turn away from him because she could have only part of him and thus condemn herself to having none of him at all.

Such questions kept Eleanor up much of the night, and the next morning she awoke late and dressed somewhat listlessly. She told Samantha that they were going to the balloon ascension despite the events of the day before, and the happiness in the girl's eyes revived her spirits somewhat.

Anthony arrived shortly after luncheon, and she went to greet him, the lurking doubts and sadness fleeing at the sight of him. She did not throw her arms around him and kiss him as she would have liked to, but greeted him formally, aware of the presence of the footman who showed him in.

"We should be ready shortly," she told him, smiling. "I shall just send a maid up for Samantha."

"Wait. There is something I wish to talk to you about," he said, reaching out a hand to detain her.

Eleanor's chest went cold. There was something altogether too grave about Anthony's face. It occurred to her that he regretted what had happened between them the other night. Now that a little time had passed, he had probably started to look at their affair through the prism of cool reason. He would have realized that there could be no future for them.

It was sensible, of course. But this time Eleanor had no interest in being sensible. She turned quickly away, saying, "Now? But we have so little time. I— I must see to Samantha and—I must change."

"Change? What is wrong with what you are wearing?" he asked.

"Oh, no, this will not do at all. I, um, this is, well, it is not what I planned to wear." She flashed him a dazzling smile. "Can our talk not wait until this evening? Or tomorrow? When we have more time?"

His mouth tightened in irritation, but he said only, "Of course. We shall speak later."

Relieved at having escaped the confrontation, Eleanor slipped off to her bedroom. She rang for her maid, wishing that she had thought up a different excuse, for now she would have to actually change into a new dress.

When she went back downstairs, the others were waiting for her. Eleanor was surprised to see that Lady Honoria had decided to join them.

"One must put forth an effort," Honoria explained with the air of a martyr. "For Samantha's sake."

Since Samantha could just as easily have gone with Anthony and Eleanor alone, this seemed an unlikely reason to Eleanor. It was more likely that Honoria simply wanted to go but could not admit that fact.

"I do hope no one has heard about the magistrate visiting the house," Honoria continued as they exited the house. "I don't know how I shall hold up my head if the *ton* all knows about the dead body in the hallway yesterday. Really, Eleanor, you must stop doing such things."

"I did not actually intend to do it," Eleanor replied mildly.

They rode to the park in Anthony's open-air landau so that they would be able to sit in their carriage and watch the progress of the balloons. As they neared the park, the number of other vehicles grew, many of them open curricles or landaus like theirs.

Before long, Anthony pulled their vehicle into the ragged line edging the large open field where the balloons were sitting. He neatly maneuvered the landau so that it was backed in, with the horses facing away from the large baskets and brightly colored balloons that might make the animals nervous.

"It will be some time before they take off, I believe," he said, jumping down from his perch and

turning to look up at Eleanor. "Would you care for a stroll around first, Lady Eleanor?"

"Of course," she replied without thinking, remembering too late that it would not do to give Anthony an opportunity to have his "talk" with her. "Samantha? Lady Honoria?"

"Oh, my, no, it sounds quite exhausting," Lady Honoria said in a die-away accent, wielding her fan. "You are entirely too active for a lady."

"And Samantha should stay with her mother," Anthony put in firmly, before Samantha, her face eager, could speak.

Samantha grimaced and sank back in her seat, resigned. Anthony held out his hand to Eleanor. She took it and stepped down from the carriage. Her stomach was curling with worry, but she put a good face on, smiling at Anthony as he offered his arm.

They strolled along the line of carriages, looking at the various balloons in different stages of readiness. It seemed to Eleanor to be a scene of chaos. She only hoped that the men manning the balloons were more in control of what was happening than they appeared.

"Oh dear, there are the Colton-Smythes," she murmured, quickly stopping and turning aside to admire the nearest balloon, a brightly-colored red-and-yellow affair.

"You do not wish to see them?" Anthony asked, humor dancing in his eyes. "We can simply turn and walk back the direction we came."

"No." Eleanor sighed. "I must offer my sympathy to them on the death of their houseguest." She shouldered her parasol, like a soldier preparing for battle, and started to turn, but Anthony took her arm, stepping neatly in her path.

"First, before we throw ourselves on the fires of that social sacrifice, I must speak with you."

This was it, Eleanor thought, and though she cast about wildly for something to say to stave off his words, her mind was utterly blank.

"Lady Eleanor, I wanted to ask you…that is to say—I have been thinking the last few days…" He glanced up at her, his eyes so warm that Eleanor wanted to cry. "I have never known anyone like you, never felt anything such as I have felt for you. I—" He stumbled to a halt, then grated out an oath.

"I think I know what you want to say," she told him, sorrow tingeing her voice. "You have realized…" She had to pause and swallow hard before she could continue. "You have realized that what happened the other afternoon was a…a grave mistake. And you—"

"Mistake!" Anthony stared at her. "You think we are a mistake?"

"No!" Eleanor looked at him, astonished by the fury flaming to life in his eyes. "I do not think that. But surely you are looking for a way to end this. To—"

"To end this? Blast it, Eleanor, will you let me speak?"

"Of course," she replied, her voice a little chilly. "Please, go ahead."

"Thank you. I am not trying to end anything, other than my supreme frustration. I am asking you to marry me."

CHAPTER SEVENTEEN

ELEANOR STARED at Anthony blankly. For a moment she wondered if she had heard him correctly. "You—I—is this a jest?"

"I have never been more serious," he replied grimly.

"But you can't—I mean—" Joy welled up in Eleanor, making her almost giddy. She wasn't sure whether she was about to laugh or cry.

"Lady Scarbrough!" Mr. Colton-Smythe's voice sounded behind her. "What a pleasant surprise! Didn't expect to see you here today. And Lord Neale."

Eleanor had never been less happy to hear anyone. It took all her willpower to paste on a grimace of a smile and turn around to face the man. "Mr. Colton-Smythe. And Mrs. Colton-Smythe. Lovely day, is it not?"

Anthony sketched the merest bow toward the other couple, but they did not seem to notice that his response bordered on rudeness. Instead, Mrs. Colton-Smythe began to babble about the weather and balloons.

Finally, as she appeared to be winding down,

Eleanor hastily interjected, "I was so sorry to hear about Signora Malducci."

"Oh, yes." Mrs. Colton-Smythe shook her head, setting her side ringlets to bobbing in a comical way that was at odds with the gravity of her expression. "Terrible thing, when one cannot walk down the street without being afraid that one will be run over. Such a careless driver."

"Did he have an explanation?"

"Not he." The other woman looked indignant. "He didn't even have the common decency to stop. We only knew about it because the lad sweeping the crosswalk knew she was our guest and ran to tell us. It was dreadful. She was still alive when we got there."

"How terrible for you."

"It was, yes."

"Was she, um, able to speak when you found her?" Eleanor asked.

"No." Colton-Smythe shook his head. "She barely lasted a minute after that."

"I regret that I did not come to call upon her earlier," Eleanor said. "I arrived an hour or so after the accident."

"Yes, it might have put her mind at ease. She was so distressed, you see, kept saying that she must talk to you."

"Do you know why?" Eleanor asked.

"I'm not sure. She was so distraught, though I did not think it warranted such worry. It seems of little

importance that she saw Sir Edmund that day. It was sad, of course, but I saw nothing untoward about what he or his friend did."

"His friend?" Eleanor stiffened. "She saw Edmund with a friend?"

"Yes. That was what she wanted to talk to you about, although I cannot imagine why it exercised her mind so much. But when she saw Mr. Paradella at the consul's—"

"Dario?" Eleanor interrupted, astonished. "Dario Paradella? But he was not at the consul's ball, was he?"

"No, I think not. He had just left the consul's house as we were arriving. He almost ran into us. We had arrived a trifle early, it is true; I know it is terribly unfashionable of us, but I do like to be on time, don't you?"

"Yes, of course. But what happened when Signora Malducci saw Mr. Paradella?" Eleanor asked, trying to mask her eagerness.

"Well, she spoke to him about Sir Edmund. She said that she had seen them right before Edmund left, and how sad it was that he had died on their voyage. But he said almost nothing, just looked at her and denied that he had seen Sir Edmund that day. Really, he was almost rude, and I had always held him to be such a polite young man. Well, I suppose one never knows."

"Was she sure of the date?" Eleanor asked

abruptly, cutting into the woman's flow of words. "Could it not have been that she remembered another day when she had seen the two of them?"

"Oh, no, she was sure of that. She saw them quite near the docks. She had gone to say goodbye to a friend who was setting sail, so she was certain of the date, because that was the day her friend left. Her carriage passed Sir Edmund and Mr. Paradello as they were walking toward the docks. She said that they were deep in conversation."

"How odd," Eleanor commented, her mind racing.

"Yes, it was, rather, and after Isabella—Signora Malducci—spoke with Signore Paradella, she was quite silent for a time. Then, when I saw that you were there, she told me that she had to meet you. She wanted to talk to you."

"Yes, I know. I am so very, very sorry that I did not come to call earlier."

Eleanor cast a look at Anthony, and he quickly took her elbow, saying to the other couple, "Dreadfully sorry. We must go now. Appointment, you see."

"But—what—" The other couple stared at them, astonished.

Anthony doffed his hat. "See you another day."

Quickly he turned and steered Eleanor back in the direction of his carriage.

"Anthony, what does this mean?" Eleanor asked.

"You know as well as I what it means," Anthony

growled. "It means we have apparently just given that list to the very man who killed Edmund."

"I cannot believe it!" Eleanor exclaimed, hurrying to keep up with Anthony. "Why would Dario have killed Edmund? They were good friends."

Anthony stopped, turning to her. "Did you know that Paradella went out with Edmund that day?"

Eleanor shook her head. "No. He had intended to go with him, but then he sent a note saying that he could not. He was...I thought he was somewhere else when Edmund died."

"Where?"

"I don't remember. His horse had come up lame, and he could not ride back into town. I think perhaps he was visiting friends who lived in the country."

"There are two things here that I find important," Anthony told her. "First, Paradella was seen leaving the consul's house, where Conte di Graffeo, a man he supposedly hated, was staying. And secondly, an eyewitness saw him with Edmund walking toward the docks on the day that Edmund died in a boating accident, supposedly alone, while Paradella claimed to be elsewhere. Yet Paradella never said a word about having seen Edmund shortly before he died, and when Mrs. Malducci mentioned having seen him with Edmund, he adamantly denied it. Why?"

"Oh, God, Anthony, this is a nightmare," Eleanor murmured. "I trusted Dario. He spoke with such

affection of Edmund. He offered me his sympathy, his help—and all the time, he had killed Edmund?"

"I don't know for sure. But I have to say that he looks highly suspicious." He paused, then added, "I think it's possible he might have been working for di Graffeo."

"But he hated the man. You should have seen his face when he saw him, spoke of him. Dario was a member of *L'unione*."

"It is possible to hate someone yet still work for them."

"He kept the count from killing you," Eleanor pointed out.

"True. He shot him. But he did not have to shoot him, Eleanor. I did not think about it at the time. I was too glad for his help. But why didn't Dario simply come forward and help me wrest the gun away from the man? It was a difficult shot to make. Why risk it? I had di Graffeo down. He could have taken his gun. He and I could have overcome the man together."

"It is hard to fault a man for a decision made in an instant," Eleanor argued. Yet she could not help but remember that her instinct had been to get the gun out of di Graffeo's hand; that was why she had grabbed the vase.

"As for his being a member of *L'unione*—what if he joined the group to spy on them, or he was already in the group and di Graffeo paid him to turn

on them? Or perhaps the count held something over Paradella's head to force him to work for him. That would certainly make a fellow hate him even as he worked for him. Remember how the count looked rather surprised when Dario shot him? And he called Paradella a traitor, which Paradella neatly treated as meaning a traitor to his country. But what if di Graffeo meant that Paradella had betrayed *him?*" He paused, then added, "We cannot get past the fact that he lied, that he was with Edmund right before Edmund died."

"I know," Eleanor agreed sadly. "And Mrs. Malducci was killed before she could give that news to me." She straightened her shoulders. "We have to find him. If he killed Edmund, we cannot let him get away."

They hurried to the landau. It took some time and a good deal of persuasion to get Lady Honoria to vacate the carriage. Samantha, naturally, was quite happy to; she would have preferred to watch the ascension sitting on the ground on a blanket, or roaming up and down the line of carriages. But Honoria valued her dignity and her health, she informed them. She was not about to sit on the ground like a heathen. They finally got her out when Anthony, exercising a great deal of charm, wangled an invitation for Honoria and Samantha to join Lady Thornbridge, one of the doyennes of the *ton,* in her own elegant carriage.

Once that was accomplished, Eleanor climbed up on the driver's seat with Anthony, and they made their way out of the crowd. It took them several minutes to negotiate the traffic. Once they were away from the park, they were able to make better time, and before long, they pulled up in front of the house in which Dario was lodging.

His rooms were on the second floor. They climbed the stairs quickly, and Anthony rapped on the door. Eleanor was sure that she had heard noises from inside as they approached, but the sounds stopped now. There was a long, breathless silence.

Eleanor and Anthony glanced at each other. She raised her gloved fist and knocked again, saying, "Dario, it is I, Eleanor. I would like to speak to you."

Now she was certain that she heard sounds within the rooms—something that sounded very much like hurried footsteps.

"Paradella! Open this door!" Anthony bellowed, and when there was no reply, he threw his weight against the door.

The second time he did so, the door popped open, and he stumbled into the room, Eleanor on his heels. They ran through the empty sitting room into a short hallway, which ended in a bedchamber. There was no one in that room, either, but a window was flung open. Anthony ran to the window and looked out.

"Bloody hell! There he is, heading around the side of the house. He's scarpered."

"Anthony, look!" Eleanor pointed with a trembling finger to the traveling bag that lay open on the Paradella's bed. There, fallen between two rows of neatly folded shirts, was a gold locket.

Anthony let out an oath and reached in to pick up the locket. He opened it; inside lay a miniature portrait of Sir Edmund. He turned and looked at Eleanor.

"You were right. It *was* Dario that night in my room," Eleanor said. "When he described to me how you could have escaped back into your room and undressed so that you looked as if you had been in bed, he was simply telling me what he had actually done." She picked up the locket and folded it into her palm. Her gaze hardened. "We must not let him get away. He cannot leave the country."

Anthony grabbed her hand, and they ran back through Dario's rooms and down the stairs to their landau. Anthony flipped a coin to the urchin who was holding the reins, and they climbed in and started off. Eleanor shielded her eyes, looking all around for any sign of Dario.

"There he is!" she exclaimed. "Turn right."

Anthony turned the horses' heads and started after him. Dario had a good head start, but their conveyance traveled more quickly than he could run. Glancing back, he saw them gaining on him. He looked around frantically, then darted out into the street and threw himself at a man riding along. The

startled horse reared, and the man was unseated, tumbling to the ground. Dario grabbed the reins and lithely swung up into the saddle. He took off at a gallop.

Anthony slapped the reins across his horses' backs, and they took off after the fugitive. Anthony's horses were prime blood, and they were able to keep up with Dario, but the bulky conveyance was less than maneuverable, and as they went around corners and wound in and out among traffic, they gradually lost ground.

Still, Dario was in their sights as they once again approached Hyde Park, where Dario took off across the grass. Anthony let out an oath. A carriage was meant for the road, not the uneven ground of an open field. He hesitated for an instant, then turned his horses onto the grass after Paradella.

Eleanor hung on to the seat as they rattled across the ground. Dario rode into a group of trees, no doubt hoping they could not follow, but Anthony drove along the edge of the grove, keeping Dario in sight. He and Eleanor ducked beneath the wide overhang of two spreading oaks, and suddenly they found themselves on the edge of the balloon ascent.

Dario had pulled up, staring at the scene before him, and Anthony seized the opportunity to regain the ground he had lost. He pulled the landau behind Dario, blocking his escape to the rear. The crowd of people kept him hemmed in on the sides, and the

balloons stopped him from going forward. Dario heard the sound of their carriage and whirled, kicking his horse, but the animal, tired from his run, merely shied.

Anthony tossed the reins to Eleanor and leaped from the carriage seat directly onto Paradella. The two men went spilling off the far side of the horse. They fell into some of the bystanders, eliciting shrieks and angry oaths. Dario's horse, taking exception to all this unusual behavior, reared.

Eleanor watched with her heart in her throat, fearful that the animal would come down on top of the two men rolling across the ground, punching and grappling. The horse, however, neatly managed to elude them and trotted away from the fray. Eleanor wrapped the reins around the whipstand to hold Anthony's horses and clambered down the side of the carriage.

By the time she reached the ground, several of the male bystanders had jumped into the fight, pulling the two men apart.

"Here, now! Stop that!" one burly gentleman said as he and his companion wrapped an arm each around Anthony's arms, pulling him away.

"Good Gad, sir, there are ladies present," another man expostulated. He had pulled Dario away, and his hand was still on Dario's arm.

His hold was too loose, as it turned out, for Dario whirled, pulling a pistol from inside his

jacket, and grabbed Eleanor by the arm, pointing the pistol at her head.

Everyone froze, staring at them in horror.

"Stay back, all of you," Dario told them.

"Damn you, Paradella, you won't get away with this," Anthony snarled, jerking his arms from his captors' now-slack hold.

"Won't I?" Dario asked insouciantly. "It seems to me that I have a very good chance of it."

"Dario, how could you do this?" Eleanor asked.

"My dear, you must know that I have no desire to harm you," Dario replied. "And as long as Lord Neale and the others let me go, I will set you free, don't worry."

"You killed Edmund!" she exclaimed. "How could you have done that? He was your friend."

"It grieved me," he told her with great sincerity. "It was the hardest thing I've ever done. But I could scarcely let him tell everyone, could I? He had found out about me, you see. I had foolishly tried to talk him into letting me see the list, and it made him suspicious. I did not realize it, but he had me followed, and he learned that I was meeting the count in secret. Being a gentleman, he offered me a chance to explain myself. I wrote that I could not meet him, so that no one would know I was with him, but then I intercepted him on his way to the docks."

"And you killed him," Eleanor finished bitterly. "Because he was foolish enough to trust you."

"Oh, he was not that foolish. He balked when we got to the boat. I had to knock him out and throw him in. Then I sailed out and threw him overboard, left the boat and swam back to shore. I have always been a good swimmer."

"You are a monster!" Eleanor cried, her eyes filling with tears of rage. "I despise you."

"Nevertheless, my dear, you are coming with me," Paradella replied.

"Never."

"Unless you prefer to die," he responded flatly. He began walking backward, his eyes on Anthony, the gun pointed at Eleanor's head as he pulled her with him.

Eleanor cast a quick glance at Anthony. She knew that he would be waiting for a chance to rush Paradella, just as he had done yesterday with the count. She must offer up some distraction that would give him the chance to do so.

She dragged her feet, making Dario jerk and pull her along. Her resistance clearly irritated him, for he burst into an angry spate of Italian, but he did not take his eyes from Anthony or his gun from her head.

They reached the nearest balloon, where the operator stood staring at them, openmouthed, like everyone else in the crowd. The balloon was filled and moored by ropes tied to stakes driven into the ground.

"Get in," Dario told Eleanor curtly.

"Into the basket?" she asked in surprise.

"Yes, of course. We are going to take a little trip."

She sidled through the narrow door, Dario edging in right behind her. The man who stood beside the balloon goggled at them in astonishment.

"Sir, what are you doing?" he cried. "That is my balloon. You cannot take it up yourself!"

"Dario, please. Think! You cannot operate one of these things, can you?" Eleanor cried.

"I will have to," he replied.

"Damn it, Paradella!" Anthony roared, striding toward the balloon. "Let her go! You have made your escape."

"I think not." Paradella smiled. "I may need Eleanor yet."

"No! No!" the balloon operator yelled, pulling at his hair in his agitation. "You will wreck it. You don't know how to operate it. Please, sir! Please!"

"Unfasten the ropes," Dario commanded. When the man hesitated, he lifted the gun higher, pressing it flush against Eleanor's temple. "Unless you wish to see this lovely lady die in front of your eyes, undo the ropes."

Moaning and fretting, the man did as he was told, unfastening first one rope, then another, working from side to side. All the time he kept up a running plea with Dario not to go up in the balloon.

Eleanor could sense Dario's impatience. If she could just distract him even more, it might give Anthony the opening he needed. He was edging

closer, and so far, Dario had not noticed. In any case, time was running out for her. She had to do something now.

"Dario, please," she said, putting as much distress in her voice as she dared. "Let me go. We will let you leave, I promise, if you will just let me out of this contraption."

"I cannot," he told her curtly.

"But you don't understand," she wailed. "I cannot go up in this! Please. I am terrified of heights."

"Don't be absurd. You are the least terrified woman I have ever met."

"You have not seen me in the right situation. You know I never went onto the roof of the Mustellis' villa, even though everyone said the view was spectacular."

"No, I did not know it."

"Well, it is true. I detest the mountains. That is why Edmund and I never went to the Alps." That was not true, of course; the reason had been Edmund's shortness of breath. But with any luck, Dario would not know that.

"You will survive it."

"No, I don't think I will!" Eleanor cried, turning her head toward Dario as much as she dared. "Please, Dario. All of us have something that we dread. I cannot go up in the air in this thing!"

"Please, sir, listen to her!" the man who was undoing the ropes yelled.

He had unfastened over half of them, and the

balloon jerked upward, tugging at its moorings. Eleanor shrieked, and the man jumped forward. Dario, startled, whipped the gun around toward the balloon operator. Eleanor threw herself against Dario, grabbing at his gun hand. He jerked his arm upward as she hit him, and the gun went off.

At that moment Anthony vaulted over the side of the basket and punched Dario in the face. Dario staggered back, coming up hard against the opposite side, and Anthony went after him, landing a hard right to Dario's stomach. But Dario turned so that the blow glanced off his side, and he hurtled forward, ramming his shoulder into Anthony and knocking him backward.

The basket was rocking crazily under the force of the two men's bodies slamming into it, and Eleanor was thrown down to the floor. She could hear shrieks from the crowd, and the agitated voice of the balloon owner over them all.

She struggled to her feet, grasping the side of the wicker basket, and as she straightened up, a rope gave way. All three of them went sliding as the basket tilted. Eleanor slammed into the side, the impact knocking the breath from her. Beside her, Anthony hit the wall, as well, and Dario landed against him.

Dario struggled, trying to lift Anthony and push him over the side. Anthony pulled back his arm and landed a powerful punch to Dario's jaw. At that instant, the last rope holding them to the ground popped free, and the balloon rose precipitously.

Dario staggered backward under the force of Anthony's blow and the sudden movement of the basket. He hit the side with a sharp crack, and the top rail of the basket snapped and fell off. Dario reeled backward, flailing his arms.

Eleanor gasped and reached for him, as did Anthony, but it was too late. Dario went over the side and fell to the ground.

"Oh, my God!" Eleanor twisted and looked down in his wake.

Paradella lay sprawled on the ground twenty feet below them.

"Is he dead?" Eleanor gasped.

Anthony came up behind her, wrapping his arms around her and looked down. "I cannot tell. I'd say his leg is broken, but I think he is moving his hand. The crowd will hold him, I'm sure."

Eleanor let out a breath of relief and leaned against Anthony, holding on to him tightly. "Thank heavens you managed to hit him."

He gave her a squeeze. "Only because you distracted him. You were the one who knocked the gun away." He kissed the top of her head. "You are going to have to stop doing this, you know. I shall be gray before my time if you keep having guns held to your head."

"Believe me, I would rather not, as well," Eleanor answered.

She glanced around her and down at the

ground, still receding from them. "What are we going to do now?"

"I don't know. I don't suppose you know how to operate a hot air balloon, do you?"

"No, I cannot say that I do," she responded. "One does something with these bags on the side, I presume."

"Mmm. I think you throw them over if you want to climb higher. To avoid trees and hills."

"Or church spires," Eleanor commented, looking down at the city below.

He glanced around. "Yes. Well, I think we are above everything at the moment. The question is whether there is a way to steer this thing."

"And how one comes back down again."

"I'm not sure that will be a problem." Anthony looked up at the balloon swelling above them. "I think perhaps that shot that went off when you hit Paradella's arm went through the balloon."

"What?" She looked up, alarmed. "You mean air is escaping through it?"

"I believe so. I also believe the leak is growing a little larger as time passes."

"Oh dear. Well, I suppose it will come down sooner or later then. Hopefully slowly rather than all at once."

"That would be my preference, as well," Anthony responded dryly, then chuckled and pulled her into his arms again. "Ah, Eleanor, life is never dull around you."

"It is glorious up here, isn't it? The children would love it. We must take them up sometime."

He smiled. "There is no one like you, my dear. Now...since we are up here all alone with nowhere to go and no chance of doing anything until we come down, I think it is time that you answered my question."

"Your question?"

"You wound me," he replied. "I asked you to marry me before we started on that mad chase."

"Oh." Eleanor looked down.

"What? Have I mistaken your feelings?" He tipped her chin up to look into her face. "Do you not wish to marry me?"

"Anthony...you are speaking in the heat of the moment. You cannot have thought... The things that made me wrong in your eyes for Edmund are still true. How can I have been too low-born to be his wife and yet be satisfactory as a countess? You know I cannot."

"You are more than satisfactory to be *my* countess," he responded. "Eleanor...I told you that I feared you were an adventuress, out to fleece Edmund. I did not care that you were an American or that you were not an aristocrat. I was wrong. Please do not hold that mistake against me."

Eleanor looked at him, hesitating. Everything inside her longed to say yes, but still she held back. "I do not want you to wake up in a month or a year or ten years and regret that you married me."

"I could never regret it. I frankly cannot imagine life without you." He took her hands in his and looked earnestly down into her eyes. "My dearest Eleanor, I have looked back on my behavior when you married Edmund, and I realize that I was a boor and a fool. But I know that deep in my heart what made me, in the fiercest way, try to discourage you from marrying Edmund was the fact that as soon as I saw you, I wanted you for myself."

Eleanor gave him a skeptical look. "What?"

"It is true. When you walked into that room, I thought you were the most beautiful woman I had ever seen. I wanted you so much at that moment that it hurt. I didn't want you to marry Edmund. I didn't want you to marry any man. I would have liked to sweep you out of that house and take you home to my bed. It is why I never visited you and Edmund. I did not want to see you with him, to know that you were his wife, forever forbidden to me. It would have been torture. I love you."

"Anthony!" A dazzling smile broke across Eleanor's face, and she flung her arms around him. "I never thought I would hear you say it. I love you, too." She pulled back and gazed tenderly up at him. "Yes, I will marry you."

He bent his head and kissed her, a long, slow, delicious kiss. At last he raised his head.

"Well," he said, smiling. "I suppose we had better figure out how to land this thing."

"In a minute," Eleanor responded, cupping her hand at the base of his neck and pulling his head down for another kiss.

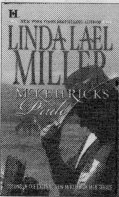

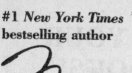

REQUEST YOUR FREE BOOKS!

2 FREE NOVELS FROM THE ROMANCE/SUSPENSE COLLECTION PLUS 2 FREE GIFTS!

YES! Please send me 2 FREE novels from the Romance/Suspense Collection and my 2 FREE gifts. After receiving them, if I don't wish to receive any more books, I can return the shipping statement marked "cancel." If I don't cancel, I will receive 4 brand-new novels every month and be billed just $5.49 per book in the U.S., or $5.99 per book in Canada, plus 25¢ shipping and handling per book plus applicable taxes, if any*. That's a savings of at least 20% off the cover price! I understand that accepting the 2 free books and gifts places me under no obligation to buy anything. I can always return a shipment and cancel at any time. Even if I never buy another book from the Reader Service, the two free books and gifts are mine to keep forever.

185 MDN EF5Y   385 MDN EF6C

Name _____ (PLEASE PRINT)

Address _____ Apt. #

City _____ State/Prov. _____ Zip/Postal Code

Signature (if under 18, a parent or guardian must sign)

Mail to **The Reader Service:**
IN U.S.A.: P.O. Box 1867, Buffalo, NY 14240-1867
IN CANADA: P.O. Box 609, Fort Erie, Ontario L2A 5X3

Not valid to current subscribers to the Romance Collection,
the Suspense Collection or the Romance/Suspense Collection.

Want to try two free books from another line?
Call 1-800-873-8635 or visit www.morefreebooks.com.

* Terms and prices subject to change without notice. NY residents add applicable sales tax. Canadian residents will be charged applicable provincial taxes and GST. This offer is limited to one order per household. All orders subject to approval. Credit or debit balances in a customer's account(s) may be offset by any other outstanding balance owed by or to the customer. Please allow 4 to 6 weeks for delivery.

Your Privacy: Harlequin is committed to protecting your privacy. Our Privacy Policy is available online at www.eHarlequin.com or upon request from the Reader Service. From time to time we make our lists of customers available to reputable firms who may have a product or service of interest to you. If you would prefer we not share your name and address, please check here. ☐

BOB07

Two unforgettable classics from
New York Times bestselling author

DIANA PALMER

Get swept away once again by these vintage tales
celebrating two Diana Palmer heroes we dare
you to forget...

Rediscover HUNTER and MAN IN CONTROL
in HARD TO HANDLE.

"The ever-popular and prolific Palmer has penned
another sure hit."
—*Booklist* on *Before Sunrise*

*Available wherever
trade paperbacks are sold.*

HQN™

We *are* romance™

www.HQNBooks.com   HQNDP77261

CANDACE CAMP

77097 AN INDEPENDENT WOMAN ___$6.99 U.S. ___$8.50 CAN.

(limited quantities available)

TOTAL AMOUNT	$ _____
POSTAGE & HANDLING	$ _____
($1.00 FOR 1 BOOK, 50¢ for each additional)	
APPLICABLE TAXES*	$ _____
TOTAL PAYABLE	$ _____

(check or money order—please do not send cash)

To order, complete this form and send it, along with a check or money order for the total above, payable to HQN Books, to: **In the U.S.:** 3010 Walden Avenue, P.O. Box 9077, Buffalo, NY 14269-9077; **In Canada:** P.O. Box 636, Fort Erie, Ontario, L2A 5X3.

Name: _____
Address: _____ City: _____
State/Prov.: _____ Zip/Postal Code: _____
Account Number (if applicable): _____

075 CSAS

*New York residents remit applicable sales taxes.
*Canadian residents remit applicable GST and provincial taxes.

HQN™

We *are* romance™

www.HQNBooks.com   PHCC0906BL

WEE BOOK INN

10810 - 82 AVENUE 432-7230
8101 - 118 AVENUE 474-7888
10328 JASPER AVENUE 423-1434
15125 STONY PLAIN RD. 489-0747